Also from Indigo Sea Press
A Novel by Rachael Stratford

Right of Trespass

indigoseapress.com

Endure and Prevail

By

Rachael Stratford

Perseverance Books
Published by Indigo Sea Press
Winston-Salem

Perseverance Books
Indigo Sea Press
302 Ricks Drive
Winston-Salem, NC 27103

First Perseverance Books edition published
January, 2016
Perseverance Books, Moon Sailor and all production design are trademarks of Indigo Sea Press, used under license.

For information regarding bulk purchases of this book, digital purchase and special discounts, please contact the publisher at indigoseapress.com

Cover design by Stacy Castanedo

Manufactured in the United States of America
ISBN 978-1-63066-326-1

Dedicated to all those who endure and prevail,
And also to those who just endure.

—Rachael Stratford

Chapter One

She gathered her books, put them in a satchel, threw the strap over her shoulder and went outside into the heat of the afternoon. Tossing her purse and books into the passenger seat of her rather well-used, but still serviceable Ford Explorer, she lifted the hair off her neck to enjoy the cooling, southerly breeze. A surge of hot air rippled past as she slid into the uncomfortably warm, vintage leather seats.

"Jeez," she quipped, "wouldn't it be nice if the air conditioner in this regal carriage worked."

A couple of miles down the highway, she took her regular exit onto the gravel road that meandered through the hills and eventually passed in front of her mother's driveway. She flipped on the radio, permanently tuned to KJOI, K-Joy, the station that played top-notch western singers 24/7. She tapped the steering wheel, her head bobbing, keeping time with Garth Brooks singing about his friends in low places.

"Oh, my," she groaned.

She just remembered she would have to cut a field of alfalfa, then pick up a few remaining bales of Bermuda left from yesterday's baling. That would keep her busy for several hours before working the evening shift as an aide at the hospital.

She didn't mind farm work at all. In fact it was enjoyable...just as long as it didn't keep her from accomplishing out-of-class assignments...or tire her until she couldn't remember what she had studied. It afforded excellent exercise without any gym fees to pay. And it seemed the mind worked better if the body kept busy. Then too, getting all that hay to feed her horse and the cattle was a wonderful bonus. How could anything be better?

1

"Well," she muttered, "it *could* be better if Mom would kick that no-good-drunken-leech, Charley, out of our house. Out of our lives. Forever!"

Glad this stretch was a "road less traveled," she leaned back and relaxed. Soon, a white Ford truck pulling a long cattle trailer appeared from around a bend and drove toward her. She caught her breath, recognizing the truck. She knew who would be driving it. Past memories, painful to remember caused her hands to tremble. Emotions hard to suppress, after years of rigid self-control, harassed her with extreme discomfort.

It was at that worst possible moment, her SUV started wobbling. Her hands tightened on the useless steering wheel. Nothing worked. The Explorer bounced and skidded. Then Anna saw the left front wheel of her vehicle speed, with the force of a rocket, down the road and into the path of the oncoming truck and trailer.

"Oh God ! Please no!" she prayed.

She felt a tremendous jolt and knew her now empty hub and axle had plowed so deeply into the gravel road it could no longer move forward. Loudly, the old Ford groaned and screeched like a living thing. Its rear climbed and flipped over her head.

In her panic, she cried out, "Is this it then?" Was this the end of Anna Shelton?

A strange calm settled over her, even though she was being slammed end over end—and there was nothing she could do about it. Momentarily upside down, she observed the underside of tall weeds and small trees along the side of the road. How strange this perspective! She hadn't stood on her head since turning somersaults as a small child. The tire and wheel bounced crazily through her field of vision, landing harmlessly in a ditch. She realized she had also flown off the county road without involving the oncoming white pickup.

Thankful she had not ensnared anyone else in her bizarre accident, her last thoughts were: *Whatever happens, it's out of my hands now.*

Fragments of awareness came and went. She was on the ground. Someone covered her with a jacket. She heard a siren in the distance. A man's voice spoke her name.

"Hang on," it said, "help is on the way."

Carefully, he brushed the hair back off her cheek. Two hands gently framed her face. Lips tenderly touched her own.

His voice broke as he whispered, "I love you so much, Annie."

She struggled, wanting to respond, but only her lashes fluttered as darkness enveloped her.

Slipping in and out of consciousness, Anna finally became aware of her surroundings. She was a patient in the very hospital where she worked.

"Well, well, well, look who woke up," declared the cheerful voice of the nurse entering her room. "I'm so happy to see you fully awake. How do you feel? ...Now don't say 'with my fingers'." She laughed. "Just jokin'," she said.

Anna was glad to see Janice Higgins. She knew her well...knew her to be friendly, competent and always reliable. Janice would give her the best of care. After all, they were best friends.

"Oh...Janice. I'm glad to see you too...to be *able* to see you," she said rather weakly. "How broken am I? How long have I been here?"

"To answer your first question, you have a concussion, three cracked ribs and a cracked radius in your left arm. Splinted as you see. Don't think they will have to cast it since that's usually done only when absolute immobility of separated parts is required. And, of course, you have several significant bruises and contusions...not to mention multiple minor ones. You have been here a little over twenty-four hours.

Anna attempted to sit up, but instead groaned loudly.

Janice reminded her of the seriousness of cracked ribs and cautioned curtailed activity for some time. "Until your body

3

mends itself," she said. "Not much we can do with cracked ribs. Usually, we don't even bind them anymore. Just find a comfortable position and stay there until they heal." She grinned. "We'll keep you on painkillers though. I know it hurts like hell. By the way, would you like something to eat? Since you've been completely out of it for a while, you must be starving. A glucose drip doesn't fill the belly."

"No, I'm not hungry." Anna answered.

"The sheriff's been here a couple of times. Wants to talk to you about the accident."

"Has anyone else been by?"

"Oh yeah! Doctor Peterson...often. Several college students. And your mom...once...for a few minutes. Said she'd be back ...but I haven't seen her...and Gabe. Gabe Whittier, that handsome hunk, who came in with you in the ambulance. He gave admitting your name and stuff and told them what had happened. Stayed for hours until he found out you'd be okay. Would you like me to falsify the report and tell him you're still in critical condition, so he will keep coming by?"

Anna gave Janice a look of reproach.

"Well, hell, if you don't want to see him, I'll do it just for myself." Janice chuckled. A few seconds later, she continued, "Aw...I'm just messin' with you, sweetie," she said.

"Was anyone else hurt?" asked Anna.

"Nope! One car accident. Only you."

Anna carefully changed position, trying to get comfortable. Gazing around the room, trying to imagine how other patients felt being bedfast, unable to help themselves, she guessed most of them found it extremely unpleasant. The inability to take a needed shower, wash her hair and brush her teeth completely ripped away any feelings of independence. She found it an untenable situation. The closed-in, restricted feeling made her want to throw things.

That would be extremely improper...just endure and prevail. And what does the sheriff want to talk about?

What was there to tell him? A front wheel just came off her Explorer. She had no idea how or why that had happened.

Drowsy and falling asleep again, she realized there was no one to mow the alfalfa field and pick up the extra Bermuda bales. How was she now going to do it herself? She must call her mom and maybe her mother could at least contact the new fellows down the road who were supposed to be looking for work.

One thing for sure, old Charley won't be giving any assistance, she reflected as she drifted off.

Anna was putting Smoky, her barrel-racing quarter horse, through a strenuous workout when a voice close to her ear, waking her from a dream, whispered, "That good-lookin' sheriff's comin' to see you. Put in a good word for me."

Anna slowly opened her eyes and said, "What? What did you say?"

"The sheriff is coming down the hall. I'm sure he's coming to see you. I said put in a good word for me. He's not married is he?"

"Janice, for gosh sakes! I thought you wanted Gabe Whittier—now it's Sheriff Henderson. Which one do you want? Or is it both?"

"Either one." Janice laughed. "Whichever one you don't want is okay by me. No...I think I'd best take the sheriff. The other guy is already stuck on you."

"I have no sway with either..." Anna began but was interrupted by the rather imposing presence of Sheriff Henderson entering the room.

Better looking than Anna remembered, he was a six foot-two, broad shouldered, long legged, muscular showcase of masculinity. Dark brown hair lightly caressed his sun-tanned brow when he removed his hat. He ran his fingers through it, pushing it back into place. His eyes were the color of milk chocolate and twice as intriguing. No wonder Janice was interested.

"Well, I lucked out. Good to see you awake. I'm Troy Henderson, Sheriff of Mechlin County," he said as he extended his hand in greeting.

Grateful his handshake was gentle, Anna replied, "Yeah, I know. Troy the Trojan. Quarterback on the only state championship team from Carnegie High. Could always slam that football right where it needed to be and kept everybody guessing what you were going to do next." Anna smiled. "I was one of your screaming eighth-grade fans."

"Really? Guess I didn't recognize your voice," he joked, "but it's been awhile. Are you well enough to answer a few questions for me?"

"Yes, I'm well enough, but I'm afraid I don't have much to tell you. I don't know what happened... other than a wheel came off my SUV."

"I'm sorry you had such a scare. It could have been fatal. You were lucky." He moved a chair closer to her bedside and pulled out a pen and small pad from his pocket.

"First, how long ago did you have that front tire put on...or removed for repair?"

"It's a rather new tire. I bought it about six months ago, I think. I can check my receipts if it's important."

"Have you had a flat fixed recently? Or had any reason to have it taken off?"

"No, I've had no reason to have it repaired—or even aired up? Why?"

The sheriff was hesitant and seemed concerned. "Well, I don't want to alarm you, but we found only two lug nuts from your wheel. And we did an extensive search up and down the road where it came off. Also, the bolts on your hub were all fine. No signs of stripping except for two. And those two had only the *tip ends* stripped...maybe a couple of threads on the ends."

"Does that mean I have been driving around with only two bolts holding that wheel on?"

"That's what it looks like. But it also seems to suggest that

6

those two were just barely holding it on. They had not been tightened down...maybe only a couple of turns. Just enough to get you started good. Get you up to speed maybe, but take you only a short distance before they stripped off."

Anna stared. What was he thinking? "Are you saying someone has tampered with my wheel recently, causing it to come off?" she questioned.

"It sure looks that way. You certainly couldn't have driven on that tire for any length of time. Where were you parked before leaving to drive home?"

"At the Carthage University Campus. I have classes on Tuesday and Thursday afternoons from 1pm until 3. I left there about 3:10 and was on my way home."

Sheriff Henderson stared at his hat, twirling it a couple of times before continuing. "I hope I'm wrong, but I would guess someone took off the taps while you were in class. Did you see anyone hanging around your car or did anything unusual happen that caught your attention?"

"No, not a thing." Anna was puzzled.

"Did you have an argument with anyone that was severe enough to cause them to want revenge?"

Anna's first impulse was to say "not recently" but realized that she would have to divulge something she did not want to—at this point. She answered instead, "No, not at all."

"Well, do you have any enemies, long standing rivalries or anything of that nature?"

"No, not any who hate me enough to wanna kill me. I usually get along with everyone except that dumb crap that hangs with my mom. But there's nothing new about our bickering...nothing more severe than usual." Anna explained.

"What's his name?"

"Charley...Charley Dugan."

"And where does he work?" asked the sheriff.

"He doesn't. Not that I know of...he just hangs around and tries to tell us what to do. Drinks like a fish...er...ah...does a fish drink? Well, he drinks constantly, eats his meals and watches TV at our house most of the time. I think he gets disability benefits or something. He says he can't do any work because of a bad back."

"So he's not married to your mom?"

"No, but that may be about to change. I was hoping not, but I guess Mom needs someone. Wish it were anyone but him," Anna confided.

Sheriff Henderson contemplated what he was told and thoughtfully continued. "Well, I don't have a lot to go on here, but I feel certain your wheel was tampered with, so I would caution you to be extremely careful. Take a hard look at things and if you have second thoughts about anyone—or if anything else unusual happens—call me immediately. Okay?"

Anna could hardly believe what she was hearing, but promised to heed his advice.

"I don't mean to scare you unnecessarily, but your life could be in jeopardy. Have you had any other near misses lately?"

"No, none at all."

"Maybe someone was releasing pent-up anger and used your vehicle just because it was there. Or maybe they got the wrong car. At any rate, you should be alert and maintain cautionary vigilance. The chances seem remote, but you could be the target."

"That *is* kinda scary," Anna replied.

"Yeah, I know. Call me anytime with anything that bothers you. How soon will you be going home?"

"Don't know yet. Soon I hope. I have to get some hay in the barn. Well...ah...no, I guess I won't be doing that anytime soon, will I?" She frowned.

"No, I wouldn't think so, but no rain is forecast anytime soon. Maybe you can find someone else to take care of it for you. Call me if you have concerns...and be careful."

"I will. Thanks," Anna replied.

After Sheriff Henderson left, Janice questioned Anna.

"Why did they call the Sheriff—Troy, the Trojan?"

"Well, you know about Helen of Troy and the Trojan horse?"

"Yeah, I do."

"Well, a Trojan is a person from Troy and known to be tough, determined and courageous. They are also suspected to be someone who might be planning serious harm for you in the future. Troy was really good at an unexpected quarter-back sneak. No, not just good—he was great! Sometimes they called him the Trojan Horse. You know the real Trojan Horse was hollow and full of warriors hiding inside until after it was rolled inside the enemy's gate before they surprised their adversaries and rescued Helen of Troy. They called Troy the Trojan Horse because he was full of surprises too."

"Ah, hah! Very apt. He's also gorgeous with machismo that really grabs you," she said.

Anna agreed. Janice was just now off duty and seemed to be in a hurry to leave.

Was she possibly thinking of catching up with the Trojan? Anna wondered.

Janice came bouncing into Anna's room the next morning with, "Howdy, howdy, howdy! How's my favorite patient?"

"If you mean me, I'm angry at my nurse right now."

"Angry? At me? What did I do?"

"You had bean soup on my menu after I told you emphatically no bean soup," Anna answered. "I had nothing to eat but bean soup for supper last night."

"Oh goodness! I forgot to have it changed. Menus are not my responsibility, actually. But beans are a wonderfully nutritious food...full of protein."

"Maybe so, but it causes a lot of...er...ah...causes a lot of...well, the Russian president."

"What? Are you okay? Did somebody give you the wrong injection or are you just out of your mind? That makes no sense whatsoever. What do you mean: beans cause a lot of the Russian president?"

"Well...his name is "pooh-tin" isn't it?" Anna tried to hide a grin.

Janice stared for a second before bursting into hilarious laughter. "You are so goofy! Besides, women don't do that."

"Yeah, I know. At least that's what I'm told."

They chuckled together.

"By the way, Doc Petersen says you are well enough to go home today. What time would you like to check out of this fabulous hotel?"

"Don't know. I'll try again to get my mom. Haven't been able to get her at all. I don't have transportation now. Don't know how I'll be able to get by without it?" Anna replied dejectedly. "Can't afford any either. I only had liability on my Explorer, so no help there."

"I get off at four this afternoon. I'll be glad to give you a lift if you need it," Janice offered.

"Thanks a lot, Janice. Guess I forgive you for the bean soup. Could I buy you a burger at the Burger Hut when you take me home? Sure would like one myself."

"Great!" Janice was enthusiastic. "It's a date unless someone else shows...like that Gabe guy."

"Then it's definitely a date!" Anna replied, rather subdued. "I'll be ready at four."

"The Doc will be by again to check you out...to make sure you're not looking cross-eyed or something, before you can check out. Be sure you ask for a prescription for a palliative."

"A what?"

"Palliative. A painkiller. You sho gonna need one, honah." Janice spoke with an exaggerated southern accent for emphasis.

Doctor Peterson entered Anna's room at about two that afternoon, after knocking on the door frame. He was a jovial, plump man about fifty with sandy hair and an owlish look.

Staring at Anna over his glasses, he asked in a loud voice, "Ready to go home?"

"Absolutely!" She answered.

"Well...let me see here."

He had her to touch the tip of her nose with each index finger separately, after closing her eyes. She endured staring at the tip of his finger as it approached the end of her nose, in addition to several other tests to check her reflexes. He asked if standing or walking caused her to be dizzy and if she had a headache.

Seemingly getting satisfactory answers, he continued, "Well, you've had a very traumatic experience, but you were lucky. I believe an obviously healthy, active young lady, such as yourself, should have a rapid recovery, as long as you're careful for a few weeks and don't try to make your car fly again."

He chuckled. His belly jiggled "Don't do any strenuous labor and when you start feeling extra pain because of some activity, stop doing it. There will, of course, be pain. I have a prescription here that will take care of that. Just take as directed and let me know if any unusual problems arise. Your ribs and arm are cracked, not broken. But give them special care until they have healed completely. I'll see you in two weeks unless you have a problem before then. You can make an appointment with my receptionist before you leave."

He extended his hand, saying, "I hope you do as well as I expect."

"Thank you, Doctor Peterson. I will follow your instructions precisely to the letter. I have felt very safe under your care."

He smiled and nodded as he turned and walked away.

Anna wanted to shout but kept it to a loud whisper. "Yes! I'm getting out of here—into the world of sunshine and singing birds—but," she cautioned herself, "don't forget the heat and all those problem you have to solve out there. Oh, well, c' est la vie—that's life."

At least being cooped up in a boring hospital room was no

longer one of her problems.

Anticipating her release from the hospital, Anna had washed the jeans she was wearing during the accident along with her blood stained shirt and undies, drying them in her bathroom. They were wrinkled and still stained, but she had no other choice. She had been unable to get her mother on the phone and had no one else to bring her other clothes.

Well, Janice would have... if I had thought to ask her in time, she told herself.

These would have to do until she got home. She only had $15.27 in her purse. That would buy her and Janice a burger. She hoped no one she knew would see her at the Burger Hut looking as she did.

A few minutes after four, Janice appeared carrying a plastic Wal-Mart bag. She stopped short as she saw Anna.

"Wowee! Who's your fashion consultant? Good job...but you're wrinkled and still stained." She laughed. "Here!" She handed Anna the plastic sack. "They're your very own. I went by to see your mother to get some of your clothes, but no one was there. I jimmied the door and got your things anyway. Hope you can overlook that bit of breaking-and-entering. It was for a good cause."

Anna laughed. "You are a piece of work, Janice. I love you bunches. And what you did is easier to forgive than bean soup for dinner. As a matter of fact, I may award you with a medal. 'Greatest thief of the year'!"

They laughed together.

"I would have loaned you some of my clothes, but I don't think my size-12 jeans would snug your size-8 butt. And ya gotta know, snug is the ultimate goal."

Anna was glad to have her own clean clothes. The blouse Janice had brought was sleeveless and loose-fitting. It had buttons down the front, making it easier to get over her splinted arm.

"Thanks so much, Janice. I owe you."

"No, you don't. Let's go."

After ordering their burgers and drinks, Anna sat sipping her Coke. She looked up to see familiar blue eyes watching her from across the room. There was a trace of a smile as Gabe slowly lifted his arm—thumb and index finger making a zero—to salute her.

Anna felt her body tense. She thought, *God, I must have nerves even in my hair. It feels like it's standing on end!*

Janice noticed Anna's slip of composure. She turned and saw Gabe. "Woo—hoo! Aren't we glad for 'snug' now?" she whispered.

Almost six feet tall with hair as black as midnight and eyes as blue as the mid-morning sky, Gabe stood and walked toward them. His bare arms were muscular and tanned, disclosing long hours in the sun. He walked with the agility and vigilance of a hunter, yet with the confident stride of a man who knew himself well and did not find himself lacking. It was obvious he made no apologies for who he was—nor what he had or had not done.

Leaving a couple of guys at his table, his eyes never left Anna's face as he approached her. "I'm glad to see you're well enough to leave the hospital. It could have been so much worse," he said.

Anna hoped she sounded more relaxed than she felt. "Thank you. Thank you for all you did. If you had not been there, I might well have been much less fortunate. I'm glad I didn't involve you in my metal crunching fiasco. Have you met my most competent nurse and very good friend, Janice Higgins?" she asked, turning to Janice.

"Well, I spoke with her a time or two at the hospital. Hi, Janice."

"Hi, Gabe. Have a seat."

"Actually, I have an appointment that I'm already late for. I just wanted to offer Anna any assistance she might need on the farm while she's unable to take care of things herself."

"I appreciate the offer, but I think we can manage to hold things together for the few weeks I'm unable to do the heavy stuff. Thanks though."

His eyes narrowed momentarily. His lips firmed into a hard line. "Well, let me know if I can help." He turned, smiled at Janice and walked away, saying, "Have a good one."

"You too," Janice answered. Wide-eyed, she stared at Anna. After a moment, she exclaimed, "What's wrong with you? You goose! You had a golden opportunity thrown in your lap and you trashed it. Why?"

Anna swallowed hard. She steadied her hands and took a sip of her Coke.

"There's history between you two isn't there?"

Janice noticed dampness on Anna's cheeks, "And he still matters to you, doesn't he? You idiot! Why turn away from that gorgeous hunk who obviously wants you too?"

Anna sniffed, cleared her throat and replied, "Janice, that's one topic I don't intend to discuss, if you don't mind."

"Well, I do mind! But another time then."

Neither Janice nor Anna said much to each other until they reached Anna's house.

"There's still no one here! You'll be all alone. Why not come stay with me?" Janice asked.

"I'll be okay. I'll be careful and if I need anything, I'll call. I really appreciate you, Janice. Thanks a lot."

"Oh, that's okay. It's my pleasure to help tend a hurt and needy goose." Janice laughed. "Please do call me if you need anything...anything at all. By the way, why isn't your mother here? Did she die or is she in a trauma center somewhere? I mean...you could use some help here...just lifting a chair or reaching into the cabinet will be hard...or impossible, you know!"

"Don't worry about me, Janice. I'm accustomed to fending for myself. And I'm really glad that goofus that hangs with her is not here. Thanks for your concern...and everything else. I'll see you soon."

"Okay. But take special care for a while. Don't do long, overextended reaches or heavy lifting. Why don't you just call Gabe? He has a long reach, I'll bet." Janice smiled mischievously. "Take care," she said and was gone.

Chapter Two

Left alone, Anna began to worry about the problems she now faced with no mode of transportation, except her horse. Hah! She tried to visualize riding Smoky to class or to work.

She had no money with which to buy a car and the paycheck she would get from the hospital tomorrow would be her last. Hired under a special plan sponsored by the hospital, especially for college students during summer semesters, she had been lucky to get the job at all. The program had been designed for students interested in a medical career. The hospital hired on a temporary basis for the summer—then after monitoring them for three months, picked those students who had the work ethic and abilities the hospital desired. After hiring all the applicants from the pre-med pool this year, they still needed a few more employees. Thus Anna had been selected even though she was an accounting major. But the summer was now over and she was without a job, without transportation, without money and handicapped by a few cracked bones. What on earth would happen to her next? It was scary.

Anna could collect unemployment compensation for a few weeks, but with that being her only source of income, no one would lend her money to buy a vehicle. What could she do? In order to buy the old Explorer, Anna had already sold two of the other horses her father had given her. She hadn't wanted to but it had been necessary. Transportation was vital. No way, however, would she ever give up Smoky! Not even if it meant riding a bicycle in the worst kind of weather. And she knew her mom would not spring for anything that would allow her to become more independent.

Anna fretted. *Mom would much rather keep me elbow deep*

in work on the farm...and that's okay. I like farm work, but she wants firm control over all I do and all I earn. At least it seems that way. ...But she sure likes her independence! Where is she now? Did she even care that I could have been killed in that wreck? How long has she been gone anyway?

Checking the refrigerator and finding nothing there except several eggs, a tub of margarine, some stale cheese and catchup, Anna supposed her mother had been gone several days.

Probably flew the coop the day after I went flying, she thought, remembering how she had flown end over end in her SUV. She felt an unexpected longing for her old, worn out Ford.

"Guess I had better check the animals." she muttered. "Good thing my legs aren't broken too."

Anna noticed a new watering container, an upside down gallon jug with a tray underneath, setting just outside the kitchen door. It was mostly filled with water. Beside it was a similar feeder for dog food. It, too, was more than half full.

Surprised, she thought, *Wow! That's a new one for Mom—to worry about my dog. She must be coming home to fill them periodically. Wonder where Miss Kitty is getting her food.* Anna wondered about her fluffy Persian cat.

A noise behind her interrupted her thoughts. As she turned, Anna saw her exuberant pup in time to avoid his launch into her arms. She slipped behind a post on the patio until she could calm the whining, jumping ball of fur with flailing legs, her Old English Sheepdog, Casey.

After he had calmed a bit, she knelt and patted him on the head, saying, "What a good boy you are! I'm so happy to see you." Rubbing him down and hugging him, she continued, "You are so smart and so shaggy. You could really use a bath too."

Anna knew it didn't matter what words she used—only the tone and affection accompanying them counted.

Casey was still whining and wanting to jump on her, but she was able to restrain him. After a few minutes of telling him how wonderful he was, she said, "Go, boy!"

Casey took off running at a fevered pace with ears flapping up and down. Mostly pointing up it seemed. His tongue began to hang out of his mouth as his breathing increased. He loved to run while she exclaimed how fast he was, encouraging him with excited tones and phrases he seemed to understand.

"Wow! What a jumper! Look at you go! Whee! Watch that! You're so fast! I'll bet you can catch *yourself* runnin' those circles!" she yelled, as he ran ever enlarging loops around her.

She supposed he would run for hours if she continued. But after several minutes, calling, "Okay, boy, let's go," they headed for the barn to check on Smoky.

She noticed, as they walked across the yard how nice it looked. Someone had recently mowed it and had done a good job of it too.

Who? she wondered.

Her mother never mowed and she'd stake her life on a bet that Old Charley hadn't done it either.

"Must have hired someone." she muttered.

Smoky was grazing just outside his lot in the pasture with his back to her. He was a jet black, gelding, somewhere around thirteen hands high—sleek and shiny—with the look of good ancestry and excellent care. He had been a smoky gray color as a colt, but his coat darkened as he grew older causing those who hadn't known, to ask, "Why the name Smoky?"

"Smoky!"

He turned and stared, his mouth full of grass.

"Come here, boy!"

After a moment, he started in her direction, bowing his head low then raising it high. Again and again, he bowed while prancing towards her, as she had taught him to do.

Anna laughed delightedly. "You handsome devil!" she shouted.

Appreciating the compliment, he stopped prancing, whinnied once and kicked his rear high into the air several times before trotting up to the fence where she waited.

Anna rubbed his face and patted his neck. "Sorry I don't have an apple, but here, I did get these," she apologized reaching into her pocket to retrieve several cubes of sugar.

She wanted to crawl through the fence so she could hug him properly, but with her fractures it was best to keep the fence between them. Smoky was a gelding not a stallion—who would be expected to exhibit more aggressive behavior. But Smoky, none the less, occasionally revealed a tendency to be fractious. He was not overly large, but very quick. It was sometimes difficult to anticipate his intentions before being bumped or pushed and Anna didn't need any more bruises just now.

Her father had bought Smoky for her as a colt when she was fourteen, shortly before his fatal heart attack. The loss of her father was a life-shattering event for Anna. Everyone had said Sam Shelton had been too young to die that way.

She had even heard one of his friends say, "It was that harpy caused it. Living with her would give anybody a heart attack."

The friend had been speaking of her mother, Josey. Anna remembered how she had always harped at her and her father both. Her mother seemed to be unable to share their happiness. Anna had often wondered why. Josey had been an only child as was Anna. But Josey had lost both of her parents—her father while serving in the military overseas and her mother in a car accident a few months later—when Josey was still a very small child. Anna knew that had to be traumatic for Josey and to add to her trauma, she was then placed in the care of her aging grandparents, both of whom died before she was twelve. She was then placed in a foster home, but evidently was extremely unhappy there. She severed all ties with the family as soon as possible and would never discuss her life with them. So far as Anna knew, her mother had no relatives she felt kinship with. So why didn't she value what she had or could have had with her husband and daughter? It was a puzzle Anna mulled over often. Was Josey afraid of losing every one she became attached to or was she just so angry and bitter she couldn't love again? As far as Josey was concerned, her past was a closed book. She would never disclose any part of it. Anna often thought she herself might have been much like her mother if it had not been for her loving relationship with her father. She determined that if she every married she would have many children and give them lots of love and care. A strong, supporting family seemed vital to her.

Before her father's death Anna had been trying to train Smoky to do special things, like take a hat off her head or prance and bow to the audience at barrel racing competitions. Everyone had laughed and said it couldn't be done. Everyone except her father.

"If Roy Rogers could train Trigger to do all that he did, Smoky can surely do some of it. Just keep trying. We'll see what he can learn," he had said.

And so Anna had kept trying and hoping.

She grieved for a long time after her father died. He had been her best friend. Smoky was her only enjoyment and the only thing that could take her mind off her tragic loss. Smoky seemed to understand her need to get lost in playing and he cooperated fully. After training for hundreds of hours and overcoming some of Anna's own uncertainties, he became the main attraction at all the rodeos Anna had entered—the showoff who drew the crowds. He "did good" for her and she loved him for it.

Anna talked to Smoky for several minutes, rubbing him as best she could through the fence. When the last of the sugar cubes were gone, she told him how much she had missed him and that she would be back soon.

As she walked around the lot to the front of the barn, Anna saw newly stacked bales of Bermuda grass and rows of freshly baled alfalfa hay. Someone had cut and baled the field she had so worried about. They had even hauled and stacked the rest of the Bermuda in the barn. Someone was on the ball and very much appreciated.

"Hallelujah!" she cried. "One of my major problems is solved! Wonder what that cost?"

After Sam Shelton had passed, Anna knuckled down and took on responsibilities she had not shouldered before. Her father taught her from early childhood how to do things and it had been her pleasure to help him take care of his numerous chores. Still, there were lots of other things to learn by herself. She had gotten information from the agricultural extension division at the university about how to plant and fertilize, about which seeds were the best for almost any crop in the area and about when to cut hay and when to bale it for the most nutritional value.

Finding her father's old equipment manuals, she had learned how to fix most mechanical problems. Even taught herself how to re-time a baler, something a lot of the older farmers complained they couldn't do.

She found it helpful to write down the date the papa and mama cows "got together," in order to determine exactly when to expect the babies. Close supervision at that critical time gave them a much better chance for survival. Anna rarely missed an expected birth by more than a day and was always watchful for any unexpected problems.

She loved the farm, the animals, the birds, the sunshine and the rain, most everything Mother Nature had to offer—even the work. If only Josey had been happy. But her mother loathed the farm as much as Anna loved it. At first she feared her mother would sell the farm, but she finally decided Josey held on because of the extra income she earned. Anna expected her mom to eventually pitch in and get involved—to help with all the necessary chores. But Josey never did.

Farm work was hard. The weather was sometimes uncooperative and crops failed often. Cattle markets were unpredictable and Josie didn't like to get dirty. Anna would be the first to admit it could be a sweaty, gritty job, but oh...how good she felt after slamming that last bale into its slot in the barn just before a loud clap of thunder sounded and rain began pelting

21

the tin on the roof. The smell of that unique aroma in the air as the rain settled the dust was a treat in itself. But, altogether, it was better than winning a football game. Maybe even better than winning the lottery. After all, it was—for the rancher—high stakes gambling...and she had just beaten the house.

It hadn't taken long before Anna was running everything on the farm and all was going well. The neighbors seemed surprised. The steer calves were sold each year and all the best heifers were kept to replace the older, less productive mothers. The herd was growing and quality of the cattle had greatly improved. The additional income Anna was producing allowed her and her mother to live comfortably. They were financially okay, but Anna knew a regular, more dependable income was needed. They might encounter a couple of bad years that could cause them to sell a large portion of the cattle and then too, the equipment was getting old. The price of new equipment was staggering.

So Anna had decided she must enroll in college after graduating high school and take as many courses as she could handle—day or night—until she could earn a degree. She would become an accountant. Eventually, a CPA, maybe. She had hopes of getting a good job. One that would give them more stability even though she still planned to keep and run the farm. Maybe, she could cut back some on the numbers in the herd and, therefore, some of the work...or perhaps hire some help if it became too much.

But there was another reason for wanting that well-paying job. Anna wanted cash of her own, some money to spend on necessary items for herself and...well...for things she just wanted. Her mother was tight-fisted with all the money Anna had worked so hard for. She gave her daughter as little of it as possible and grumbled about that.

"It's my place and my cows. And you need to earn your keep," she stated sourly when Anna questioned why she couldn't have a little extra.

If she got a paycheck in her own name, Josey could not say it was hers and keep the better part of it. Anna had looked forward with great anticipation to her graduation and a good job with a steady income all her own.

What she hadn't counted on was meeting the blue-eyed captain of the football team, who had them both looking at other options by the end of their junior year—options that might require Josey to hire and pay for help or else learn to run her own farm. It wouldn't be easy for Anna to leave the farm and her mother, but the magnetic attraction to Gabe and their emotional involvement became an overpowering force that had to be reckoned with.

Breaking from her reverie, Anna found herself wandering out in the cattle pasture, watching the herd graze. The calves were mostly around five months old now, looking fat and fit. Cows, chewing their cuds, watched her as they rested in the shade. Others paid her no mind at all. How had she arrived at the pond? Past memories had absorbed her thoughts so completely, she hadn't been cognizant of what she was doing. She supposed it was a necessary part of healing, before she could eventually put the past aside and get on with her life.

Seeing Gabe that afternoon and actually talking to him, triggered all those hurtful thoughts and angry feelings again. It tore at her heart to find they reappeared, seemingly as strong as ever. Despite knowing she would never rid herself of the disturbing emotions he stirred in her, she knew she would never let him close again. He had shattered her heart and her life, put her in such despair she was physically unable to function for months. She thought she would never recover. But, slowly and after great effort, she pulled herself together and was now able to convince the world and herself that it was all behind her—over and done with. She prayed that was true.

She had first met him at her then-best friend's birthday party. And Carla had made it known to all that he was already taken, tattooed with her brand. He was gorgeous enough to break a girl's heart at first glance, but Anna respected her friend's claim as sacred.

He had enrolled as a junior at Carnegie High that fall and was reputed to be "one hell of an athlete." Carla and Anna felt lucky to have him in their class. Gabe Whittier was his name and his family had just bought a cattle ranch close by.

Carla told Anna his father was a financial adviser with Edward Jones and Company in Oklahoma City, about thirty miles away. She thought Gabe was going to help run the ranch, which could be a good investment and generate income for Gabe as well as his father.

He became the starting quarterback on the football team and was indeed one hell of an athlete. Though the team never "won state" while he quarterbacked, he was thought to be as good or better than "Troy the Trojan." Everyone seemed to agree his teammates had fallen a little short of the support Gabe needed to gain the championship title. In addition to his athletic prowess, he was friendly, witty, an excellent student and a popular one, always willing to pitch in and support a good cause. Everyone liked him.

Since Anna and Carla were best friends at the time, they usually double dated. They also studied together many evenings, so Anna got to know Gabe pretty well. Anna couldn't help coveting her best friend's sweetheart, but she kept hands off and pretended not to notice his presence—as far as she was able.

She tried to limit any direct conversation with him to nothing more than a casual, "Hi, Gabe" or "How ya doin'?"

After a few month, however, Carla met Billy Freemont, Gabe's exact opposite. Loud, boisterous, and pushy, always drinking and cutting classes, he ran with a bunch of hoodlums. He was good looking in a greasy, tough sort of way. After a few wolf whistles, sexy winks and slaps on the butt, Carla finally confirmed the proverbial axiom—girls like the bad boys. Carla started dating Freemont. Anna disliked him and his crowd and stopped double dating with her. Soon she saw little of Carla at all.

Not long after the break, Gabe had asked Anna to accompany him to a movie. Her heart raced.

She hoped her voice wouldn't crack as she casually waited a few seconds before answering, "My schedule is pretty tight, but...yeah, I guess I can squeeze in a movie."

It was a joy to be with him. He was funny, considerate and attentive. And furthering her appreciation of him, he bought the large size of popcorn and soft drinks. He didn't seem to be hurting from the loss of Carla. On the way home, he addressed the subject.

"You don't run with Carla any more do you?" he asked.

"No, I really don't care for Billy or his buddies."

"Neither do I," he responded.

Anna couldn't help herself. "Do you miss her?"

"Truthfully? No. Not in the least. As a matter of fact...," he had reached for her hand and gave it a squeeze. "I had always wanted it to be you I was dating, not Carla. I wasn't sure you would date me because of your friendship with her...and I just kept dating her to be near you."

Anna had been holding her breath, not knowing if she could believe what she was hearing.

"You must think I'm crazy...or at least a 'wuss'," he continued.

Anna finally burst out laughing.

He looked at her quizzically and said, "Well, I guess that *is* rather bizarre."

"No! No, Gabe, I was just laughing because I wanted to be with you too and was trying so hard not to show it."

They laughed together. He put his arm around her and pulled her close. It felt wonderful. Wonderfully right.

Always a couple after that, they had become seriously interested in a lasting relationship by the end of the school year. Gabe had wanted to become an architect, but loved ranching as well. After several helpful discussions with his father, he had decided to attend the university at night. He could hire a crew and build a few houses even now, before taking a degree and still run cattle on the side. He had started taking classes—day and night—whenever he could fit them into his schedule during summers, even a few night courses during his senior year at high school.

It was at the beginning of their senior year that Gabe had asked Anna to marry him. She was ecstatic! But she knew her mother would object strenuously.

"Mom'll have a conniption fit, but I don't care. I'll marry you anyway...nothing would make me happier!" she answered joyfully.

It was true. Josey had a screaming fit, saying all kinds of bad things about Gabe. "I am your mother and I absolutely forbid you to marry him!" was her final edict.

Anna knew it was not Gabe her mother had objected to, but rather the fact that Anna would leave her. She would have no one to do her work. She needed Anna. Anna thought she looked absolutely terrified.

"Mom, we won't be getting married until we have both graduated. That's almost a year away. Even then we won't be going far...we'll still be here for you. All your needs will be met. And I love him dearly!"

Anna had tried to soothe her mother's anxiety. Nothing seemed to work. She was quite sure the fact that she loved Gabe completely meant nothing to her mother.

"No! It won't be the same. You're still a baby. I need you here. You'll not abandon your mother, I forbid it." She raved on and on.

Anna wondered, *If I promise to give her all the money I earn will she sanction our marriage?*

It was the slave labor she provided her mother that Josey wouldn't give up, not the enjoyment of her daughter's company. Anna's anger rose.

"You cannot forbid me. I am an adult...of legal age and I will marry him whether you approve or not. So get over it!" Anna told her more harshly than she had intended.

It was only the first of many such arguments. As the year progressed, Josey tried lots of tricks even pretending to have health problems, such as: an inability to see or to walk or drive—anything she thought might influence Anna to reconsider.

Mostly, Anna ignored her ravings, but occasionally had told her in no uncertain terms the marriage would happen. She tried to make light of Josey's objectionable behavior when the topic came up with Gabe. She hadn't wanted him to think he was the objection.

While Anna's and Gabe's personalities seemed to complement each other's, Carla and Billy had been having a stormy relationship. It was an on-again, off-again affair that evidenced the "off" side more than once with Carla sporting a black eye and other telltale bruises at school. She skipped more classes than she attended and was failing most of her subjects.

Gabe and Anna had been doing great. They had a goal in mind. Gabe was a straight "A" student, while Anna had all "A"s with the exception of one "A-." Going about their business with a dedicated perseverance, they hardly partied at all, though Anna always went to Gabe's football games and they found time for an occasional movie or burger at the Burger Hut. Copious amounts of time studying together had been fun and much had been learned about each other's likes and dislikes. Anna believed they were well suited for life together.

There had been a great turnout at commencement exercises when the school year finally ended. Gabe gave the valedictory address and Anna was salutatorian of their graduating class. It had been a time to celebrate. Their dream of a small, but beautiful, wedding was about to be realized. They were both excitedly anxious and eager for the day they had worked so hard to prepare for. All their friends congratulated them for their achievements and their upcoming nuptials. Most senior class parents were there at the final ceremonies. Josey, for her part, claimed to be unable to get out of bed.

All students were to return the following day to clear out their lockers and pick up their grades. Anna waited until most of the students would be finished, thereby avoiding the crowd. She cleaned out her locker, leaving the key in the lock and hurried toward the gym. Rounding the row of lockers, she stopped—astounded! Her books dropped with a crash. Unable to believe what she saw, her hand flew over her mouth and a low guttural cry sprang from her throat! Gabe stood with his arms around Carla, who was kissing him on the mouth.

Hearing Anna's books drop, they turned, pulling apart. An anguished "No!" escaped her lips. She fled, fighting tears, leaving her books where they had fallen on the floor.

Gabe ran after her, calling for her to wait. "Anna, please wait! Honey, don't go! Let me explain!"

Anna ran faster than ever. There could be no explanation capable of wiping away the raging torment that ripped through her.

She drove home faster than was safe. Gabe almost beat her there. He slammed on his brakes and was out of his car, grabbing her arm before she could enter the house.

"Anna, what's the matter with you? You know how much I love you. Can't you at least listen while I explain?"

She hesitated. Gabe began immediately.

"Carla's pregnant with Billy's baby, but he won't acknowledge it's his. She's beside herself, not knowing what to do. She doesn't want her parents to know—or anyone else, really. So she wanted to know if I knew of a doctor and if I could lend her some money. She didn't know of anyone else to ask. I told her no, but I cautioned her to make sure she knew what she really wanted before doing anything she might regret. Billy may come back and want the baby. Who knows? She's probably better off if he doesn't. Hell! She waylaid me before I knew what was happening. And... yeah...I guess I felt sorry for her, but good god, she means nothing to me, Annie. Please, sweetheart, trust me enough to at least verify it with her. She promised she'd come by tomorrow and explain, even though she's embarrassed to let you know."

Anna relaxed a bit. Wiping the tears from her cheeks, she felt the weight of betrayal lift as embarrassment replaced it.

"I'm so sorry." She tried to smile. "You just seemed so together...wrapped up in each other. When she kissed you on your mouth I wanted to die."

Gabe had put his arms around her. Holding her close, he said, "Always know I love you, Annie. There'll never be anyone to take your place. Not ever!"

Turning her face up to his, he kissed her gently. She put her arms around him and apologized again. "I'm sorry Gabe. I feel like a fool. It was just so sudden and so... right there in my face, I just lost it."

He hugged her tightly. "Let's go get a soda."

"I look a fright. And I need to feed the livestock. Besides, I'm still shaking. And I know you need to tend your cattle as well."

"Okay, sweetheart, tomorrow then."

He kissed her again, saying "I love you, Annie. Life's nothing without you."

He reached in his car and handed her the books she had dropped and left behind. Then he smiled, his mouth forming a kiss as he winked and drove away.

God, he is so gorgeous, she thought. She could hardly believe her luck. He was to be her husband...and she wanted him...forever.

Josey had miraculously recovered from yesterday's mysterious malady that had held her bed-fast. She had watched Gabe and Anna through the window and was in Anna's face the minute she opened the door, demanding to know what had happened.

"Wha'd that worthless piece of crap do? He hurt you didn't

29

he? He made you cry! I told ya it wouldn' work. You're not gonna marry em! He's no good—tryin' ta break up our family an all.... Wha'd he do?"

"Not now, Mom. I need some time to myself and I need to tend to Smoky and the cattle."

"You tell me what I wanna know!" Josey shouted. "I'm your mother and I gotta right ta know!"

After all that had happened, Anna could stand no more.

"Shut your mouth. I'll tell you in my own good time or not at all!"

She had thought, as she walked away, *this is like an episode of Jerry Springer—not the way I want to live. I have to try and be nicer to her.*

The loud blaring of a horn pulled Anna from reliving her past. She hadn't wanted to remember any of it, but she was glad to be spared remembering the rest. It had been soul withering and memories of it sometimes caused weeks of despondency. She wondered why she had to descend into hell occasionally and let those horrible thoughts and feelings plague her into oblivion.

She turned from staring at the herd of cattle to see her mother's older—but still nice—Lincoln Town Car slide up to the front of their garage.

"Hey, git up ta this 'ere house! What're ya doin' anyway?" Old Charley yelled, as he got out of the driver's side of her mother's vehicle.

Not wanting to talk to Josey or Charley, Anna turned back to watch the cattle graze. She spied Daisy, a special cow she had turned into a pet, ambling her way. Daisy had given birth to a calf about a month before, somewhat out of sync with the schedule of deliveries for the rest of the herd. It was Daisy's first calf and she had been slow to breed. She had a difficult delivery, but Anna had been there every moment to make sure all ended well.

The calf was a beautiful red heifer with a white spot in her

30

forehead and white stocking feet. She was becoming as much a pet as Daisy. Anna must name her.

Daisy stopped in front of Anna and started sniffing around for a treat.

"Oh, shoot! I don't have a thing today." Anna apologized, feeling around in her pocket.

She found a forgotten sweet potato picked up from her walk through the garden. Breaking it into pieces, she offered them to Daisy, who swallowed them almost without chewing—which would come later. Mama cow stood very still as Anna rubbed her down. Several minutes later, Daisy turned to nudge her baby away from nursing and pushed her towards Anna. Baby didn't know what to expect. She moved off to the side. Daisy followed, getting on the other side of her, she butted her again towards Anna, who didn't know what was going on either. She had never before seen Daisy butt her baby.

Finally, the calf stopped in front of Anna. Then Daisy, seemingly satisfied, started contentedly licking her all over.

Anna laughed. "Oh...it's show time! Do you want me to rub her too?" she asked.

It sure wouldn't hurt a thing to show Daisy how much she appreciated her baby. Falling to her knees, she started rubbing the calf and talking to it solicitously. After Anna and Daisy had done a thorough job of washing and brushing Daisy's baby, Daisy started grazing and slowly moving back towards the herd.

Later Anna walked back past Smoky's pasture. He had grazed farther away and didn't notice her. She started walking towards the house. She was not in a hurry. She didn't want Old Charley to think he could in any way tell her what to do.

About 30 minutes later, as she neared the house, the door flew open.

Old Charley, with several days of scraggly beard, loudly exclaimed, "I thought you wuz beat up bad. Looks ta me like yur a doin' fine. Why ain't supper ready?"

Anna ignored him altogether and to avoid him, went around

31

the house to enter through the front door. There sat her beautiful fluffy cat, Miss Kitty. Anna picked her up and while cuddling her, told her what a beautiful kitty she really was. Miss Kitty sniffed at Anna's breath and purred contentedly.

"Ah hah! You now know I had a hamburger for lunch, don't you? Well don't expect one for dinner. The cupboards are bare."

After a few minutes, Anna and Miss Kitty entered the house. Her mother was checking out the refrigerator when they walked into the kitchen.

"Well, how come there ain't nothin' in here to eat?" she demanded.

"Mom! I just got out of the hospital this afternoon. I have no transportation and very little money. What do you think I am? A magician? But where were *you*? Why didn't *you* leave *me* something in the frig?"

"You 'er in the hospital. I thought you 'er bad hurt and they'd take care a ya a lot longer than they did.. How wuz I ta know you'd get home 'fore I did?"

"Thanks a lot. I'm glad to know you thought about my welfare," Anna replied.

Old Charley was listening from the doorway and butted in, "Well, ya cud a bought some grocers instid a gettin' 'em sorry ol' dog dishes ya got. And it must have costed plenty to get that hay baled and put 'n the barn."

Anna immediately wondered who had bought and filled Casey's water and food containers and taken care of the hay. Old Charley had just told her it wasn't her mom. She already knew he would never have made such a nice gesture.

"Gimme some money and I'll go git some grocers," Dugan continued.

Josey looked in her purse and took out a ten and a five dollar bill. Looking at Anna, she demanded, "Gimme what 'cha got and it'll maybe be enough."

Taking a deep breath, Anna handed over her last bit of cash—$3.37.

Charley was gone about forty-five minutes, returning with a small bag of potatoes, a loaf of bread, a jug of milk and a six pack of beer. Though it was difficult, Anna held her tongue. It cut to the bone to think she had in any way contributed to Old Charley's alcohol consumption. Now she knew why Dugan had volunteered to go and buy the groceries.

Josey told Anna to call her when supper was ready. She had been, "ridin' all day and needed a rest."

"Mom, I'm not sure I can grip these potatoes firmly enough to peel them. I have a cracked left arm and I'm not supposed to lift anything heavy or exert any pressure until it has healed. Besides it hurts."

"Aw...I'm sure that won't hurt ya none. Taters don't weigh nothin'."

She left, heading for the bedroom.

Anna peeled the potatoes without too much discomfort. She found an onion, a can of beans in the cupboard and boiled the eggs she'd found in the refrigerator. It might be okay for supper, but she wondered what they would have for breakfast.

She found Old Charley asleep in the recliner when she went to call her mother to eat, the third can of beer loosely gripped in his hand.

Good, Anna thought, *maybe he'll sleep and not eat a thing.* But when Josey called him, he hurried to the table, not even washing up first.

Anna was desolate. She longed for her dad. How had they let things fall into such a deplorable condition? Her mom had not always been so hard to live with. When Josey was very small she remembered how pretty her mom looked and how nice it was to hear her laugh. Except Josey had never liked the farm and wasn't about to give up her idea of moving to town and throwing more parties. Her mother and father began to quarrel often. It grew worse. Finally, they stopped quarreling. They didn't speak any more. Her parents had slowly grown apart. They became strangers to each other.

Her father would have been appalled to see the present relationship between Anna and her mother. He would never have believed that Josey would tolerate a man such as Dugan—that she had accepted his behavior and began to treat Anna as he did. She had even, at times, started talking like Charley. Did she have no pride?

Anna couldn't bear to live with her anymore. She had to escape! But how? Life wasn't giving her many opportunities at the moment.

Chapter Three

The next morning Anna foraged in her almost depleted garden. Finding a couple of large butternut squash, she washed, sliced and baked them with margarine, sugar and cinnamon for breakfast. Served with toast, they would have to do.

Janice called early to inquire about Anna's well-being.

"Thought you might be needing your paycheck. I'm off today and can play the chauffeur if you need one," Janice offered.

Anna thanked her and promised she would be ready at 10 o'clock when Janice would arrive.

She did indeed arrive at 10—her hair freshly cut and shampooed. Cropped so short that it barely touched her cheekbones in front. Soft black curls loosely covered her scalp.

"Oh, how beautiful! I love your new do! You look like that lovely actress...uh...I can't think of her name right now. But you look gorgeous!"

Janice laughed, obviously pleased.

As Anna was preparing to leave, her mother handed her a piece of paper.

"What's this?" Anna already knew.

"It's a grocery list. Don't cha know we're completely out 'a groceries?"

"Yes, Mom, I know. But, I can't buy all the groceries This will be my last check. I need everything I can save until I get a job and figure out how to get a car or truck...something to drive. You have dad's insurance and the money from the cattle we sell. Can't you at least buy part of these?"

"The cattle are mine. Ya live here! Ya gotta pay fer yur keep."

35

"I know, Mom, but I do all the farm work and take care of your cows. It's a lot of hard work. That should count for something! Especially, when I have had an accident and need help. And what about Old Charley? Does he pay for what he eats? Why not? He doesn't do a darn thing around here!"

Dugan stepped forward and took the offensive since he really had no defense.

"If ya hadn't been drivin' suh dang fast or paid more 'tention to what yu're a doin', ya wudna had no wreck," he declared. And if'n it's money ya need, we kin sell that damn horse of yourn to buy the grocers."

Anna began to panic. She couldn't bear to lose Smoky. Especially not now after everything else she had lost.

"You can't sell my horse! You have no right. He's mine. My dad gave him to me. Besides, Smoky hates your guts. He'd kick your teeth out!"

Seeing Charley's chipped and darkened teeth, as he swaggered, Anna thought that might be a blessing.

"Oh, I'd have someun' else load 'em. D'ya thank I'm not smart enough to figger that out? 'Sides, we do have a right ta sell that durn critter."

Janice, who was standing by silently clinching her fists, was unable to stand it any longer. Reaching in her pocket, she pulled out her phone, "Why don't I just call the sheriff and he can tell you in a very few minutes if you have the right to sell Anna's horse."

Charley jumped erect, staring at Janice. Anna could see fear in his eyes.

He's afraid of the law! He must be wanted for something. I need to ask Sheriff Henderson to check his record.

"Well, now, who pulled yore chain? Git offen this property. You got no biznez 'ere," he demanded.

"I have as much right here as you, dirtbag! And I'll go when I'm ready!" Janice said in a very even, firm voice. She started punching in numbers on her cell phone.

Charley backed off. "Now there ain't no reason ta git the law out here. We ain't gonna sell 'em rat now."

Janice continued to let the phone ring. Someone answered and she asked, "Could I speak with Sheriff Henderson, please? This is Janice Higgins."

Charley quickly left, walking around to the back side of the house. Was he afraid the sheriff might want to speak with him on the phone?

Janice finished her phone conversation, "No, I need to speak with Troy directly. Please have him call me." She left her cell number.

Josey went in the house and closed the door.

Janice took Anna's good arm and with a tight, mischievous grin and a glint in her thickly lashed brown eyes, said, "Come on Chiquita. Let's make tracks."

Anna dejectedly got into Janice's pretty, red Mustang—tears in her eyes, staring at the grocery list she still held in her hand.

"That'll take most of your check, won't it?" Janice asked, looking at the long list.

"Just about."

"Why don't you buy what you need for yourself and let the rest go?"

"It wouldn't work. If I just bought a little, I'd still have to share it and it would all be gone in no time at all. Then, I would just have to buy some more or do without."

"Well, hell! Just move in with me!" Janice became enraged.

"I can't pay my share, Janice. And I can't leave Smoky. They *will* sell him. I have to find a job and I have to somehow get a vehicle so I can get to work and back."

"Okay, we'll find you a job. We'll get a copy of the Gazette and see what's listed in the classifieds. If you get a job, I can drive you to work for a time, maybe. We'll figure it out."

"Janice, you're a dear friend and make my life livable. I don't want to impose, but looks like I have no choice right now. And I do need transportation to and from the university to take a couple more of my last exams. I'll make it up to you."

At that moment, Janice's cell phone rang. It was Sheriff Henderson. Anna listened to half of the conversation.

"Good mornin', Sheriff" Janice answered. "Yeah, I did call. Anna Shelton needs to come by and file a complaint for harassment against this goober that hangs with her mom. I said *needs* to. She may not want to, but a big guy like you with the help of my very persuasive powers might get that job done. Ya think?"

Anna could hear the sheriff laughing.

"Sure can...be there in about twenty minutes. Thanks a lot." Janice hung up, turning to Anna.

"Janice," Anna began, "I need to think about this. What happens to my mom if I drive Old Charley away? She's so unhappy now. If she has no one—not even Charley—what then?"

"Maybe Old Charley's the reason she's so unhappy," quipped Janice. "Besides, she treats you like a stepchild instead of a daughter. No...not even that good. Why should you care about her unhappiness?" Janice questioned.

"I don't know.... She's my mom and she hasn't always been this way. I just feel maybe somehow she could be different."

They pulled up in front of the sheriff's office. Janice killed the engine, removed the key from the ignition, saying, "Come on Punkin'. You have to do this. Otherwise I won't be able to sit and drink in the intoxicating aura of that absolutely enchanting hunk of manhood called Troy, the Trojan!"

"Janice for god's sake, behave! I'm in a crisis here. Be serious...if you can. And just let me do the talking about Old Charley. Okay?"

That was fine with Janice.

The sheriff didn't normally take complaints himself. Whether it was because he wanted to talk with Janice—as much as she wanted to talk with him—or whether he knew about

Anna's problems and wanted to help, Anna knew she and Janice were being given special treatment.

Anna folded her arms in front of herself and took a deep breath. She felt uncomfortable, as if she had been pushed into making a serious decision not yet carefully considered.

"Have a seat," Henderson said, motioning to the empty chairs in front of his desk. "Could I get you something to drink? Coffee or maybe a soft drink?" Anna sensed the offer was not something he normally did for just anyone.

"I'd like a cup of coffee if it's not too much trouble," Janice replied. Anna abstained.

"Cream and sugar?" he asked.

"Here let me relieve you of that." Janice offered.

They stood together at the coffee bar, filling cups and adding condiments to suit their own tastes.

Sheriff Henderson sat down with his steaming cup and shuffled a few papers, before picking up his pen and asking Anna, "Do you have any other clues about who might have sabotaged your SUV?"

"No," Anna replied, "and I'm not so sure I need to be here. It's just that Old Charley is constantly at our house and always verbally abusing me. I guess he's there with my mother's approval though at times she seems to dislike him even more than I do... if that's possible."

"Have you asked her if she wants him there?"

"Ah...no...I just assumed if she didn't, she'd run him off."

The sheriff made a note.

"My main concern right now is he's threatening to sell my horse. You may have seen Smoky do his thing if you've ever attended any rodeos around here. He's special. My dad gave him to me before he died. I don't want Dugan to sell Smoky, but my mom would probably let him. How do I stop him?"

"Yes, I have seen you put your horse through his paces. It's a beautiful thing to watch. And to answer your question...you're an adult and Smoky's your horse. Neither of them has a right to take him without your consent, but we can't do anything until he has committed a crime," the sheriff explained.

"By then it may be too late. I might never see Smoky again."

"I can drop by and talk to them if you think it will help. Explain that they really don't have a right to sell him."

Anna hesitated, wondering if that would just exacerbate the problem, so Janice spoke up. "Yeah, that sounds like it could help a lot, don't you think so Anna? I saw how scared he looked when I started dialing the sheriff."

"Yes, I noticed that too," Anna said. "I think he must be running from something he's done that's illegal. Could you possibly check him out?"

"Sure can," the sheriff replied. "Maybe we can get him out of your life by transporting him to another state or something...if he's wanted elsewhere." He made more notes. "Has he done anything else that might be cause for us to arrest him now?"

Anna looked away and started tapping her foot.

Sheriff Henderson waited a minute before commenting, "Seems like you need to talk about something," he said.

"Uh...not really." Anna hedged.

"Come on Anna...while you have the chance, let the sheriff help you," Janice urged.

"Well...I...uh...should have reported it when it happened, but I didn't want to hurt my mom. She should be told I suppose, but it wouldn't make any difference. He'd still be hanging around. It was about six months ago, I guess, and I don't know if it would be called illegal."

"Why don't you tell the sheriff and let him decide?" Janice encouraged.

Sheriff Henderson nodded his head and patiently waited for Anna to continue.

"Well, I was cleaning out Smoky's side of the barn and didn't know anyone else was around. I bent over to pick up some feed sacks and he grabbed me."

"Where did he grab you?"

Anna took a breath trying to figure out how to phrase the answer. "In the most intimate place possible." She was embarrassed.

"That SOB!" Janice exclaimed, indignant. Her nice, even tan darkened with obvious rage.

"What did you do then?" asked the sheriff.

"I was so startled, I jump and screamed. I called him a bastard and told him to get out? He just laughed and said no one was there to stop him. My mom had gone to get her hair done. Then he slammed me up against the barn and began trying to take off my clothes. We fought and I did a lot of screaming and...yeah, some pretty flaming bad words too."

"Casey, my dog came running to see what was going on. He didn't like what he saw and started barking and jumping at Old Charley. Charley would kick at him so Casey never got close enough to actually bite him."

"I got loose and started to run, but he grabbed me and slammed me up against the side of the barn so hard it knocked the breath out of me and I fell. Just then, Smoky came running around the barn and took over. He was one mad horse. Old Charley started running, but Smoky was biting and pawing and knocked Old Charley off his feet several times. He finally made it to the ladder and climbed into the loft. He had some pretty significant bites and bruises. When Mom got home, he told her Smoky was a mean and dangerous horse and needed to be put down. He swore he had done nothing to provoke Smoky."

"I should have told Mom then, but I didn't think she would send him packing even after what he'd done and it would have just caused her grief.... Then too, you know what they say about killing the messenger. I didn't think it would improve my relationship with Mom. I did tell Old Charley I would kill him if he ever touched me again. He never has, but he does everything he possibly can to make me miserable."

Sheriff Henderson was rapidly writing on his notepad. Astonished and amazingly speechless, Janice was just staring at

Anna, who was feeling some relief to have finally shared her secret.

"Now you have some idea why Casey and Smoky are so precious to me," she said.

"Well...you can file charges of attempted rape," the sheriff began, "but because so much time has passed, prosecuting attorneys would be reluctant to take the case, especially since it is *attempted* rape. You could add assault and battery since he knocked you down. But there is no evidence and no witnesses. All that sort of stuff causes more of a heartache than it's worth to most women.... Still..."

"No, I don't want to go through all of that. If you can just keep a record so that if anything else happens, maybe it will help to show his character. But I really would like to know if he has a criminal record."

"Of course, and I will speak with him if you like. It might cause him to quit harassing you, but I would like to check his record first. I need to know what I'm dealing with," Sheriff Henderson explained. "If he's wanted for some crime, I may not need to talk to him about this at all, but just arrest him on the other charges. It's usually the best plan with the least fallout. But I want to caution you again to be alert and watch for any possible indication that he or someone else may be trying to hurt you."

Reminded of her accident, Anna considered the possibility Old Charley had messed with her wheel.

He's certainly capable of murder, but why would he want me dead?

Anna could think of no reason he might profit from her death.... And she was in no way a threat to him. Was she? Everyone knew Anna had no sway over her mother and could never get Josey to kick Dugan out.

Does he just hate me that much? she wondered. It didn't seem logical.

On their way out, Janice brought up a subject she knew the sheriff would be interested in. "I hear you quarter-backed for a

42

state championship team at Carnegie High," she said.

Seemingly surprised and maybe pleased, Troy smiled. "Yeah, that was some time ago."

"Do you attend many of their games now?" Janice asked.

"Oh, yeah. All of them. Always buy season tickets."

"Really? Where should I go to get season tickets? I'd love to see Carnegie take state again. Do they have a quarterback as good as you were?"

"Probably do have," he replied. "Just call the principal's office. They'll fix you up."

"Great! Thanks," she said, extending her hand.

Anna thanked him and said she hadn't really wanted to come in, but was glad she had. She felt better just talking to him about what had happened.

As they drove away, Anna said, hiding a grin, "I've never seen you so eager to shake hands before."

"Yeah, I couldn't wait to get my hands on him." Janice laughed. "Is there any way to find out where his seats are located?"

"Sure...ask him."

"I was pretty obvious, granted. But I don't want to go that far." Janice chuckled.

"Well, then, I don't know. But if anyone can find out, I'll bet you can. And, no he's not married. Guess you already knew that though."

"Yep, why do you think I've been so upbeat lately. I can't just sit around on my laurels and wait for someone else to snatch him up. And you should heed my advice and think about not letting Gabe slip through your fingers either. He's too great a catch to be single for long. Besides, I think he's really hung up on you...I mean like...totally."

Anna continued looking out the window and said nothing.

"I'll drop you off at the grocery store and while you fill that monster list, I'll get a copy of the Gazette and pick up my dry cleaning. I'll park in the lot beside the grocery store—as close to

43

the door as possible—when I'm finished. Are you okay to buy groceries or is that going to be too difficult for you? I can go with you if you need me."

"I think I can do it by myself even though I'm getting tired and it hurts when I breathe. I'll take a 'pal'."

"Take a what?" Janice asked.

"A 'pal'...a painkiller...didn't you call them a pal...something. 'Pal' is all I can remember for sure."

Janice laughed. "Yeah, I guess you could call them pals alright."

"I hope I don't keep you waiting too long. It will take some time." Anna continued.

And it did. Anna knew Janice would have been waiting a long while before she had finished her shopping. When she pushed her cart around the corner and into the parking lot, she spied Janice's car. Someone was seated in it beside Janice. As she neared the trunk of the Mustang, the two of them got out and came to help her.

Oh,no!

Janice unlocked the trunk and Gabe asked if he could help her put the groceries in the car.

"Thank you," she said, "It would really help. I didn't think it would be as hard as it was. It just took so long. If you'll excuse me, I need to sit down."

"Of course." He hurried to open the car door for her then finished helping Janice with the groceries.

Anna thought Janice had a guilty expression on her face and wondered if she had been making a move on Gabe just as she had on the sheriff. What did it matter? She would never be involved with him again anyway. She just wished she could put aside all the feelings he stirred in her and not feel this jealousy that was bothering her at the moment.

When they had finished, Janice got into the car, saying, "I bought a Gazette for the classifieds."

"I might have enough money left to pay for the paper," Anna offered.

"No, you won't. My treat. Besides, I was looking for football schedules. Do you want to stop by the Burger Hut and have a Coke while you look through the ads? You might want to check on a job while you're here in town. If you're not too exhausted."

"I'm really tired...but I need to check them out anyway. Tomorrow may be too late. The job might not be available. I guess all the groceries will be okay in the car for a little while."

They drove to the Burger Hut and Janice got their Cokes while Anna found a booth and opened the paper.

"Not much in here," she said as Janice approached with the drinks. "Just ads for a cook's helper, a mechanic and an algebra tutor. I could tutor for algebra, but it would only be a temporary thing. Wonder how much it pays? Maybe the student could come to me, which would eliminate the need for a vehicle for a bit." Anna was disappointed.

"Well, well, look who's here!" Janice remarked.

"I didn't expect you either," said Gabe, "I was just ready for lunch. Have you guys eaten?"

"No, we haven't and I'm hungry! Are you offering to buy?" Janice asked.

Anna wanted to crawl in a hole—if one could be found.

"Sure am." Gabe watched Anna, waiting for her reply.

She shook her head "no," but before she could voice her objection, Janice intervened. "Come on, Anna, don't cheat me out of a free burger and conversation with the best looking guy in the county."

Anna rolled her eyes and shook her head again.

"Yeah, she'll have a burger with mustard, no pickles and she likes extra onions...odor free if they have them." Janice chuckled.

"Yeah, I remember," Gabe replied, still watching Anna, waiting for her answer.

Anna remembered too. That was exactly the way they both liked them.

She chuckled, "Alright, if I can return the favor sometime. They do smell delicious." She didn't want to be indebted to him for anything...not even a burger.

"It would be my extreme pleasure," he said.

Anna hadn't intended to accept his offer, but with Janice's urging and the wonderful smell of the burgers, she had acquiesced and thanked him graciously. Burger Hut burgers were always the best.

Gabe seemed pleased as though he had just won a point and the possibility of more.

After returning with a tray of burgers and fries, Gabe asked, "What's new in the Gazette?"

"Not much, I would guess. Haven't had time to read it yet."

Anna was reluctant to admit that she was in desperate need of a job and was just searching the want-ads. But Janice wasn't reluctant at all. She jumped into the breach and explained Anna's whole situation and problems to Gabe. Anna sat silent and mortified—determined to strangle her later.

Gabe was astonished by what he heard. "Really!" he said, "How lucky can I get? My secretary, Mrs. McClusky, is retiring and I was going to put an ad in the paper next week. Why don't you come in and make application? I already know your skills and the pays pretty good. Besides, I can save the price of a classified ad," he joked.

She wanted with all her heart to jump up and shout "Yes!" But it would be an untenable situation, not one she could handle for any length of time. There would be too much stress being around Gabe. No, it was not a good idea.

"Well, I...uh...don't think I can do that. Not...uh...not now anyway. I have to find a way to get a vehicle and ...." She was stalling and they knew it.

Janice interrupted, "Oh, I can take you to work for a while," she offered.

Gabe has a better idea. "That wouldn't be necessary. I know you, Annie, and how dedicated to your principals you are, I

46

would be willing to advance the down-payment on a vehicle of your choice and you can make payments each month out of your salary. And you can start when you feel well enough. Work only half days at first maybe. You will need to familiarize yourself with our procedures and stuff, and when you feel ready, then take over full time. I'm sure Mrs. McClusky would be willing to give us a few extra days if it becomes necessary...which I doubt."

"Well, I will think about it...I'm not sure...." she began.

Gabe must have realized what the problem was...that she would find it hard to work with him.

"I really need someone I can trust in the office at all times, since I'm going to be out in the field checking on the workmen and the construction about 75% of the time. I know you would be perfect for the job."

It made a difference. Anna began to think perhaps she could handle it if he were gone most of the time.

"Well, uh...maybe I will make an appointment with Mrs. McClusky and come in for an interview. And thank you. Thank you very much."

"Great." Gabe was smiling. "Don't wait! I'll need someone right away."

Janice fastened her seat belt, started her car and as they drove away from the Burger Hut, she slapped the steering wheel and excitedly exclaimed, "Woo-hoo! How's that for a blessing? Talk about manna from heaven! Nothing could have been better."

Anna was skeptical. "Janice, did you set this up?" She felt close to tears. She wasn't sure if they were tears of joy or tears from worrisome fretting.

"Hey, Chiquita, I'm good, but not that damn good! Sometimes it's the luck of the draw or the hand of the Master. This answers all your prayers. You even get to keep your horse! Don't look that gift horse in the mouth." She chuckled. "And you'll get to be with the gorgeous love of your life"

Anna hesitated a moment. "That's what really bothers me," she said.

"I know. Don't let it. Take it a day at a time and solve the problems as they come...if they do."

It sounded sensible. Anna would be a fool to not check it out.

When they reached Anna's house, Janice unlocked the trunk and Anna reached for a bag of groceries.

"No, you don't! You go in and rest. Send Old Charley's butt out here to help carry these in and let your mom put them away. You've had a full day. And call me. I'll take you for your interview at Whittier Enterprises and also to take your finals. Make that interview for tomorrow. The sooner the better."

Anna thanked Janice profusely. With tears in her eyes she smiled. "Okay, bossy, I'll give it a try. I love you, Janice. You're so good to me...in a pushy sort of way."

They laughed together.

"Someone needs to teach you how to treat yourself," Janice said, "Call me."

Chapter Four

Anna called the university and found that she could take both of her exams on Tuesday afternoon. It was a lucky break if Janice could give her a lift at that time.

Janice answered her cell on the first ring, "Yeah, Chiquita, What's goin' on?"

"That was quick! I just found out I can take both my exams, one immediately after the other on Tuesday afternoon. Is it possible you could dump me there about 1 o'clock?"

"Yep, dump you and pick you up later! Did you make an appointment with Whittier Enterprises?"

"No, not yet. I was trying to get it all lined up so you would only have to make one trip."

"Doesn't matter! I can take and pick you up any morning as long as I'm finished by 10:30. Just do it. Don't wait."

"Okay, is Monday at 9 alright...if I can get it set for then?"

"Sure. I think they'll be very flexible in their scheduling for you. Gabe knows a good employee when he finds one."

"But that only gives us an hour and a half to get you back to the hospital. What if it's a long interview?"

"Well, then Gabe can take you home."

"No, maybe I should wait until Tuesday even if it makes for a long day."

"No, do it as soon as possible. I'll call the hospital if I'm going to be late. I'm never late, so they'll know it was unavoidable. It'll be okay."

"Oh, gosh! Janice, thanks so much. I'll call back as soon as the appointment is made."

Anna called Gabe's secretary and asked for an interview as early as possible on Monday morning.

Mrs. McClusky was very obliging. "Certainly, I get here at 8 o'clock. Would 8:30 be okay for you? Gabe has already told me to expect your call. He's impressed with your academic record and I'm looking forward to meeting you."

"Thank you very much, Mrs. McClusky. I'll be there by 8:30." Anna hung up wondering what else Mrs. McClusky knew about her past relationship with Gabe.

An 8:30 appointment turned out to be fine with Janice. Anna's spirits soared. It appeared things were going to get better after all. She decided to go for a walk with Casey and take Smoky some sugar cubes.

As she ambled toward the barn, extending her arm and snapping her fingers, laughing at Casey trying to figure out what made the noise, Anna remembered the apple trees she had planted at the far end of the fall pasture. How long ago had that been? Several years. She wondered if they might have produced apples this year. Maybe it was time to check them out and, anyway, she would enjoy the walk.

Anna would need a bag to carry them in, if by chance she found a few. As she went back into the house, she heard Dugan complaining. She had not heard him or her mother grumble much since she had delivered the groceries.

Guess full bellies quiet the tongue, she thought.

"She didn' buy me not one can a beer!"

"Looks like you could at least buy your own beer."

Surprised at Josey's response, Anna wanted to clap her hands.

"Listen, you bitch! You know better than to sass me!"

Old Charley's reply angered Anna, but puzzled her more. What did it mean? It implied her mother knew she would be made to suffer if she crossed him. Just what would he do to her? Steal her money? Beat her? Leave her? Anna had no clue, but she would remember the threat.

Anna searched for a sack with handles that would be easier for her to carry. She rummaged around in the bag drawer long enough to irritate Dugan.

"Why don' cha git outta here and be quiet?" he fussed.

Anna said nothing, but took the paper bag by one strap and flipped it through the air, causing it to open with a "pop" close to Old Charley's face.

He jumped out of his chair and yelled, "Listen, you smart aleck bitch. I'll teach ya sum manners."

Anna was glad to hear a horn honk out front because she realized she had probably gone too far. Through the window she saw the sheriff's cruiser turning around in the drive.

"It's the Trojan Horse, Sheriff Henderson. I wonder if he wants to talk to me or you?" she asked, looking at Old Charley. "Maybe you'd like to tell him how you are going to teach me some manners."

Dugan's face went white. He sat back in his chair and for once had no caustic reply.

Walking up to his patrol unit, Anna greeted Mechlin County's finest as he turned off the ignition. "Good afternoon, Sheriff. Would you like to come in and meet my mother and Old Charley?"

"No, not at this time. I just wanted to tell you what I have discovered about Charley and to ask a favor. I didn't find much. He does have several arrests for assault and battery, drunk and disorderly conduct and passing hot checks here in Mecklin County. I couldn't find a driver's license number for him. Does he drive?"

"He drives my mom's car some. I don't think he has a vehicle of his own. He just showed up one day and has been here most all of the time since. I don't know if he has a driver's license."

"I need to do a thorough criminal background check on him and in order to do that I will need a driver's license number, a social security number or even a finger print might help. Maybe he has an out of state driver's license. We have fingerprints from previous arrests here, but they're unreadable. Do you suppose you could safely—and I stress safely—help me get any of those

51

things?" the sheriff asked Anna.

Anna detected a reluctance in his question. Obviously he didn't want her exposed to danger."I think so. I'll certainly do everything I can and let you know." Anna replied.

They chatted for a few minutes and Sheriff Henderson seemed pleased to learn Anna might be going to work at Whittier Enterprises.

"Gabe's a great guy and a good business man. It'll be a nice place to work," he said.

Later, when Anna took the long walk to look for apples, she was overwhelmed to find the trees loaded with golden fruit in various stages of ripening.

"Oh, my gosh! What a blessing! I can't believe what I'm seeing!"

She remembered Janice's earlier statement of "manna from heaven." It seemed apropos. Maybe things were indeed "looking up."

She gathered her bag full and hurried to the house. She'd get the tractor with the front-end loader already attached and go back to pick all those up from the ground and all she could reach that were ripe. She would need a ladder and some help to gather those in the top of the trees.

Anna couldn't remember the name of the apples. They were called "Priceless", "Pristine", "Princess"...or something like that. Most apples start ripening from mid-August through late September, even early November, but these were advertised to be the earliest ripening apple of the year. And indeed they were. How wonderful!

After gathering all the apples except those in the tops of the trees and some still too green on the lower branches, Anna had the loader full of yellow beauties that smelled and tasted like a slice of paradise. She easily had two full bushels. Janice would love them and so would Smoky. This was the first year they had produced. She hadn't really expected any...or at least not many. It would soon be time for her to switch the cattle to this fall pasture and they would have eaten everything as far up as they could reach. Anna was so glad she had taken the time to inspect the trees.

Even Josey was well pleased to see the enormous pile of apples. Anna was so happy, she ignored Old Charley's sarcastic comments.

"Why didn' ya git 'em sooner? Sum 'ub 'em are too ripe."

Anna was sure Smoky wouldn't care a bit. He'd love them all. She filled both crispers in the refrigerator and a large bag for Janice with the less ripe ones on the bottom and the perfectly ripe ones on top.

"I'll make a pie for supper and put the rest of these in the cellar where it's cooler," she told her mother. "Just for snacking, I'll leave a few of the riper ones in a bowl in the refrigerator. There are some more on the trees that need to be picked now and more left to ripen."

Maybe I'll even make some apple butter if they are ripening faster than we can use them, she thought. *I am so glad I planted those trees. I wish I had planted some peach trees too. Maybe I'll just do that.*

As soon as possible Anna hurried to share her find with Smoky. He very much enjoyed his apples and the rub-down Anna gave him. She wanted to take him for a gallop, but knew she couldn't—just yet.

"I'm pushing my recovery as it is," she told him. "I'll be back, sweetie and bring you some more apples."

He nickered as she turned and walked away.

Anna had to rest for a time. When she felt able, she arose and made an apple pie and a tossed green salad. She cooked pork chops with Spanish rice and some green beans for supper.

After they had eaten, Josey filled her glass with more tea and went out to relax in a lawn chair under the shade of the mimosa by the back kitchen door. Dugan brought his empty glass with a complaint as usual.

"Why'd ya gimme this little ole glass?"

Anna saw an opportunity. She had been doing the dishes and quickly dried the smallest glass of the bunch. Holding it mostly covered by the dish towel, she handed it to Dugan.

"Here, try this one," she said.

Old Charley grabbed it and immediately slammed it down on the cabinet.

"Aw, hell! That 'uns even littler than t'othern," he grumbled.

"Oh...well, here's a big one." Anna gave him what he wanted and got the ice for him in order to hurry him out of the kitchen.

After he left, Anna covered her hand with the dish towel and carefully picking up the small glass by its rim, slipped it into a larger one. She would put them in a small bag and tape it up for Sheriff Henderson. She hoped that would preserve Old Charley's fingerprints as the sheriff had requested.

Anna finished cleaning the kitchen and, looking out of the kitchen window, saw her mother reading the paper Janice had purchased. Dugan was apparently asleep in his chair. Here was an opportunity to look though his stuff for a driver's license or something the sheriff could use to run a criminal background check. Did he even have one scrap of personal belongings? Anna had never seen him bring in anything at all. She hurried into the bedroom where he supposedly slept and stopped short!

"Mon Dieu!" she muttered. The French version of "My god" seemed less indelicate than the English, so Anna preferred it and hoped most people didn't know what she was saying if they heard her.

The room was a mess. She had made it a point to never enter his room and therefore had never cleaned it at all. From the looks of it neither had Josey. Old clothes, socks and a pair of boots were scattered on the floor. Smashed beer cans, candy wrappers and empty cigarette packs overflowed the wastebasket. Two ash trays were full of butts. Ash powdered the nightstand and spilled onto the floor beneath it. The TV screen was so dusty she wondered how he could watch it.

Quickly, she opened the nightstand drawer and found only some matches and a pencil. Next she checked the dresser drawers and found them mostly empty. One had socks, unmatched, with holes in the heels, some underwear and T-shirts. Another drawer contained several pairs of worn blue jeans. Two drawers were completely empty. There was nowhere else to look. Well, maybe the closet. She found several shirts, patched but not ironed hanging crookedly on wire hangers there.

Look under the bed—even if it's an unlikely place to hide anything important, she instructed herself.

She discovered a small battered suitcase, the brick-red color of Oklahoma soil, pushed up against the wall underneath the headboard. It appeared to have been left out in the weather for a time and had absorbed some "Okie" mud. Anna hurried back to see if Dugan were still asleep before opening it. Good thing she had checked. Old Charley was awake and getting up out of his chair. She ran back to his room and grabbed up the tattered case. Swiftly she took it to her own bedroom and hid it at the back of her closet. She would have more time to search it thoroughly while he slept.

Anna readied her things to leave early the next morning for the interview. She took her time with small busy-making chores.

When all had settled down and she thought they were asleep, Anna went into her room and locked the door. But before she could get the case from the closet, she heard a loud thump and then a scraping sound. Her pulse quickened. Who was moving around just outside in the hallway? Anna found only Miss Kitty there, who—looking up—started meowing her displeasure at having been locked out of her favorite place to sleep. She had jumped off the small table in the hallway and was industriously scratching to be let in. Anna picked her up whispering that she should be quiet and carried her into the bedroom. She laid Miss Kitty on her bed and relocked the door. The cat purred contentedly and was soon fast asleep.

Old Charley didn't have much to search through. A very

careful inspection of his belongings turned up only a disability1099 from the Social Security Administration with his number on it and the Houston, Texas address where it had been sent. The name on the document was William Charles Dugan. There was another empty envelope with the same address but the name was Willie C. Dugan. The return address on it was just a post office box in Houston.

Anna copied the information for the sheriff and packed Charley's meager possessions back as they had been, then snapped the case shut and hid it in her closet. She would try to put it under Dugan's bed while he was having breakfast in the morning—or maybe he would take time to shave his grizzly beard.

Very tired from a rather busy day, Anna took a pain pill and hoped she'd be able to sleep. She was somewhat keyed up for the interview with Gabe's secretary.

The following morning, Anna and her cat bolted upright when the alarm clock loudly jangled the hour of seven. Miss Kitty plopped off the foot of the bed before peering around to see what had happened.

"Bless you, sweet darlin'," Anna wanted to comfort her.

The wonderful aroma of coffee filled the air. Anna went down the hall and into the kitchen where her mother sat sipping a cup, looking out the window. The bathroom door was closed so she assumed that's where Old Charley must be.

"How long has he been in there?" she asked her mother.

"'Bout five minutes, I reckon."

"I have an interview at 8:30. Janice will be picking me up about 8. How long do you think he will be in there this morning?"

"Don't know."

Anna knocked on the door. "Are you about finished?" she asked.

"I'm a shavin, an I'll take my time," he growled.

Anna decided to take a chance. She went back into her bedroom, retrieving the suitcase, and slipped into Dugan's room. She quickly shoved it under his bed and slammed it up against the wall close to where she had found it, then hurried out just as she heard the bathroom door open.

Miss Kitty had followed Anna and was just coming into Dugan's room. Anna almost stepped on her in her haste to get out of Old Charley's messy digs. Miss Kitty hissed and ran into the hall.

"Hey! Wha' cha doin' in ma room?" Dugan demanded, wiping shaving cream from his face and neck.

"I was just trying to catch Miss Kitty. She needs to go outside now," Anna replied, scooping up her cat who squirmed and climbed over her shoulder.

Even though there was still plenty of grass and no need for hay, grain or any extra rations, Anna liked to take Smoky an apple or something special when she could. So she ran to the barn and found him there, waiting patiently. He stiffened his front legs, and scooting backwards bowed his head over them, then stood and whinnied as she approached. She loved that horse. He was a beauty and so smart. She patted him and rubbed his neck then kissed his forehead as he attacked his apples with gusto.

"I'll be back to see you later. I promise."

Smoky turned to watch her hurry away, still munching his treat.

Anna had a few extra minutes after dressing and putting on her makeup, so she decided to eat something even though she didn't really want it. She buttered a piece of toast and ate it while she drank a small glass of orange juice. Janice found her ready and waiting.

Thrilled with the bag of apples Anna gave her, Janice exclaimed, "My lord! I can never eat all of these before they spoil."

"The bottom ones are greener and they are good keepers anyway. Just put them in the crisper, they'll keep a long time."

After a few moments, she added, "Why don't you bake an apple pie and invite the Trojan Horse for supper? He might be impressed with your domesticity. And most horses really like apples." She chuckled.

"Hey, that's a great idea...except I don't bake. Maybe you could make it for me."

"I can, but then he would be impressed with *my* domesticity, wouldn't he?"

"I guess...well, no, why don't you come and teach me how to make an apple pie, but let me actually make it? Okay?"

Anna laughed. "I guess that's the least I can do...you've helped me so much. When?"

"Well, let me see if I can figure out a way to invite him without seeming like a love-starved, man-chasing moron. What if he doesn't even like apple pie?" she fretted.

"Ask him," was Anna's quick reply.

"I'll work on that." Janice said thoughtfully, seemingly going into her planning mode.

Anna had hoped Gabe would not be present when she was interviewed by his secretary, but his late model, red Hyundai was parked in the President's reserved spot in front of the building. She wondered if he would ask her questions about her life and goals this morning. Maybe he would have business outside the office before Mrs. McClusky had finished with her.

Mrs. McClusky turned out to be as nice as she looked. Neat and attractive, she didn't appear ready for retirement. Perhaps she wanted to do fun things while she still could. Anna noticed very few wrinkles and no sagging neck line though her hair was a lovely silver. She wore a dark gray suit with a soft pink blouse—that reflected the pink in her cheeks—and a warm welcoming smile.

The interview was mostly just filling out papers that would give the employer needed information for complying with regulations such as paying insurance, withholding FICA and sending W2s and so forth. Mrs. McClusky's attitude seemed to be that of a curious conversationalist not a prospective employer. But Anna had prepared a resume beforehand and gave it to her before she started filling out the forms.

"I don't have any experience as an accountant or a secretary yet, as you will see. I've just been involved in widely dissimilar activities, such as: a summer librarian, a nurse's aide, a camp counselor and even a candy striper. But I have mostly been running my mom's farm while I have been attending the university getting my degree. I guess what I'm saying is—I am a rank beginner in this area and have no experience whatsoever."

Mrs. McClusky smiled, "We can teach you our system in a short while, I think. If your grades are any indication, you already know well how to apply the principals of accounting and are a fast learner."

Anna appreciated Mrs. McClusky's expression of confidence and relaxed a bit.

"Gabe would like to discuss some of the company policies with you, now that I have all the information I need."

She stood and reached out for Anna's hand, taking it in both of hers. She gave it a squeeze and a pat instead of a shake, then pointed down the hall to the door marked "Gabe Whittier, President."

"I'll just buzz to let him know you're on your way."

"Thank you very much Mrs. McClusky. You have made this a pleasure."

Anna started down the hall towards Gabe's door and the part of the interview she knew would be more disquieting. She tapped lightly on his office door.

"Come on in."

She turned the knob, biting her bottom lip, and was surprised to see him in a suit and tie sitting at his desk going through several sheets of paper he seemed to be correcting as he read.

Gracious! Is this the usual office attire? Anna wondered. She had never seen Gabe in a suit and tie before...unless you counted the tux at the prom.

He smiled as he got up from his desk. "Have a seat. Please. Can I get you something to drink?"

"Uh...no...thanks." She slipped into a chair in front of his desk.

Gabe sat down—not behind his desk—but in the chair facing her. "It's so good to see you. I'm glad you decided to give us a chance to show you what we have to offer employees."

"Thank you for allowing me the opportunity." After a pause, she ventured, "You look so different in a suit and tie."

He chuckled, "I have a meeting with some executives of a new company wanting to expand into Oklahoma. They're considering a new apartment complex over on Hickory Avenue and are letting bids on the project. I'm not too sure I'm interested at this time." After a moment, he continued, "Anna, I don't need to see a resume. I know all I need to know about you. You're the kind of person I want in my employ. So if you'll accept my offer, you're hired."

He told her the amount of the annual salary, how much vacation time and sick leave she would get and talked about all the other perks they offered. He also said they helped certain employees through a crisis if they were the kind of workers they wanted to keep. So if she needed transportation, the company would purchase a vehicle of her choice and take monthly payments for it from her salary.

"It's a wonderful offer, Gabe. How could anyone refuse. I just don't want to get the job for any reason except on merit and I need to make that clear up front."

"Of course, Anna, I understand. I'm eternally gratefully for your testimony at the hearing. By refuting your mother's damaging accusations, you probably kept me from a hurtful court battle and maybe even prison. But, no, that's not the reason I want you to work with me. You are trustworthy, diligent, productive and like a bulldog when it comes to solving a difficult problem. You persevere until it's solved. Who wouldn't want you? It's like William Faulkner said in his acceptance speech for the 1950 Nobel Prize...and we so often repeated in high school...we must endure and prevail. And you do, Anna.

Anna felt a tightening in her throat. She blinked her eyes and fought to maintain a calm demeanor. "Thank you for all the compliments and the job offer. I do need a job desperately."

They talked about her schedule for remaining exams and her ability to work full days at the present. They decided she would come in for half days for a short period of time or until she felt she could handle all day on the job.

"I appreciate the offer to finance a car for me. It's a most unusual perk. I would like to take advantage of it and will decide as soon as possible on the vehicle and get back to you. Thank you so much. You have saved my life."

"You're entirely welcome. Happy employees are good employees. We like to help where we can."

She stared at him for a moment before continuing. "Someone was extremely helpful and bought food and drink dispensers for my dog, mowed our lawn, baled our hay and stacked it in the barn while I was in the hospital. Do you know the person who did that?"

He hesitated and with a slight grin said, "Well, if you can tell me who actually did it, it's quite possible I might know them."

She knew he avoided admitting that he was behind it all, but it was obvious.

"I see. Take that out of my salary too, please. I don't want to feel like a charity case."

She felt so much gratitude for him that it frightened her. Was she being sucked back into a relationship she swore she would never again be part of?

Remember to be like that bull dog he mentioned...just endure and prevail, she told herself. And she resolved that she would.

He accompanied her to the door, as she rose to leave, and put his hand on the doorknob. She expected him to open it for her, but he hesitated, looking at her for a long moment. She thought he was going to reach for her and was terrified by the realization that she wanted him to. But he only opened the door.

Stepping back he said, "I will be out of the office most of the time, but if you have any problems or anything bothers you, please let me know. I want you to enjoy your work here."

"Thank you very much for all your help. I'll try not to let you down."

"I know that, Anna," he said softly.

Janice was waiting when Anna walked back into the reception area. As she looked up, she caught a glimpse of Gabe in his suit and tie.

"Woo-hoo! Don't you look snazzy?" she called out.

Gabe turned and laughed. "Hey, Janice, how are you?" He walked into the reception area.

"I'm great! But I'd be better if you'd take me to lunch. Is that why you're dressed so cool...to take me to lunch?"

Everyone laughed. "It would be my great pleasure, but I have a meeting and I have to run," he said.

"Okay, but some opportunities don't come around twice, you know?" Janice persisted.

Gabe hugged her. Still laughing, he said, "I'll have to catch you later," and was out the door.

Anna wondered why she couldn't be more casual in her relationships. More like Janice, but maybe not quite so outspoken. She thought Janice was a little "over the top" much of the time, but everyone seemed to like and enjoy her—as Anna, herself, did.

As they were driving away, Janice glanced at Anna. "Why so sober? Did you not get the job?"

"Yes, I was offered the job and it's a good one with exceptional perks."

Janice slapped the steering wheel. "I knew it! I knew it!" she exclaimed.

Anna said nothing. She sat, looking out the window, thinking that taking the job might be a mistake.

"Well, then, why so glum, chum? If you're angry because I asked Gabe to take me to lunch, you know I wouldn't have gone without you. Don't you?"

"Janice, once and for all, please know that I do not need or want you to snare Gabe for me!"

"Well, why not? You're crazy about each other. Any moron can see that and it sure looks like he's willing. What the hell is wrong with you?" Her friend was baffled and irritated.

"That, as I have said before, is not a topic for discussion. Please leave it alone."

Almost throwing a gift bag at Anna, Janice said, "Well, crap! Okay, here! I went shopping and they had some great sales at Margaret's Boutique. I bought a lot of nifty stuff, but the greatest of all wouldn't fit me. It was your size, though and so gorgeous, I couldn't resist. Here's a congratulations-on-a-new-job or graduation or whatever-the-hell-makes-you-happy present. Don't know why I bought those. You'll never wear them or at least no one will ever see you in them! That's criminal! It's almost like never unveiling the Mona Lisa."

Anna felt ashamed.

"I'm sorry Janice. It's just something I can't talk about, ever. Please understand. But thanks. You're a wonderful person and I am so lucky to have you as a friend."

"Okay, Chiquita, I'll try to leave it alone. It must be gargantuan to cause you to walk away from a guy like Gabe."

Anna said nothing, but opened the bag Janice had given her.

"Oh! My gosh! How beautiful! You're right, they are irresistible! Thank you so much. A set like this might make even me put them on and parade down Main Street."

"Yeah. That'll be the day!" Janice countered.

The bag contained a matching set of panties and bra, made from beautiful white lace flowers with revealing, peek-a-boo holes where the petals fastened together. Small seed pearls, scattered here and there, shimmered like dewdrops in the moonlight.

"Thanks, Janice. You are too good to me." Janice said nothing, so Anna offered further, "I guess I could frame them like the Mona Lisa and hang them behind my desk in the office."

Janice burst out laughing. "Yeah! That'd work. Every guy that came into your office would be seeing you in his dreams with those beauties on."

At least Janice was laughing. Anna wanted to cry.

Anna reviewed for her exams until late in the night. Miss Kitty contentedly slept beside her. After some more reviewing the next morning, Anna felt prepared for her exams even though she had missed several of her last classes while she was in the hospital.

Janice picked Anna up and took her to the university as planned.

"What will you do while I'm taking my finals?" Anna asked.

"I'm going to have lunch, wash my car and buy some flour, spices, butter and stuff to make an apple pie. Maybe, some steaks too. And if I see that Trojan, I'm going to buy his lunch and invite him to dinner ASAP."

They laughed together.

"I'm so sorry to be such a bother, but as soon as I get some transportation of my own and a paycheck, I will pay you back," Anna said.

"Forget it. That's what friends are for."

"If I can just get to work and back for the rest of this week, I think I'll have a vehicle. Think I'll get a truck. The mileage is not as good as that of a car, but I need one on the farm. It would help a lot."

"Your choice, Punkin'. And before I forget, I have to go to a conference in Oklahoma City on Thursday or Friday this week. I'll let you know. Maybe your mom could take you to work. If not Gabe can pick you up."

"Oh, no!" Anna began.

"It's only one day, Anna. You can handle it."

Endure and Prevail

I guess I'll have to...just endure and prevail. Anna sighed her acceptance.

A bit of encouraging news lifted Anna's spirits when she got home that evening. Dugan had decided he needed to visit family or friends somewhere in Texas. He had reservations on a bus, leaving early on Thursday. Josey would take him to Oklahoma City where he would pick up his tickets and be gone by 8 that morning.

Anna wondered what had prompted his trip, and she hoped he would never return. She was surprised that Old Charley would have friends—mean as he was. It would be so good to be rid of him.

The next morning was Wednesday. One more day and Dugan would be gone.

Anna fretted about what to wear. It was going to be wonderful earning money of her own. She could buy something nice to wear to work. She mostly lived in blue jeans. But she would like something more suitable for office wear. She remembered Mrs. McClusky's outfit and Gabe in his suit and tie. God! Was she a hick or what?

The sun was shining. The whole world seemed bright and beautiful. Anna felt more confident and Mrs. McClusky was as nice as before. She explained things in logical, easy to understand terms. The work was easy and the Whittier systems were sensible and flowed smoothly, making it easy to follow. Anna was surprised at the size of the company. It had grown substantially, thanks to Gabe's hard work. Of course it had helped that his father backed him. He had started on firm footing and had continual monetary support as well as good advice.

Much to Anna's relief, Gabe didn't put in an appearance all day. Janice was there waiting to pick her up and drive her home.

Somewhat tired from her first day at unfamiliar tasks, Anna took a nap in the afternoon. Unusual for her, but she awoke feeling so great that she was glad she had. She decided she needed to check on the animals. She noticed Casey's dish as she went out the kitchen door. It was still full of food. She looked around and called several times, as she headed for the horse pasture, but he never showed.

Where is that goober? she wondered.

Anna spent quite a bit of time with Smoky. At first he seemed agitated, but settled down after she fed him a couple of apples and currycombed him completely. He looked absolutely beautiful—freshly brushed and shiny.

"You're a handsome devil," she told him.

He shook his head up and down several times as though agreeing with her.

She patted his nose softly, saying, "I'll be back," as she walked away.

Counting her mother's cows, Anna spied Daisy and her baby. She called. They left the herd and came to her. She had sliced a couple of apples for them, and fed them both pieces of golden sweetness that they swallowed in a hurry—obviously enjoying their treats. After a few minutes, Daisy took her baby and leisurely grazed back toward the herd.

Anna returned to the house where Miss Kitty was waiting. Casey was still nowhere to be found.

In spite of Anna's afternoon nap, she felt sleepy and tired, so after bathing and washing her hair, she laid out her clothes for the next day. She chose a pair of pale celery colored, linen slacks and a creamy off-white silk blouse with a braided straw belt. It was probably the closest thing to appropriate she had. It would be good not to have to wait on Dugan to get out of the bathroom. He'd be gone before she got up the next morning. With that pleasurable thought in mind, she went to bed early and fell asleep immediately.

When the alarm went off, Anna put Miss Kitty outside and made coffee. She had plenty of time. Maybe she could share a cup with Janice when she came by to pick her up.

She put on her makeup and a little extra curl in her long dark hair. She thought of Janice's new haircut and wondered if maybe she should change her style as well. She lifted the thick dark brown curls and remembered Gabe's words. "A woman's hair is her glory they say and yours is absolutely glorious! I love the golden and red highlights when you are in the sun." She decided to leave it as it was. As she began dressing, she discovered all of her knee-hi stockings were in the laundry basket.

"Oh, jeez! I can't wear panty hose with slacks," she muttered. "Now what?"

She had some thigh high stockings and lacy garters...somewhere. She rummaged through her lingerie drawer until she located them. While she searched, she saw the new panty and bra set Janice had given her. They were indeed irresistible. She decided to try them on...she had extra time. Janice was right...they even made *her* look pretty nifty.

Just as she started to switch into more practical undies, the phone rang. It was Janice.

"Oh, hi, Janice. I have a few extra minutes this morning. Would you like to come in for coffee and toast?"

"Yes, I would like to come in! Hurry up and unlock the door." Janice seemed somewhat distressed.

"Wait a minute. I'm not fully dressed yet."

"Open the door anyway! I need to use your bathroom! Now!"

Hearing a knock, Anna ran, unlocked it and threw it open.

"I know you're in a big hurry, but I need...oh, my god...oh, my god...I'm so sorry...I thought you were someone else!" she cried, slamming the door.

Judging by the stunned expression on Gabe's face, he was as surprised as she.

"Wow," he said, softly and then was rendered speechless, until she slammed the door in his face which seemed to jar him awake. "Well, who *is* the lucky bastard?" he questioned, angrily.

"Just a minute!...Just a minute!" Anna had completely lost

her composure. Hurriedly, she jumped into her clothes and went back to open the door.

And that was the precise moment she saw Sheriff Henderson drive up. Anna wordlessly went back to get the glass with Dugan's prints on it and the other information she had gathered about him. Gabe was standing by the cruiser talking with the sheriff when she walked out into the yard. Seeing Anna, Gabe left the patrol car, walked to his pickup truck, got in and waited for her.

Anna handed the bag through the window of the sheriff's vehicle, explaining what it was and told him she hoped it would help.

"And by the way, Old Charley left this morning for somewhere in Texas. I hope he never comes back," she said.

"I totally agree." He smiled at her. "You look especially nice this morning...you've an extra blush in your cheeks."

Oh, my gosh! Does he think Gabe spent the night?

Anna was mortified. She imagined her cheeks were now pinker than ever. "Thank you, sheriff. I guess it's because I was in a hurry. Gabe just came by to pick me up and I didn't want to keep him waiting."

"Then I won't delay you. Keep in touch," he said as he waved and drove away.

Reluctantly, Anna approached Gabe's truck.

"I'm so sorry, I had no idea you were...."

"Looks like you were expecting the Trojan Horse? Did I spoil your party?" He sounded upset.

Staring at him for a moment before fully comprehending, Anna strongly objected.

"Oh, my god, no! Janice was on the phone and told me she was in a hurry to use my bathroom and for me to immediately open the door. So I did, though I was not presentable."

Gabe turned away. Was he trying to hide a grin?

Anna felt anger rise within her. What exactly had Janice done and was he a part of it?

"Just what were you talking to the sheriff about? Reporting me for indecent exposure?" she demanded.

"I didn't see anything indecent about it and you looked pretty damned presentable to me," he said, giving her a long look.

"That Janice! Why would she do such a thing to me?" Anna was furious.

"Don't judge her guilty until you know her side of the story. I did see her pull into your drive and when she saw me, she backed out and left like the devil was after her. Maybe she *was* in a hurry to find a bathroom. Anyway, she called me earlier and asked me to pick you up. She had to go to a meeting in Oklahoma City this morning," Gabe explained. "I check on my cows about two miles down the road from here almost every morning. I guess I'm a little earlier than expected," he continued.

"She never told me to expect you." Anna was still not completely convinced.

"Maybe that's why she was dropping by...to let you know. She was on her way to Oklahoma City, but she probably had a few extra minutes."

Anna felt foolish. "I'm sorry you caught me in such a state of undress..." she began.

"I'm not," he replied, barely above a whisper.

She stared out the window saying nothing.

Chapter Five

Almost a week had passed with no sign of Casey. Anna had walked every foot of their property and driven every mile of road on all sides of their farm and had not found a clue as to where he had gone or what had happened to him. Maybe someone had just wanted him enough to steal him away. But that didn't seem likely. Casey was not too friendly with strangers.

Anna remembered he had gone missing on the day before Dugan left. Old Charley hated Casey and the feeling was mutual. Had Dugan taken him away? Or killed Casey? He would have had to use Josey's car to remove him in either case, because Anna's search had turned up no body. Anna would ask her mother if she knew anything about Casey's disappearance. She hoped that wherever Casey was, he was okay—healthy and happy.

"What do I know about that dumb dog?" The question was answered with a question. But Anna detected a tightness in Josey's voice and a veiling of her eyes as she looked away.

"Did Dugan kill him or take him away? He would have had to use your car?"

Anna thought her mother's face paled as she turned and walked away.

"You better not accuse Charley of sump'n you can't prove! He's not a man can control his temper and he's meaner 'n a snake." Josey still had not answered the question.

"Mom, you can't let Dugan rule our lives and he's not even here now. Maybe he won't ever come back."

"You don't know nuthin' bout Charley. Just leave it be. I don't know where yer dog is." Josey adamantly declared. As an afterthought, she added, "Charley *will* be back!"

Anna shivered at the thought of having to live with Old Charley, that pitiful excuse for a human being, again. And, for some unexplained reason, she was apprehensive—wondering for a moment if he had even gone to Texas. Maybe she should mention Casey's disappearance to the sheriff.

Well maybe not.

She didn't want to seem like a nervous ninny—seeing malicious mischief in everything that happened. He might think a missing dog was an insignificant problem.

Her work at Whittier Enterprises was a blessing. Anna loved every minute of it and Mrs. McClusky was pleased with her progress.

"There's not much else I can teach you. You have learned quickly and well...and you are exceptionally particular about all you do. I'm sure you will be able to handle all the work proficiently. But if I have forgotten something, you can always call me. Sometimes the workload increases for short periods. Sometimes I even get behind. If that happens to you, don't panic. Call me if you need to. I am more than happy to come in and lend a hand." Mrs. McClusky was a lovely person and Anna appreciated her immensely.

To her great relief, Anna rarely saw Gabe at all.

Her injuries from the rollover accident were healing rapidly. She still needed a pain pill now and then, but she was very careful not to abuse her body and was confident it wouldn't be long before she was totally back to normal again.

She was ready to go out and look at vehicles. Excited and full of questions, she wondered if a brand new truck or a good used one would be the wisest choice? The tag, title, insurance and taxes would be more expensive on a new one, but there would be a good warranty and less likelihood of problems. How would that even out? If she bought a used one, could she spot any defects that might become a major headache after several months? Anna needed help. She wished again for her father and his expert advice.

As Anna was preparing to leave for lunch, she asked Mrs. McClusky about a few extra minutes if she should be late because she was trying to choose the proper truck.

"Of course, dear. I will be here and we are well caught up on all our reports. Just take your time. It's a big decision, I know."

Gabe entered the office to hear Mrs. McClusky's reply.

"Oh, you're choosing a vehicle today."

"Yes, I thought I'd better get something soon and stop having everyone else chauffeur me around. I have to say I'm apprehensive about it though."

"I'd be happy to go with you if I can be of some help," he offered.

Anna was embarrassed and confused for an instant. Gabe's presence would rattle her and cause her to be less able to make a good decision.

"Um...I think I'll just look today. I'll let you know if I decide."

"Okay. Where will you be looking first?" he asked.

"I thought a truck would be more useful to me. My dad always favored Fords and I see you are driving one, so I thought I'd check the Ford dealer first."

"Good enough." Gabe smiled. "If you decide on one today talk to Bob Flannagan there. He handles purchases like this for our company. He can take care of your transaction on the spot."

"Thank you so much. I'm always so amazed at how well you are organized."

"It pays off in the long run." He smiled. "Let me know how it turns out."

She felt his eyes following her as she turned and walked out of the office.

The Flannagan Ford dealership was only about three blocks from Whittier Enterprises so Anna elected to walk. She was hurrying along when she heard the slightest honk and looked up to see a slow moving cruiser marked "Mechlin County Sheriff" pull up to the curb beside her. She smiled and walked towards him as Troy rolled down his window.

"Can I give you a lift? You seem to be in a hurry."

"Yes! I would love a lift." Anna replied as she opened the car door and slid inside. I'm just on my lunch break and am going to look at trucks at Flannagan Ford's. I'm rather uncomfortable about doing it by myself though."

"That's exactly where I'm heading. I need to talk to Bob about one of our patrol cars. I would be happy to give you any assistance I can, if you would like."

"Oh, wow! Thank you. Thank you so much. I do need some help in deciding. I can't make a mistake here. Gabe has been so helpful and generous." After a moment's hesitation, she continued, "What do I call you? I feel rather awkward calling you Sheriff all the time."

He chuckled. "Call me Troy. That's who I am. You don't have to call me Sheriff unless I have to arrest you." They laughed together.

They looked at several vehicles and compared mileage projections, warranties, prices and everything else they could think of. And Anna had already decided upon the one she wanted before Troy finally suggested the very one she had chosen.

"Oh, great!" she said. "I'm so glad you agree with me." They laughed.

"I didn't really think you needed my advice," Troy said.

It didn't take long for the paperwork to be taken care of and her truck—a new, white Ford F150, six cylinder, extended cab—was rolled into Flannagan's shop to be serviced. It would be ready for her at the end of the day.

Anna was ecstatic. There was no end to wonderfully good and helpful people. Life was good.

"Could I buy you lunch before you go back to work?"

"Oh, no. Thank you so much. I have already taken up too much of your time."

"I'm going to stop for lunch myself. Just a quick sandwich, maybe."

"I appreciate it very much, but I'm already late. I need to get back and finish up some loose ends. I need to be diligent." She grinned. "They have been so good to me—I can never repay their kindness."

As she was getting out of the cruiser, the sheriff asked, "Has anything unusual happened or have you heard from Old Charley?"

"No, we haven't heard from him...that I know anything about. But my dog, Casey, is gone. Dugan hated him and he went missing the day before Old Charley left."

"Hmm, it could be connected. Let me know if he shows up."

"I will. Do you mean Casey or Dugan?"

"Either one." They both chuckled.

Anna walked toward the office door. Gabe stepped out and held it open for her.

Troy rolled the window down on his cruiser and stuck his head out. A gentle breeze stirred the soft curls across his forehead. He raised his voice and said, "By the way, that apple pie you baked was absolutely out of this world. I wanted to eat the whole thing by myself...at one sitting."

Anna laughed. "Thanks, Troy. I'm glad you liked it."

She hurried past Gabe who looked first at her then at Troy and started toward the sheriff's car.

"Sorry I'm late." Anna apologized to Mrs. McClusky.

"Hardly at all. Did you find what you wanted?"

"I think it will be very useful. I hope I didn't make a mistake. The sheriff happened by and helped me compare notes and decide on the best truck for the money. It was a blessing."

"Oh, good." Mrs. McClusky smiled. "I knew you'd be okay though. Gabe called Bob Flannagan and told him to make sure you got a good deal because you were a special employee of ours and he'd best treat you fairly." She laughed softly. "They are very good friends."

"Oh! I didn't know. I thought I was on my own." Anna wondered how Gabe would feel about her taking the sheriff's advice, but reasoned it was a fair bargain or Mr. Flannagan would not have approved it...after talking to Gabe.

Anna could hardly wait for the end of the day to get her new truck. She had signed all the necessary papers with Mrs. McClusky and Gabe had gone to the Ford dealership, paid for it and asked that the truck be delivered to her before 5 o'clock. She had wanted to thank him, but he never returned to the office.

The smell of new leather invaded her nostrils and lifted her spirits as she opened the door and slipped behind the wheel of her new vehicle. She decided she would buy a new ladder, as well, to finish picking the apples left on the trees in her winter pasture. Their old ladder was rickety and coming apart. It might cause her to fall. As she slid the new 16-foot ladder into her truck bed, she was glad she had taken Troy's advice and purchased a bed liner. She wanted to avoid all the scratches and dings she possibly could.

Janice didn't answer her phone when Anna called to ask for help climbing trees to gather fruit, so Anna went about her regular duties taking care of the animals. In addition, she put diesel in the tractor, checked the fluid levels and pulled it into the pasture, putting the new ladder in the front-end, bucket loader. She couldn't help wondering and worrying about Casey. She prayed he was okay wherever he was.

Later, Anna called Janice once more. After several rings, Janice finally answered. She had been tied up with an emergency at the hospital and would be there for at least a couple more hours.

"I would love to help you pick apples, sweetie, but it will be dark soon and I am working tomorrow."

"Thanks anyway, Janice. I'm sorry you have to put in so much overtime. Guess who helped me pick out my new truck today."

"Gabe!"

"Nope! It was your handsome Trojan!"

"What? How did that happen?"

"Fortuitous! He needed to go to Flannagan Ford about one of his patrol cars. I guess you told him I had made the apple pie. He told me he really liked it. You will have to give it one more shot. And don't burn yours next time. I'll let you go. I know you're busy. Call me soon." Oh, wait, by the way, what's the big idea? ...Telling me to open the door because you needed to use my bathroom in a big hurry and when I did, there stood Gabe. Worse than that...I was standing there in nothing but my undies."

Janice laughed. "It was not intended, but we'll talk about it later. Actually, I thought that worked out quite nicely." She laughed again. "I've got to run. See you later."

Still not completely convinced it was not intended, Anna hung up. They would discuss it later.

Anna asked her mom if she would help her gather the last of their fruit tree bounty.

Josey refused. "I ain't climbin' no trees."

"No, Mom, you won't have too. Just take my full buckets and carry them to the tractor or maybe steady my ladder if the ground is not level. Just be there in case I need you."

"I ain't walkin' that far and I sure ain't ridin' no dumb tractor."

Anna decided since it was almost dark anyway, she'd wait until morning and do the picking by herself. She would have plenty of time and lots of sunshine. She would not be rushed or careless and could at least see what she was doing.

The first thoughts entering Anna's mind the next morning were of Casey. *Where in the world could that sweet puppy be?*

She hoped he had returned sometime during the night, but as she exited the house his dish was still full of food, sitting by the kitchen door in its customary place.

After finishing breakfast and her regular chores, Anna grabbed a bucket and the tractor keys. "I'm going to pick the rest of the apples, Mom. Wouldn't you like to come with me?"

"No, I already told you no and why I wud 'n. Ain't cha

gonna do the dishes first?"

"Mom! Can't you do them this morning?"

"Don't think you can get out of your chores just 'cause sump'n else comes up!"

"Okay, Mom. There aren't very many. I'll do them when I get back." Anna knew it was useless to argue with Josey.

The sun was shining beautifully and the breeze was delightfully warm. It was good to be alive. The birds thought so too for they filled the air with their own special refrains throughout the yard and barn lot, flitting from tree to tree. Anna stretched luxuriously. How things had changed in just a few weeks.

She heard the hum of an engine and saw Gabe's truck going east.

Going to check on his cows no doubt. I owe him so much for my improved state of affairs. I'll try to be the best employee he has ever had, Anna promised herself.

She started up the old Fiat tractor and drove across the pasture to finish gathering their bountiful harvest of apples. She took the ladder out of the front-end loader and set it up, making sure all connections were in place and it was firmly on level ground. She didn't want a malfunction of any kind. Things were going good and she wanted them to stay that way.

When all had been picked up from the ground, Anna climbed to the top of the ladder with her bucket. It was almost full as she reached as far as she felt it was safe when the ladder twisted beneath her. She stood very still, but the ladder continued to twist. She needed someone to help. She turned loose of her bucket and grabbed for a limb. Beautiful golden apples spilled all over the ground. She heard the hum of an engine. It must be Gabe. How she wished him to stop and steady her ladder. Presently, the ladder, too, fell. She had caught handfuls of small branches, but they were not large enough to hold her. She reached further into the tree and caught a larger limb. After a few minutes, however, her arms began to tire. What was she going to do now?

"Hang on just a little longer." It was Gabe—running hard, she could tell. Then he was underneath her. Breathlessly, he instructed, "Just let go. I'll catch you."

Anna was reluctant. The ground seemed so far away. What if she hurt her already damaged ribs? She searched for other branches with her feet. But she could hold on no longer. Her fingers slipped. She fell—in a sitting position—into Gabe's arms.

She had not fallen far, no more than maybe fourteen feet, but the force was enough to knock Gabe to his knees. Holding her tightly, he eased her onto the ground on her back.

"Are you hurt?" he asked, concern in his eyes.

"Just my pride and a few scratches." She was embarrassed and struggled to get up, but he hovered over her, an arm on both sides of her shoulders.

"Were you getting more apples to bake another pie for the Trojan?"

She stared for a moment. "No...actually I baked that pie for Janice. She burned hers and needed some help. He was coming to her house for dinner."

Gabe seemed to like what she had said. Pausing for a moment, he continued, "You are determined to beat yourself up aren't you?" he muttered.

"And you are always there to save me it seems. I am so indebted to you and I am so sorry to be such a klutz."

"You're anything but that," he said, watching her intently. Then he slowly lowered his head to touch her lips with his.

Anna closed her eyes and felt the touch of him strike up chords of longing held at bay for years. Joy unbidden made itself known and her arms automatically went up around his neck. His kiss was tender and lasting. She clung to him wishing it to last forever.

When he finally released her, he whispered, "I still love you, Annie, and I think you love me too. Please don't throw away what we have. Why can't we solve whatever problems you feel you might have with our relationship and begin again...where we left off?

"Before Anna could answer, they hear a loud "Vrip...vrip...vrip" of a siren as Mechlin County's Sheriff pulled up and exited his cruiser to climb the fence and join them. His face showed concern as he hurriedly approached.

"Are you guys okay?" he asked.

"Yeah. We're okay now," Gabe answered.

Troy laughed. "Then what are you doing rolling around in the grass?"

"Well, her ladder collapsed and I saw she needed help so I came running...just in time to catch her." Gabe seemed a little irritated.

"Yes, I could see you here as I turned the corner down there." Serious now, Troy continued, "I'm glad you're not hurt." He picked up the ladder and examined it carefully.

Anna was getting up, rubbing her scratched arms and said, "That's a new ladder. I bought it just yesterday and I thought I had it latched together correctly."

"You did. Look here," Troy commanded as he pointed to braces on the ladder. "These have been cut almost completely into. With Anna's weight on them they broke. This is no accident! Someone is trying to hurt you, Anna."

"It had to have been cut last night. I left it in the front-end bucket parked close to the barn. But who and why?"

"That's what we have to find out, sweetheart," Troy said, sensing her discomfort and wanting to put her at ease. He put his arm around her and continued, "You must take every precaution and suspect everyone. Someone wants to hurt you. We'll watch very closely." He squeezed her close before letting her go.

Gabe stood quietly, obviously uncomfortable with the unnecessarily intimate care Troy was offering Anna.

After a few questions about any suspects or unusual happenings, the sheriff made his departure and Gabe offered to help Anna retrieve her spilled apples.

"I don't want to bother you. I can take care of this mess, but I thank you for what you did."

"I'll stay and help gather all those from the top of the trees," he offered.

Reluctantly, Anna agreed. "I really hate to let them waste. They are very good apples. If you would like some, take all you can use."

Gabe's gaze swept her face and somewhat disarrayed wisps of dark curls that clung to her forehead and cheeks. "Would you maybe bake me a pie, so I can brag to the Trojan how good it was?"

Anna stared for a moment, then blinked her eyes, before laughing and saying, "It was a caramel apple pie and yes, I'd be very happy to bake you a pie and even an apple cake. They are delicious."

Tension seemed to leave Gabe's face as he smiled and reached for her. She tensed and handed him the bucket she had picked up. She turned away, and began to pick up the golden fruit.

"Would you lift me in the front loader to pick the rest from the top of the trees?" she asked.

"No, I don't think that's safe. I'll just brace the ladder firmly against the tree and I can reach almost all of them that way."

When all were gathered, Anna offered Gabe a bucket full of the best.

He accepted. "I'm sure Mom and my family will love them and I'm still looking forward to that pie you promised."

"I'll bring it Monday. Will you be there?"

"I'll make it a point to be," he said.

Gabe took a step closer to her. Earnestly seeking an answer, he spoke hardly above a whisper, "Annie, what keeps us apart? What is it that you fight?"

She looked away, unable to answer—obviously wanting to.

"You testified to my innocence. You knew I wasn't guilty. I've asked you to forgive me even though there's nothing to forgive. I can't understand what keeps us apart."

"I did testify to your innocence, but...." She hesitated and could not proceed.

"But what Annie? Your testimony is what freed me. What's wrong?"

Anna buried her face in her hands. Barely audible came her reply, "I lied. I couldn't remember." Her voice broke. I couldn't remember and if you were innocent I couldn't help you if I told the truth...that I couldn't remember. So if you were guilty, so am I."

"Oh, my god, Annie. You lied for me?"

"I knew in my heart you couldn't have done it!" she cried. "I couldn't let you be falsely accused, but I am haunted by what I did. I really had no proof and then I wondered if I had loved you so much that I let it cloud my vision. I can't put it to rest. My mom was so sure and she keeps reminding me of my transgression, as she puts it, until I'm not sure of anything. If only I could remember. I sometimes wonder if I can't face the truth—so I refuse to remember.

"Oh, Annie, Annie, Annie. I swear to you by all that I hold dear, I am innocent. Your mother lies! I'm sorry to call her a liar, but she is. She never wanted us to marry. She has kept us apart. Please, oh god, Annie, know that I tell you the truth."

Anna's hand covered her mouth. Tears fell silently down her cheeks. Finally she spoke. "I pray to God I'll remember. I can't forgive myself such a lie if..."

Gabe, with hurt in his eyes, questioned, "If I am guilty you mean?"

She turned to go. He reached for her, lovingly pulling her into a tender embrace. "I love you with all my heart and I need you, Annie."

She sobbed uncontrollably for some minutes before lifting her head and whispering, "I love you just as much Gabe, but what kind of a marriage would it be if I wondered...even if just occasionally. I wouldn't be fair to you or to me and our marriage would suffer."

She pushed away, turned her back on him and left. He stood silently as he watched her leave, before dejectedly walking back to his truck parked on the roadway, the door standing open as he had left it in anxious haste.

Anna battled with her conscience. She had been so devastated by the events that afternoon several years ago. Maybe she couldn't remember because she had never comprehended what was actually happening at the time. She had paid no attention to anything after hearing the words that tore out her heart and shriveled her soul. If that were the case, she would never know with certainty the truth of the matter that had hounded her for years.

Tired and emotionally drained, she cleaned the kitchen and did the dishes she had left earlier. She needed to rest and went to her bedroom to lie down, even knowing she could not sleep. Thoughts of Gabe tormented her. She couldn't bear to hurt him, but which would be worse—to marry him, questioning his good character until finally he learned to despise her, or to turn her back on him and forever deny the love they shared. It was a torture she could hardly endure.

As she lay hating herself for not being able to put it aside and to accept and love Gabe as she yearned, she heard a whining. She jumped to her feet and ran to the back door.

"Oh, mon dieu! Casey! What on earth happened to you!" she exclaimed.

Her precious Old English Sheepdog was whining, barking and jumping on the back screen door, a quivering mass of cockleburs from head to toe. He had already eaten most of the food in his dish and all the water was gone from his watering container. He was so thin and dirty, she would never have recognized him elsewhere.

She slipped out the door and tried to pet him, but where? He was completely and solidly covered with burrs. He seemed to understand that she could not hug his "stickery" body so he resorted to licking her hands and arms, and when he could reach it, her face.

"My lord! You must have come a very long way through rough country with lots of burrs.

I will take care of these as soon as possible. But how can you rest? Your skin must be one solid pin cushion!"

She talked to him all the time she was gathering things to rid him of the sharp spikes that gouged him all over. It was going to take a lot of time, but at least he was home. She refilled his food and water dishes and laid a thickly padded comforter on the back patio for him. She gathered her scissors and a bag for the trimmed hair, then knelt and began to search for a place to start. She was unable to get the point of the scissors between the burrs and Casey's skin. His hair was too thickly matted. Horrors! What could she do? She hurried to her bedroom and returned with a small pair of thin-bladed, sharp-pointed manicure scissors. They would work, but she would have to be extremely careful.

Casey was exhausted. He must have felt safe for he lay very still for hours as Anna patiently clipped away, inch by inch, the tightly packed objects of his pain. Occasionally, he lifted his head and licked her hand before sighing heavily and once again lying back, motionless.

Anna worked for three solid hours before she had to take a break. Her legs and back, especially her left side ached abominably. Casey slept and moved around some, but was always ready to lie very still when Anna was ready to once again begin the trimming process.

It took all the time and energy Anna could muster to rid Casey of his unwanted, prickly, clinging antagonists. In two days, Casey was free of them altogether. She bathed him to his delight and laughed at his weird appearance. He looked as though he had been shaved all over—as in fact he had. He was dearer to her than ever as she reflected on what he had endured and the distance he must have traveled to get back home to her.

And Casey was so appreciative of the care she had given him that he rarely left her side...or maybe he just felt safer there.

Anna wondered who had taken him and why. Maybe someone from a distant city had taken him, and he had gotten away. But there was always the possibility that Old Charley had deliberately dumped him somewhere, thinking he couldn't find his way home. Anna decided to call the sheriff and report that Casey was back.

Anna asked her mother again what she knew about Casey's disappearance.

"I told you already...I don't know nothin' bout that dumb dog."

But she didn't seem to be happy that Casey was back. And Casey didn't seem to want to be around her either. He even growled at her once when she walked close by and woke him from a nap.

Anna needed to check her mother's car trunk. Maybe there would be some of Casey's hair there or something. Had they put him in the trunk and taken him to Oklahoma City and dumped him when Dugan left? He had disappeared the night before Dugan left. Where could they have hidden him overnight? How would she ever know? And what would happen if she could prove it?

Not much, she decided.

But Casey would remember his torment and those who had caused it.

Chapter Six

Things were going smoothly for a change. After several days, Anna could even see a difference in Casey's hair. It was growing and looked softer with maybe a little curl in some places. He was looking good again. Maybe gaining back some weight. He had always been so pretty; his hair—many shades of gray and splashed here and there with white, curling softly—was set off nicely by the bright red collar around his neck.

Where is that collar? she wondered. If she knew that, maybe she'd have a clue about who took him.

As she promised Gabe, she baked a caramel apple pie and an apple cake with caramel icing that seeped into the cake itself. Gabe rather taciturnly thanked her for the gifts and cut the pie to share with those who came into the office, but took the cake home with him.

"Thank you very much, Anna, for the delicious desserts," he said the next day without enthusiasm. Obviously he was upset with her. "Mother would like your cake recipe."

She rarely saw him for several days at a time and he was very aloof when he did show up at his office. Since Mrs. McClusky was no longer there they had to communicate with each other, but his manner had become quite formal and there were no smiles to soften his demeanor. Anna knew that he had on several occasions worked after hours because letters and other instructions were left on her desk and the cake recipe for his mother was gone. Was he deliberately avoiding her?

She knew she had hurt him by not trusting him completely, but she couldn't force herself to fully believe him, any more than she could force herself to love anyone else.

Anna had managed to get her mother's keys as she slept one afternoon and checked the trunk of Josey's car. She found nothing out of the ordinary—no hair, no mud or anything. As she started to close the trunk, the keys slid from her fingers. She bent to pick them up and noticed a bit of red underneath the spare tire. It was hard to dislodge, but with a small stick and some determined prodding, she dislodged Casey's red collar. It had his name, address and her phone number on the attached brass plate. Of course! Whoever found him would have called—most likely—and Casey would have been home again. It had been removed by someone. Who? Most likely Dugan.

How did Dugan manage to take off his collar? Casey would never have allowed it. Did Mom do it then? She wondered.

Anna called Troy and reported what she had found.

"Thank you for letting me know. And, Anna, I don't think I would reveal that you have found his collar to anyone at this time. Don't confront Josey or accuse Dugan. It might just accelerate their attacks on you, if in fact they are the ones who are doing these things. Please be careful and trust no one. I mean absolutely no one."

Who else could I suspect? she wondered. *I think he means Mom and didn't want to say so.*

Anna thought of every person she had contact with...several of Gabe's workers, Janice, Troy...himself, a few casual acquaintances, and...no...surely he didn't mean suspect Gabe too.

Several days later, on a sunny Friday after work, Anna decided she was in the mood for a Burger Hut burger. As she pulled up to the "Hut," she saw a beautiful, young girl with strikingly lovely, long black hair exit the building, carrying a paper container in her hand. She was wearing an orchid dress with a tight bodice and full skirt. White heels and a white strand of beads around her neck complemented the overall color scheme.

How absolutely exquisite, Anna thought.

As the girl passed in front of her truck, she looked directly at

Anna. Her eyes were a deep violet, fringed with long thick lashes. *It must be the reflection from her orchid dress, or maybe colored contact lenses,* Anna thought. *I have never seen such gorgeous eyes.*

As she watched, the girl screamed and jumped back from a dirty, greasy, long-haired man who had obviously been drinking. He had stuck his filthy fingers into the girl's sundae and took the cherry from the top of it along with a goodly amount of whipped cream. He plopped it into his mouth and chewed lewdly with guttural sounds, indicating it was delicious. He grinned widely, exposing crooked, tobacco stained teeth.

Obviously shocked, the girl threw her sundae in his face, saying, "Here take it all you slime-ball-low-life."

A face full of ice cream covered with hot fudge wiped the silly grin from his face. He turned back and grabbed her arm.

Menacingly, he pulled her to him, saying, "Oh, I can take it all, sugar!"

At that moment, Gabe stepped out of the door of the Burger Hut. "Get your filthy hands off her!" he shouted.

The guy laughed. "You're too late, Whittier. I already got her cherry!"

A few long strides put him quickly within reach and Gabe's powerful right swing to the side of his head knocked the assailant flat to the ground.

"Shut your filthy mouth!" Gabe spat through clenched teeth.

Anna recognized the greasy fellow as Billy Freemont, Carla's lost love. He had a buddy with him, who jumped into the fray and hit Gabe from behind. Gabe staggered, but regained his balance. He turned to face Billy's much bigger, but just as filthy companion.

The girl in the orchid dress jumped on Billy's back, who had managed to get up and was now attacking Gabe—punching him between the shoulder blades. She screamed and grabbed a handful of hair with one hand while beating him about the ears with the other.

Anna, who at the beginning of the confrontation called 911 and asked for the sheriff's hot line, had Troy on the phone.

"You're needed at the Burger Hut in a quick hurry! Two bums are trying to beat up Gabe!"

"I'm already there!" he said.

Anna heard his siren. In truth he was there in about a minute. He must have been just around the corner. But lots of blows can fall in one minute. Before the sheriff was there, two men had jumped out of their truck and with a few slams and grabs had pushed both Billy and his friend up against the wall and was holding their hands behind their backs.

"Hey, Gabe," one of them said, "Don't try to take on two at a time, buddy!" He laughed.

Troy cuffed the dirty buggers and stood talking to everyone involved. Billy and his crony were more subdued when confronted by law enforcement.

At one point, Anna heard Billy yell, "I didn't know she belonged to you, Whittier!"

"She doesn't belong to anyone, you bastard! She deserves respect in her own right!" Anna recognized righteous anger in Gabe's voice.

After a bit, Troy approached Anna, who was still sitting in her truck.

"I'm sorry. I should have called the police department instead of the sheriff's office, I guess, since this is in the city limits." Anna apologized.

"That's okay. As a sworn officer, I can make arrests in the city. And I was already here. Besides we use the same jail. I'll just turn it over to the police. Did you see everything that happened?"

"Yes, I did," she replied and told him in detail everything that had occurred, adding, "and that guy, who put his dirty fingers in her sundae to grab the cherry, is none other than Carla Spencer's lover, who disappeared. If you remember her."

"Yes, I do indeed. I remember her well. Thanks, Anna, your

story matches Gabe's exactly."

A deputy pulled up and was putting the two into the back seat of his patrol car when Billy noticed Anna talking to the sheriff.

"Oh, ho! Protecting him with more lies, are ya?"

Anna was furious. "You don't even know what I said and already it's a lie! Sounds just like you Freemont!"

"Get them out of here. Lock 'em up!" Troy demanded.

Anna heard him tell Gabe to go by the police department if he wanted to press charges.

The pretty girl, her hair somewhat disheveled and with grease on her lovely dress said, "Well, I will if he doesn't! That butt-head accosted me first!"

A little feisty, thought Anna, appreciating the girl's spunk.

The girl wiped Gabe's cheek with a napkin and slipped her arm around his waist as he put his around her and together they walked to his car.

Anna felt a shattering loneliness overtake her as she stared at their retreating backs. So they had been together all along! She hadn't known there was anyone else. But she had known it was bound to happen. A man couldn't be expected to live like a hermit—especially a man like Gabe. She'd known he could have his pick of many sweet things, and some he had dated for short periods of time, but nothing permanent had developed—at least nothing she knew about. But how could anyone resist such a lovely girl as the one who had so fiercely defended him today.

It had to happen sometime! Like death though, Anna had always thought of it as being somewhere in the future and hopefully far away. Maybe a miracle would happen and she would not have to face the agony, but postpone it inevitably. She had been a fool—unable to accept a compromise and had now lost—irrefutably! She would once again have to endure and—if not prevail—at least survive. But, why? What for? Nothing seemed to matter. The love of her life was gone and all her hope had vanished with him.

Why was she just now so devastated? She had told herself all along that she would never be in a relationship with Gabe again. Oh, how she had deceived herself! She had to have had a hidden hope because now she knew the true feeling of no hope—and it crushed her.

She had tossed and turned, crying most of the night. She still felt lost, empty inside and had no desire to face the day. Why hadn't she married him years ago and solved the problems as they arose? She was glad it was Saturday and not a work day. Her eyes were swollen almost shut and her nose was so stuffed she could hardly breathe.

"What happened to you? You look like you wuz run over by a truck." Josey stared over her cup of coffee.

"Must be allergies, I guess," Anna replied.

What did it matter? No one cared anyway. She wasn't hungry and had only a cup of coffee before going to seek consolation, the healing power of trusted friends—Casey and Smoky—who accepted her as she was.

She decided she was probably well enough to start riding again. Maybe she'd even do some barrels. Barrel racing had been an enjoyable endeavor and Smoky had obviously liked it too. She must find something to do or lose her mind. She didn't want to regress back into the condition she had descended into years ago—when she first felt Gabe was lost to her.

Throwing the saddle on her horse was somewhat painful. She wondered if she were pushing the envelope, but the saddle was already on....

"So ride!" she told herself.

Smoky cantered for a little while, but wanted to run, so she gave him his head and hung on. Casey, who was trotting behind, gave up and returned to the barn.

After a circuitous run around the pasture and back, Smoky was breathing hard. She unsaddled him and gave him a good rub-down, then fed him several apples.

We need to do this more often, she thought. She knew Smoky would be willing.

It was time to put in the winter wheat. And work was the best way to keep one's emotions under control. So she spent the rest of the day pulling a pasture drill across the north pasture in order that Josey's cows could have some "green" during the winter months.

After a meager supper, Anna did her laundry and mended a few items. She needed some new clothes and now maybe she could afford them. She would go shopping next week. Hopefully, that would help busy her mind as well.

She had not been able, of late, to spend much time with Janice,who always seemed to have a date. Anna knew without asking that she would be "tied up" on the nights Troy, the Trojan, was off duty. Anna was glad for them, even though it left her more lonely than ever.

She washed and cleaned her truck. A lot of dust settled on it as she drove the gravel roads. She was pleased with her new Ford and wanted to keep it in good condition.

On Monday morning, Anna had a lot of work to do at the office and was thankful for it. Deeply immersed in her duties, she jumped and gave a small, startled cry when a voice behind her said, "I guess Gabe's not here, is he?"

She turned to see Bill Grant, one of Gabe's construction workers, standing in front of her desk.

"No, I've not heard from him yet this morning. Is there anything I can help you with?"

"No, I guess not. After a moment's hesitation, he smiled, "Unless you have another one of those scrumptious pies in the kitchen." They both laughed.

"Not today. Maybe again next week," she said.

"That was really the best apple pie I have ever tasted."

"Thanks. It's the caramel...most people like caramel, I think."

He was looking at her curiously. "Aren't you that gal that used to ride the black horse at all the rodeos? The horse that did all the tricks?"

"I guess that would be me. My horse is black and he does do tricks and I did ride and run the barrels."

"Yeh! And you were really good too. Why don't you do that anymore?"

"I just got so busy that I let it slide, I guess. Then I had an accident and now that I'm better, I may start again."

"That would be great. My friend, George Cummings, is in charge of getting things together for the next rodeo, in about two months. He needs a good crowd-drawing act like yours. Could I have him give you a call?"

"Ah...well...I haven't ridden or trained my horse in quite some time. I'm not sure we could be ready in two months. ...Well...sure. Have him call me if he's interested."

Anna knew the grind and hard prep would keep her extremely busy and her mind occupied and there was no work she liked better than training Smoky. She should give it a shot.

"Great!" He replied. "And let me know when you bring another pie." He laughed.

"Oh, okay, how about next Tuesday?"

"I'll check it out! See you then."

As promised, on the following Tuesday, Anna brought another caramel apple pie to share with any of Gabe's workers and clients that happened into his office.

Bill Grant showed up as expected since he also had to pick up a special order that day. He had finished his pie and was lingering over the rest of his coffee in front of Anna's desk when Gabe walked in.

"Hey, Bill, what're you doing here?" he asked.

"On my lunch hour and picking up some special hardware...and enjoying myself immensely. Where did you find such a talented gal to run your office?"

With a slight frown, Gabe said, "Graduated high school with her."

"High school! That long ago and you are still letting her run loose? You must be nuts man. I mean...she's the best pie-maker ever and can train and handle a horse like...as good as any man...and better'n most. She runs a farm and your office like a pro and there's not a better looking filly in the whole state." Turning to Anna, he asked, "How come none of the guys that come in here haven't lassoed you in yet?"

Anna, somewhat dumbfounded, hesitated before answering.

Gabe spoke up with the answer. "Cause she's in love with me, Bill! Isn't your lunch hour about over now?"

"Oh, ho! I see. Well, yes, I'd best be going now. Thanks a lot, Anna. The pie was delicious. And Gabe don't wait too long to stake your claim here, 'cause a bunch of the guys are not going to take your word for how much she likes you." He laughed. "See you later, boss man," he said, as he waved his hand and hurried out the door.

Anna and Gabe stared at each other for a moment before Gabe broke the silence.

With a shrug, he said, "I had to say something to get him back on the job."

He almost grinned. Serious again, he continued, "And he's right, you do everything well. And I really appreciate your efforts. You know I would...." He waved his hand, as if recognizing the futility of any comment he might make, went into his office and closed the door.

His visits to the office became even more infrequent and when he did come by the visits were brief and to the point—very business-like. Anna longed to see him, even though it was best that she didn't. She had, however, seen him on several occasions with that beautiful girl. They had been playing tennis at the park when she had driven by, going to the grocery store. They had been eating across the restaurant when she happened to go out for lunch. They were just going into a movie theater when she picked up a prescription next door for Josey's high blood pressure.

She was a gorgeous girl and always impeccably dressed. It reminded Anna that she intended to go shopping for herself.

There's no time like the present, she thought. *I wonder where she finds her beautiful clothes.*

After work, Anna went to all the better dress shops to check their sale items. She tried on everything that looked good to her and ended up with an arm load of pretty things. Some had not even been on sale. She wanted to look nice and feel good, if she could do it without being too extravagant.

She bought a black "coat-dress" with narrow white trim around the collar and cuffs and all the way down the front on both sides of what appeared to be a coat over a dress, but was not. It made her look tall and chic. Black patent pumps added a little to her height and the "flip" hair-do caused one of Gabe's guys to say, "You look just like Marlo Thomas in that old TV series way back when."

She also purchased a light beige pant suit with a sleeveless jacket that sported a wide belt and large patch pockets lending it a military or safari look. She would wear it with a long sleeve, white, silk blouse. She liked it very much. In addition, she had chosen several dresses with fitted bodices and full or circle skirts that fell gracefully around her legs as she walked in high heels— that she had never been inclined to wear before.

She began to receive many compliments and second looks from lots of guys. She appreciated the compliments, but her days were still empty and lonely.

Why on earth did I think I would be happier wearing newer, nicer things? What's it going to take to shake this horribly dark cloud that covers my every moment? She knew what it would take and also knew it wasn't going to happen. She had been a fool and nothing she could do would change that now.

Anna accepted the challenge when George Cummings asked her to ride in his rodeo. He was delighted when she agreed to appear and let Smoky show off his skills. He put her on the program in two different spots. One was running the barrels and the other was putting Smoky through his presentation.

She threw herself into hours of practice with Smoky and they were making good progress. She set up the barrels—only three for this first rodeo. The first two barrels were 60 feet from her starting point and 90 feet, horizontally, across from each other. The third barrel was 105 feet away from and on a line perpendicular to and in the center of a line between the first two barrels.

Smoky was to run from the starting point around the right-most barrel, clockwise, then counter clockwise around the left-most barrel and proceed around the last barrel counter clockwise and return to the starting point all within 17 seconds or less to get a good score. That calculated to be approximately 420 feet plus the turns—and all that without knocking over a barrel. Anna figured it had to be done within 13 to 14 seconds to take home the trophy and the check for first prize. She wondered if she and Smoky could still do it. It would be difficult with no more time than they had to practice.

I guess I can chicken out at the last minute if I know we're not ready, she thought.

She had decided to give it a go and began putting Smoky through rigorous paces every available moment, hour after hour, day after day.

Smoky gave it his all, as though he knew their schedule was tight...or maybe because he knew he'd get an apple after every session. Anna encouraged and coaxed him, cutting off every second possible with each practice run. She also sandwiched in the bowing and prancing routines, smoothing out the rough edges. She added a few of his old tricks, but tried to pick the easier ones because of the limited time factor. Her hopes rose as their abilities climbed. Maybe—just maybe—they had a chance to take the trophy. If not, well...they would steal the show with Smoky's tricks.

Casey watched them train. Sometimes falling asleep or

sometimes barking encouragement. He was almost as pretty as ever. His hair was growing out nicely and curling beautifully. On occasion, though, he seemed nervous and watchful. Anna studied him carefully, wondering about the source of his agitation. Eventually he would settle down and seem normal again.

Uneventful days passed as Anna took advantage of every extra moment to improve Smoky's skills to run the barrels—along with all of his tricks. She decided she needed a more crowd-pleasing costume for their big night. Since Smoky was all black and his bridle and saddle blanket were red, she chose white for contrast. She went to the Western Wear House and tried several shirts with matching pants and finally chose a long sleeve, western-cut shirt with gold sequins covering the front and back yolks and cuffs. The white pants fit well and had a little stretch in order to allow Anna some ease with which to manipulate her horse around the course. For a final touch, she purchased a pair of white boots. The price tag was more than she wanted to pay. She consoled herself with the realization that if she won, the cash prize would more than cover the cost of everything. She intended to win. Most contestants wore western hats, but Anna decided not to. Hats bothered her and she didn't need any distractions.

On Thursday morning, Anna received a pleasant surprise. The phone rang for the "umpteenth" time and she answered as usual.

"Good morning. Whittier Enterprises."

"Good Morning. This is John Campbell."

"Yes, Mr. Mayor. I'm sorry Gabe isn't in this morning. Could I help you with something? Or have him to call you?"

"Nope. I'm not calling Gabe. I'm calling you. Would you lead our annual fall parade on Saturday? Some like to call it the Labor Day parade, but it never falls on Labor Day. We always have it on a Saturday—never on a Monday."

"Um...I had forgotten it was this week." Anna was hesitating. She had wanted to practice with Smoky all weekend as the date for the rodeo was not far away.

"You still have that black stallion, don't you?"

"I still have Smoky, yes." She didn't correct the mayor about Smoky's breeding capabilities.

And, yes, I'd be honored."

She had quickly decided that Smoky really needed some exposure to crowds and all their noise. It would be good for both of them.

"Good! I'll fax you the route so you can check it out if you need to. The parade starts at 10 and should last about an hour. We'll start from the county fair grounds and end up back there, so you'll have plenty of space to park your trailer. I thank you a lot and we'll get your picture in the Carnegie Gazette so wear somethin' pretty.

Anna laughed. *Did he think I was going to wear raggety jeans or something,* she wondered.

"Okay. Thank you, Mr. Mayor. It'll be fun."

"I'll see you early Saturday. You'll need to be there a little earlier than 10 to get all lined up properly."

"I'll be there by 9:30. Will that work?"

"Yes, I believe that will do fine. Thanks again. I knew I could count on you."

Anna guessed she would have to wear her white western outfit to both the parade and the rodeo. She hoped Smoky wouldn't spook. It had been quite a while since he had worked in a crowd. But, he should be okay. He had quite a bit of experience. Hopefully, he would remember it and not panic. She hoped she would do the same. She felt good about being "back in the saddle again."

On Saturday morning, Anna fed and saddled Smoky, hitched to her trailer and hurriedly finished dressing, taking special care with her hair. She had asked Josey to come watch, but her mother declined. Anna was at the fairgrounds, ready and waiting, when the others started arriving to line up for the parade.

The mayor had wanted Anna first in line, but she argued that

Rachael Stratford

it would be difficult, if not impossible, for her to gauge the
steady rate of 10 miles per hour, hoped for—to be finished in the
projected hour. "I really need to be positioned behind a pace-
setter, like a car with a speedometer, since my horse doesn't have
one." Anna joked. "I will have to determine and adjust Smoky's
canter and the number of trips across the street so Smoky can
bow to the crowd on both sides. It will be extremely difficult for
me to do that and set the pace. I would have no idea what
forward rate I was achieving. But I can follow and adapt to an
established speed."

"You're right," agreed the mayor. "Why don't you take the
position immediately behind the three cars carrying the city
officials and Carnegie business men?"

"Sounds good. I'll do my best to keep up and you might tell
those behind me to adjust their speed until I get the proper timing
and number of trips—back and forth—adjusted properly."

"I'll do that. Thanks, Anna, and good luck."

The mayor, the city manager, the president of the First
National Bank and the publisher of the Gazette were the first in
line—riding in a red convertible with the top down. Two more
convertibles followed, filled with important business men and
city officials. Anna should have known Gabe would be one of
them. He was seated in the second car with Sheriff Henderson,
Bob Flannagan, the Ford dealer, and the principal of Carnegie
High. If Gabe noticed her, he gave no sign.

She positioned herself well behind the last car with enough
space in front of the first float to allow time for Smoky to do his
prancing and bowing. She would have to give her undivided
attention to staying in sync with the movement of the parade. It
gave her no time to notice any one person in the crowd.

Still she heard voices she recognized: Janice's, "Woo-hoo!
Don't you look snazzy!" Old classmates saying, "Way to go,
Annie!" Or just, "Hey Anna!" Employees from the hospital
where she had been employed and neighbors all yelling, "Good
to see you back." Or "Lookin' gorgeous, gal."—all

encouragement of some kind. One young boy yelled, "Hey, Anna, can I ride Smoky?" It was good and heartwarming. It reminded her how much she had enjoyed the parade in the past. Even though she couldn't see the persons who had called to her she waved her acknowledgment of them—in their general direction. One group of especially vocal young boys kept giving wolf whistles as she passed and one yelled, "Boy! I'd love to have that!" Anna assumed he meant Smoky for she had brushed and clipped him the night before. He glistened in the sun. She had polished his saddle and bridle and he was absolutely beautiful. And he seemed to know it. He pranced smartly and bowed low and perfectly. She was sure he enjoyed the "oohs and ahs" and clapping of his fans. If he tired before the end, he never showed it. His step was quick and spirited. Anna was proud of him. Did he know he had apples waiting for him? Anna rather believed he just enjoyed the admiration he was receiving.

Anna took Smoky home, unsaddled him and rubbed him down with care while he munched his apples. How she loved that horse! She hoped he would win the barrel racing contest at the rodeo.

"I'm so proud of you." She hugged his neck and kissed his forehead. "And you are such a handsome devil."

He raised and lowered his head up and down several times as though agreeing with her.

She chuckled. "Now if you could just learn a little modesty, you'd be the perfect horse." She patted him lightly on the rump as she left, saying, "I'll see you later."

He nickered his goodbye and went back to munching apples.

Chapter Seven

The parade had been a great success with a nice write-up in the Carnegie Gazette. And as promised by the mayor, there was a good picture of Anna on Smoky waving to the crowd—all of whom seemed to be waving back.

On Sunday morning, Anna bought a paper and was enthusiastically reading the press report about Carnegie's annual parade to Josey at breakfast. Josey didn't seem to be interested and before Anna had read half of it, her mother got up and started for her bedroom.

"Mom! Don't you want to hear about the parade? It was so much fun. Smoky and I got a big kick out of it."

"I don't feel just real good. Think I'll lay down fer a bit."

"What's wrong? Can I get you anything?"

"No, I'll just rest and take an aspirin."

"Do you hurt or are you nauseous or what?"

"I feel a little sick, but my arm hurts and I'm just s' tired I can't go"

"Let me know if I can get you anything," Anna offered.

Josey slept until the middle of the afternoon, when Anna came in from practicing with Smoky and woke her. Anna fixed her some lunch, but her mother ate very little.

"Is there anything special you'd prefer? You didn't eat much."

"No, I'm not hungry."

"Does your arm still hurt?"

"Not as much, but m' stupid hand keeps goin' ta' sleep."

"I can take you to the emergency room. It could be your heart."

"No! Now don't go gettin' all upset over nuthin'."

"You don't know that it's nothing. Well...okay, Mom, if you will make an appointment to see the doctor soon," Anna replied.

Josey didn't answer, so Anna decided she would call Josey's doctor Monday to make an appointment herself.

"Bring me a cup a coffee, will ya?"

"Sure, Mom. I'll make a fresh pot."

The following morning Josey was up and had a normal breakfast with Anna.

"Do you feel better this morning?"

"I don't hurt any, but I'm still real tired. I'll just rest today."

"I can take you to the emergency room if it gets worse or to the doctor's office as soon as we can get an appointment."

Josey said nothing, but took her coffee, lay back in her recliner and flipped on the TV.

Anna thought perhaps that was a factor in Josey's condition. She had never gotten any exercise to speak of and, though she was not obese, she carried extra pounds and her eating habits had not been the best. A lifetime of inactivity and poor eating habits surely had taken its toll on her body. Plus she had been a heavy smoker for about ten years after Anna's father had died—before she finally gave it up. Anna suspected a heart problem and wondered how bad it might be.

As soon as Anna reached her office Monday morning, she called Dr. Milton's receptionist.

"Hi, Vera. This is Anna Shelton and my mom needs an appointment as soon as possible."

"We're booked solid for the whole week," Vera said. "What seems to be the problem?"

"She has pain in her left arm and her hand keeps going to sleep. She's somewhat nauseous and extremely fatigued. I'm afraid it may be her heart."

"If you think this is an emergency, we should send her to the emergency room at the hospital."

"Well, she's feeling better this morning and insists that she will not go to the hospital, but I would like the doctor's opinion as soon as possible," Anna explained.

"I can put you down for the next available appointment and call you if someone cancels before that."

"Okay, if it's the best we can do. And yes, please do call if there is a cancellation. In the meantime, I will keep close tabs on her and if it seems to get worse, I'll take her to the emergency room."

The day was busy and full of people coming and going, wanting information or parts or ordering something special. Most all of them had seen the parade and commented on Anna and Smoky's performance. It was a good feeling to get feed-back and all of it was complimentary, but all of the questions and comments cut into Anna's productivity which unsettled her a little.

She call Josey mid-morning and again on her lunch hour to see how she was feeling; and to let her know that she had made an appointment for her with Dr. Milton.

"I'm okay. I just got up to make a fresh pot of coffee and I may have a sandwich here in a minute."

"Mom, I made some vegetable soup late yesterday. Why not heat that up and try a bowl of it? It's your favorite."

"Naw, don't think I want soup."

"Okay, I'll be home as soon as I get off. Call if you need anything."

Josey hung up without responding.

Anna had hoped for Gabe's comments on her participation in the parade, but he never even came into the office all day.

A few minutes before 5 o'clock, Anna called Josey to see if she could get her something special. Her mother didn't answer the phone.

Probably asleep and didn't hear it ring, she thought.

Still she became apprehensive and hurried home a little faster than usual. Casey met her at the door and Anna ruffled the hair on his head in passing as she hurried inside.

"Mom?" she called as she entered the back door.

There was no response. Anna rushed through the utility and toward her mother's bedroom. She glanced into the kitchen as she passed and saw Josey lying on the floor in front of the refrigerator.

"Oh, my god! Have you been there since lunch time?" she asked.

Josey didn't answer. Without hesitation, Anna called 9-1-1. She checked to see if Josey was still breathing. She was. She opened her eyes and groaned as Anna lifted her head and shoulders.

The 9-1-1 operator answered.

"I think my mother has had a heart attack and I need an ambulance now!"

"What is your address and full name."

"Oh, god!" Anna had never thought about how to give her rural address to someone in case of an emergency. Her address was a rural box number. Struggling, she got her wits together and hurriedly went through the mile by mile directions. How else? "We're three miles north of Highway 159 at Cedar Valley Road, then back east 1 and ½ miles...on the north side of the road. There's a big sign over the gate that says 'Cedar Valley Horses.'" Her dad had sold some of the best in the country.

"Are you Anna Shelton?" the operator asked.

"Yes, yes, but can't this wait? I need an ambulance now! I don't know how bad my mom is! She wouldn't go to the hospital...I should have made her!"

"The ambulance is already on its way. I just need some information. What is your mother's name?"

"Josey. Josey Shelton. What should I be doing? She is breathing, but she won't answer me. Why did I leave her by herself?"

"Just cover her with a blanket and keep her warm. The paramedics should be there within minutes. Just hold on until they are."

Anna tried to get a response from Josey.

"Mom, oh, my gosh! How long have you been lying there on the floor?"

Josey didn't reply, but closed her eyes and clutched Anna's arm.

Sirens from the emergency vehicle could be heard coming down the road and eventually into her driveway.

"They're here. Thank you so much for your help."

"Good luck." Anna heard the operator say before the click as she hung up the phone.

Anna followed the paramedics to the Carnegie Hospital and waited outside the emergency room for some answers. Janice came with the doctor who brought her the news. It was both good and bad.

Janice immediately put her arms around Anna, saying, "She's going to be alright, sweetie."

"Thank God!" Tears filled Anna eyes as she thought, *There's nothing like sympathy to start the tears flowing when you have been hurt.*

With effort, Anna took control of her emotions and reached out to shake the extended hand of the accompanying physician.

"Hello, Anna. I'm Dr. Lindsay. I met you when you worked here earlier this year. I just examined your mother and she has had a heart attack. We don't think it's critical, but we won't know the extent of the damage until we have the results of all the tests that were run. That should be sometime tomorrow. We will move her into the coronary care unit upstairs for a time—until we know exactly what the damage is and to closely watch her vital signs for any further trauma."

"Thank you very much, Dr. Lindsay. I'll just be in the waiting room outside the CCU, if you need me for anything."

They moved Josey to the coronary care unit. Anna spent the night in a recliner a short distance down the hall from the CCU in the small waiting room. She wanted to be close by until she was sure Josey was stable.

Since Josey was in good hands and reportedly not in any immediate danger, Anna went home early the next morning. She showered and dressed for work, but not before she took a couple of carrots to Smoky. He ate them, but didn't seem to be impressed. Casey seemed to be nervous. He kept running a short distance away from the back door, toward the barn, barking.

There must be a raccoon or a skunk out there bothering him, Anna thought.

And it could be a skunk of the human variety—one who meant her physical harm. She felt the need to protect herself. But Casey settled down after a few minutes and ate his breakfast with gusto.

Wonder where dad's old shotgun is? I must ask Mom. I need to learn to handle it properly.

Anna was tired and knew it was going to be a long day. She would do her best to stay awake. She ate a large breakfast with lots of protein and drank an extra cup of coffee, hoping the caffeine would help.

She was well into her regular duties when Gabe came in at approximately 9:30.

Surprised, he exclaimed, "I didn't expect to see you this morning. How's your mother?"

"She's going to be alright, they think, but they are keeping her in the CCU. And since there was nothing I could do there, not even be in a room with her, I thought I might as well work."

"I hope she's going to be okay. If you need to take time off just let me know. Mrs. McClusky will probably be available."

"How did you know about her heart attack?" she asked.

"We were at the Burger Hut late last evening and Janice came by. She told us she was at the hospital when your mother was brought in. I'm sorry you had to find her there on the floor like that."

Anna wondered, but thought she knew, who the "we" and "us"—that he referred to—would be.

"Yes, it was an unnerving experience. I don't know how long

105

she had been there on the floor. Not too long I would guess. The TV was on and the cup of coffee on her tray was still warm."

"Did you get any sleep last night?"

"Not much. I slept a little in the recliner in the CCU waiting room. I wanted to be close in case of any significant change. But I'm okay. I had extra coffee." She smiled at him. When he didn't smile back, she continued, "Here are several invoices that require your approval and signature before I can pay them—if you have time this morning," she continued.

"Of course," he said taking them from her as he turned and went down the hall to his office. "Remember, if you need to leave, just let me know." he reiterated.

"I will. Thank you very much." she replied, thinking, *My how formal we are for such old acquaintances.*

It pained her considerably. Why couldn't they be friends? After due consideration, Anna decided Gabe was probably right. It would be easier to deny any attraction to each other than to openly acknowledge it while denying any possibility of it blossoming into a full loving relationship.

Anna went to the hospital on her lunch break and learned that Josey's heart attack was still not thought to be too severe. She had been given a "clot buster" to dissolve any coagulation problems. There was apparently no extensive damage. They would keep her in the CCU for about two days just in case. And maybe a couple more days on the floor to watch her enzyme levels and run echocardiograms to keep tabs on the functioning of her heart. Sometime soon a heart catheterization might be in order to find any occluded vessels. And then, if appropriate, put in a stent maybe. Or if that were not feasible, do bypass surgery.

If they can convince her to let them do it, Anna thought.

In the meantime, Josey would take nitroglycerine tablets, a vasodilator, to relieve the angina. Josey would have to take them until a more permanent solution could be achieved or perhaps forever.

Josey was non-committal.

"If I'm just gonna lay here, I can do that at home," she complained.

"Yeah, Mom, but they need to monitor what your heart's doing and see how the medicine effects it and stuff like that. Besides you need someone to stay with you and I really need to work if it's at all possible. Okay?"

Josey didn't answer.

"Can I bring you anything at all. I guess you don't feel like reading or doing any puzzles right now, but I'll bring you some of that stuff later today. I'm on my lunch break so I have to run. Have them call me if you need anything special. Okay?"

Josey still didn't answer.

"Mom! Did you hear me?"

Josey's mouth tightened, but she nodded her head slightly—in the affirmative. There had never been any display of affection between the two of them so—instead of kissing her forehead, or something of that nature, as she would have her father's—Anna patted her hand, saying, "I'll be back after work, Mom."

Anna had finally named Daisy's baby. The little calf was very active. She would often run circles around Anna, pitching and bucking.

"Show-off," Anna had laughingly said to her, "You're a ring-tailed-tooter aren't you?"

The name had stuck. Thereafter, Anna called her Tooter.

Smoky would attempt to lead Tooter across the arena by himself in his performance at the rodeo. In order for him to know exactly what he should do and precisely where he was to start and stop, Anna needed to teach him on the spot. She asked George Cummings, the chairman of the rodeo committee, if she could have the arena to practice from 6 o'clock until dark every day for the time remaining before the rodeo.

"I see no reason why you can't do that. We have no other events scheduled there." he said.

"Will it be alright if I use stall number seven? It's close to the front and Smoky has always used it, so I think he would feel right at home there."

"By all means. I'll put that on the roster."

"Also, I have lots of 'props' like: a table and chair, a special hat, some dishes, a coffee pot and stuff like that. It will be rather inconvenient for a me to take all that home and bring it back with me every day. I would like to leave them in the corner of the stall if that will be okay. I wouldn't want anyone to pick them up and remove them, thinking they were trash or discarded items. I can make a sign saying it's property to be used in the rodeo and to please leave it where it is," Anna explained.

"Sounds good. I think that'll work. There shouldn't be anyone messin' around here until they start cleaning and preparing the fairgrounds to accommodate us at the time of the rodeo. I should think your equipment would be safe there."

"I will be training two boys to help set up my stuff when I need it and to remove it when I am finished with each item. I will need to use your sound system's portable microphone, since I will be talking to the crowd and to Smoky...saying things that the crowd will need to hear in order to appreciate what we are trying to do."

"No problem. We do have several 'mikes' that you can choose from. You should come by and pick one up soon and try it out...sometimes we get one that doesn't work very well."

"Okay. Thank you. I will drop by tomorrow to get one."

"Thank you very much for consenting to help us out with our rodeo. We needed something special that the people of Carnegie—even the whole county—would just have to come and see. Oh, and since we have already agreed on the price, you can pick up your check after the rodeo at the grandstand, if you would like."

"That'll be great. I'll do that and I hope we don't disappoint you. It was kind of short notice, but I think Smoky will do fine."

Every day, when Anna went home, she loaded up Smoky and

went to the fairgrounds to practice. It was hard work, but she brought him home every night so he could be in his own pasture all day. He seemed to enjoy the extracurricular activities.

Anna hired the two high school boys that Troy recommended as being capable, trustworthy and in need of a job. One, Sammy Grisham, actually worked a few hours each week at the Flannagan Ford dealership, just down the street from Whittier Enterprises. He evidently scrubbed all their showroom floors once a week. Anna had seen him walk past her office—his brown hair carelessly blowing across his forehead—on his way back to school after finishing his work for the day. It was usually about noon when she saw him, so she guessed he had a few hours between classes, which he used to earn a little extra. His mom was a single mother with four children to support. The other boy was a graduating senior named Doug Garfield, who needed to save money to help with his upcoming college tuition. He was clean-cut, confident, quite talkative and had no qualms about letting anyone know what he liked or disliked. Quite a bit larger than Sammy, he had eyes almost as black as his hair. Both were glad to have the job and delighted to watch Smoky in training. Sammy was somewhat shy, but extremely eager to please Anna. He was only a freshman at Carnegie High. He reminded Anna of herself when she was much younger—shy, eager to please and wanting to do more, but afraid of failing.

On the first day, Doug asked Anna if he could ride Smoky around the arena.

"No, I'm sorry. I don't want anyone else handling him until after the rodeo. Perhaps after that, okay?"

"Okay!" he said enthusiastically. He had something to look forward to...maybe brag about.

Sammy's eyes lit up too, though he said nothing.

Josey progressed as well as the doctor predicted and was home in about five days. Anna didn't want to leave her alone so she hired a lady to be with her while Anna was away. Josey put up with it for a couple days then told Mrs. Sawyer not to come back.

"That's just a waste of my money and I'll not have it!" she told Anna.

Anna was apprehensive but she reluctantly agreed. She called her mom often to check on her– until Josey complained about that too.

"Quit calling me suh durn much. I can't sleep or nothin'. I'm always havin' to git up an answer that stupid phone."

Anna cut back on the calls and only phoned at times when she thought her mother was least likely to be sleeping. Every moment possible was spent with Smoky, running the barrels or training Daisy and her baby, Tooter, to lead. That took more time than expected. Anna debated whether or not to ask Josey if she would like to attend the rodeo. It would be difficult to concentrate on the considerable number of things needing her attention inside the arena if Anna were distracted—worrying about Josey sitting out there on the bleachers. Finally, she decided there were no options—it was the thing to do. If Josey said "yes," Anna would just have to find someone to sit with her or at least sit where they could watch her.

"'Now, why would I like t' go set through one of those dang thangs? They're always the same ever year...always the same."

That had settled it. Anna was glad she had at least asked.

It was finally show time. Anna tried to remain calm. She didn't want Smoky to pick up on any nervous energy she might generate. He didn't seem to be nervous at all...just eager.

When they arrived at the arena, she unloaded him and put him in stall number seven, rubbing his neck and patting his soft nose for a minute. He nickered quietly and crunched the sugar cube offered him, while Anna checked through her paraphernalia to make sure it was all there. It was.

She needed to register and find out if the boys hired to help her were there yet. It pleased her to learn she was third in line— out of five contestants—in the barrel racing. It was easier than starting first and not as nerve racking as having to wait until the last.

Her performance with Smoky was the last event of the evening. He needed to be walked about some between his running of the barrels and his show for the crowd. It was not expedient to let him stand in his stall for long periods of time. An agitated horse usually did not perform well. She wondered if Smoky remembered running the barrels here before. At home Anna had moved the barrels around in their pasture just to see how Smoky would do in a different setting. He did great. Hopefully, he would do as well tonight.

All the barrel-racers in the women's contest were saddled up and ready to ride—mounted in a line according to their number of appearance in the event. Anna knew two of the other contestants from past competitions and spoke in passing, but didn't engage in conversation with them. It tended to distract her.

Her focus was solely on Smoky. She leaned over and rubbed his neck and spoke to him softly. He watched the first two riders with interest. She could feel his muscles tense as the number two horse left the starting line in a cloud of dust. Anna held a tight rein so he didn't "jump the gun" and start before he should.

When it was their turn, he was more than ready. When Anna nudged him in the flank and said "Go boy," he did.

His take-off was instantaneous. She preferred to give him his head as much as possible—let him run with the least amount of interference from her. If she tried to guide him too much, the restraint seemed to slow him down. Besides he knew exactly what to do, so why should she hinder his performance by trying to get him to do what he would anyway? He could almost win the race without a rider.

When he cleared the first barrel, Anna whispered "Good job!"

The first loop had been flawless and extremely close to the barrel,—indicating a fast time. After he was around the third barrel, Anna leaned over and yelled, "Now! Go boy!"

And he did. She thought it might be the fastest time he had ever run the barrels, but who can judge as close as a second's difference? She hoped he had done it in less than 14 seconds. He hadn't, but was close—just over 14—14.4 seconds. Anna thought that was close to the record time.

One of the first two women in the race had run it in 16 seconds and the other was timed at 18.1 seconds, so at that point Smoky held first place.

Anna put Smoky back in his stall, rubbed his neck and told him how great he had been. She looked in a bag in the corner of the stall and found him an apple.

"You were so great and I'm so proud of you. Did you know that?" she asked him.

He nodded his head up and down and if he were answering her question? She laughed and kissed his forehead. She loved her wonderful horse.

The last two racers came in much slower than the first two. The final contestant was apparently a newcomer for she knocked over two barrels. Anna felt sorry for her. She knew how embarrassing it was to do that, although it was mostly up to the horse and his experience.

Anna could scarcely contain her elation and excitedly whispered to Smoky, "You just won another trophy old boy."

He nudged her sharply on the shoulder. She wasn't sure if that were a congratulatory slap or a request for another apple. Anna heard one of the first two contenders, as they passed Smoky's stall say, "Aw, hell, I knew she would win. Who can beat that stallion?"

Anna chuckled. "Would she feel even worse about her loss if she knew you were only a gelding?" she asked Smoky.

He ignored her.

Guess he doesn't want to discuss anything that personal, she thought.

It would be quite some time before Smoky would be required to perform his one-horse show. There would be bronc riding, bulldogging, bull riding and calf roping contests before he could "do his thing". That would probably take two to three hours. Anna would not leave Smoky alone for that long though she would have enjoyed watching the other events. She unsaddled him and exchanged his bridle for a halter—a bridle without a mouth bit. He could eat much better without a bit in his mouth. And besides, his tricks would require that he wear a halter later. She led him outside the back door of the barn and walked beside him as he nibbled the short grass along the outer edges of the arena and whinnied at the other horses.

When all the other challenges had been met by all contenders, except for the last three bronc riders, Anna took Smoky back in and saddled him, gave him another sugar cube and kissed him on the forehead.

"Now you can show off! Be a good boy and strut your stuff like we practiced."

He nickered low.

The two boys she had hired to assist her with her "props" were waiting at his stall and had the necessary items lined up as planned. Each had a copy of the order in which Smoky did his tricks and knew exactly what was needed and when. How easy it was to forget some important part of the process because of the excitement—just being in front of such a crowd. So Anna had written all of the instructions in detail on cards the boys could carry in their pockets. So much effort went into pulling off such a production and mistakes were so easily made. But audiences were not tolerant of mistakes. And she didn't like to be embarrassed.

When the announcer said, "And now, ladies and gentlemen, a highlight of the evening—Miss Anna Shelton on her stallion, Smoky."

His last sentence, "Let's give her a warm welcome!" was inaudible because of the roar of the crowd. Most of them already knew Anna and Smoky and were ready to see what they would do that evening.

Smoky charged into the arena as the band played loud and fast. Anna was standing on his back behind the saddle, her feet in special stirrups there. She was holding onto a flagpole with the American flag flying back over her head. The pole was anchored firmly to a device attached to the saddle, so she felt confident she was safe—even at Smoky's rapid pace. The hard part would be getting her feet out of the straps and herself back into the saddle gracefully.

Smoky ran across the arena up to the grandstand and stopped at a metal flagpole set in the ground. Anna managed to dismount without mishap and took Old Glory with a short, magnetic section of the pole from the saddle, extending it to Smoky. He grabbed the flagpole and lifted it high in the air—to the top of the stationary pole. Strong magnets of one grabbed onto the metal of the other taking it from his mouth and holding it firmly. The Stars and Stripes were flying beautifully.

"Good boy! Now let's welcome all the folks."

She remounted and checked her microphone to make sure it was on. It was. Smoky cantered midway down the arena and stood in front of the bleachers with his head held high.

"Welcome, ladies and gentlemen. We're glad you're here. Since practice time was somewhat limited for us this year the program is a bit shorter than usual, but we hope you enjoy the show. Bow to the crowd, Smoky, and let's get started."

Smoky leaned back on his haunches a little and bowed low. The audience whistled and clapped.

"Okay, Smoky, I hear Daisy's baby bawling. As a matter of fact, I can't hear anything else because of her. Will you get her and lead her to her mother so we can get on with the show?"

Smoky shook his head up and down several times. The crowd laughed. Anna dismounted, slapping him on the rump as Doug Garfield, the high school senior she had hired to assist her, whistled from the far corner of the arena, where Daisy's calf, Tooter, was bawling. Smoky took off and stopped short of the gate to her pen. Doug held out the end of the rope that was

114

attached to Tooter's halter and opened the pen. Smoky took it in his mouth and cantered back to the pen where Daisy was waiting. Anna had tied a knot in the end of the rope so Smoky would be less likely to drop it. When Smoky reached the pen he dropped the rope and pulled on another, shorter one, attached to the gate. It opened. Tooter didn't have to be coaxed. She immediately went into the pen with her mother and stopped her infernal noise. Smoky rooted his nose against the gate until it shut and latched, then came running back to Anna.

The sound of clapping hands filled the air.

"Good job!" Anna praised him. "Do you want to help me pick up the hat off the post?"

He shook his head up and down. The spectators laughed.

She mounted Smoky. Sammy Grisham, her other assistant, had put a special hat on the top of a rather short post located mid-way down the arena. Anna was to lean down and scoop up the hat from off the post as Smoky ran by at full gallop. The first pass was perfect. She set the hat on her head.

"Let's try that again. Run by the post and I'll drop it off."

Smoky was game. Anna dropped off the hat and Smoky lined up at the starting point to run by it again. But before he quite reached the post, he slowed up and snatched the hat off the post himself. That left Anna grabbing thin air. The crowd laughed.

"Okay, Smarty, you know that's not the way it works. Put the hat back you goober."

Smoky did as he was told. He ran back and dropped the hat back onto the post.

Laughter and clapping filled the air.

Anna had sewn a golf ball, in a small pouch, to the top of the hat so Smoky could grab it easily and lift it off the post.

"I guess we're finished here. You kinda showed me up didn't you? Well, just let me get my hat."

She dismounted and started toward her hat. Smoky ran ahead of her and plucked the hat off the post then plopped it down on

Anna's head. The laughter was loud and prolonged. Some stomped their feet.

"Think you're smart, don't you?"

He moved his head up and down. The people all laughed again.

"You've just about worn me out. I need to rest and have a snack." You just go over there and watch that big clock. Let me know when it's 10 o'clock because we need to say goodbye to the nice folks who have come to see you perform."

The boys had set up a table with a white cloth on it and a chair next to it. There was a small cabinet behind it with several items on top. Anna looked inside and took a few things, including a bottle Coke, from it and set them on the table. She removed the cap from the Coke and turned back to the cabinet. Smoky had started towards the clock some distance away, but when Anna turned her back he quickly went to the table and put his mouth over the bottle and holding it carefully between his teeth raised the Coke high in the air.

Anna turned to see Smoky drinking her Coke. The crowd couldn't believe it. There were "oohs" and "ahs"mixed in with "oh-nos" and "look-a-thats" and lots of yells and whistles.

"Smoky! This is not a tea party for horses. We humans sit down at tea parties. Go and watch the clock."

He immediately dropped the bottle and started toward the clock. Anna laid a sandwich and an apple on the table and turned her back to pour herself a cup of coffee. When she turned back, Smoky was sitting on his butt with his front feet flat on the ground in front of himself—the position a horse has momentarily, when he starts to get up on his feet after a nap. He sat fairly close to the table, obviously seated for a tea party. Anna couldn't help but laugh. He could have been an overgrown dog sitting on his haunches, waiting for a special tidbit. The crowd went wild. Screaming and laughing, they stomped their feet and yelled for so long Anna thought they'd never stop.

When they did, Anna said, "Smoky, get back over there and watch the clock."

He jumped to his feet and started once more toward the clock. Anna turned her back to get sugar for her coffee. Smoky ran back to the table, grabbed the apple and hurried to the clock. He stood directly in front of it—not looking right or left—just chomping on his apple. The audience thundered their delight. Anna could hardly contain her joy. Looking at the clock herself, she knew it was time to say goodbye.

Immediately, Smoky jerked the clock from the wall and hurried to put it on the table. The alarm went off as soon as he had laid it down.

"Wow, we were so on schedule tonight, weren't we? Perfect timing."

Smoky shook his head up and down. Actually, the alarm was from another clock that Anna had just set when she had her back turned, but the crowd loved it.

Anna mounted Smoky who cantered in front of the bleachers, stopping every 100 feet or so to bow, while Anna waved looking for familiar faces to make it more personal— something she always avoided doing until after the show. It tended to make her lose concentration.

"Thank you all for coming. Hope you enjoyed the show. We'll see you again next year."

Probably no one heard her since the applause was deafening and filled with yells and laughter. Anna felt great and it was all because of Smoky. She loved that horse.

She and Smoky picked up Old Glory and left the arena the way they had entered—he cantered while Anna stood on his back, waving and smiling at the crowd. Entering the barn and dismounting, she tied Smoky's halter reins to the number seven stall, and headed to the judges' stand to get her checks and Smoky's trophy. Then, after loading him up, gathering her miscellaneous "props" and paying the boys—it would all be done with. It had been wonderfully rewarding. She had immensely enjoyed everything about it, but was relieved it was over.

It seemed all the other competitors had already loaded their animals soon after their own performances and were evidently out on the bleachers. The barn was empty.

She had taken only a few steps, when she heard someone say, "You done real good. I got a horse I'd like fer ya to ride."

Anna turned and when she saw Billy Freemont, Carla's lost lover, the statement he had made took on an entirely different meaning. She chose to ignore the suggestion. She knew Billy had no horse.

"Freemont! When did you get out?"

"The day I got put in. D'ya think I cudn' afford bail?"

Anna hurried in the opposite direction, saying, "I have to catch the judges before they leave."

He caught up with her and said as he grabbed her hair from behind, "Just wait a damn minute. I'm not through with you!"

"Get your filthy hands off me!" she screamed.

He grabbed her shoulders and spun her around.

"Now just listen! If Gabe had my girl, ain't it fair I git to have his?" he leered.

"Gabe never had Carla! And even if he had you gave her up...denied your own baby. What low-life does that?"

He slapped her hard and slammed her up against the wall. Anna's head was spinning. She shook it to clear the buzz. She wished she hadn't tied Smoky so tightly. She needed some help and he was pulling at his reins but had not been able to get loose.

Anna went limp for a moment. Billy thought he had whipped her into submission. He took a step closer.

"Now let's just be a little friendlier with each other."

His grin made Anna's stomach turn over. He reached as though to put his arms around her. *Stupid ass! Did he think he had won so easily?*

She reached up as though to put her arms around him, instead, she caught both of his shoulders and putting all her strength into it, she gave him a jolting knee-kick to the groin.

"There, you son of a bitch! That's as close as *I'll* get to

118

riding *your* horse!" She screamed at him.

Billy swore and fell to his knees as people came pouring in from all doors in the barn. Troy was first—running towards her with his hand on the holster that held his Beretta. Janice was close behind. Rodeo officials and her two hired boys came from the front along with many others she did not know. How had they known? She was so glad to see them she began to cry.

After Troy cuffed Billy and deputies led him away, the sheriff put his arms around Anna and asked, "I heard him hit you. How bad are you hurt?"

"I'm okay. Just a little rattled. I'm so glad you're here."

She surprised herself when she kissed his check.

Janice hugged her close and said, "Somebody ought to shoot that bastard!"

"How did you know to come?" Anna asked Janice.

"Your 'mike'. You forgot to turn it off."

"Oh, my," Anna said as she remembered what she had said to Billy. She laughed, hoping it didn't sound too hysterical. Trying to control her emotions, she added, "I hope the kids didn't hear my foul language."

Janice laughed. "Are you kidding? Most of them already use worse, don't you imagine?"

Anna hugged Janice with great appreciation.

"I've got to catch Mr. Cummings and pick up Smoky's trophy and my checks before he leaves. Call me tomorrow will you?"

She hurriedly turned and slammed into Gabe's chest.

Oh, no! My blood pressure is already off the map! I can't handle much more, she thought.

He had a worried look on his face, but it showed anger as well. Really it was a mix of things that were hard to sort out. His arms went around her and held her tight. His hands gently pressed her head to his shoulder. He just stood there holding her and never said a word.

Anna fought fresh tears. It felt so wonderful to be in his

arms—so warm and safe. She wanted to stay there forever and forget all the things she needed to do. But then Anna saw that pretty girl, the one who was always with him, walk up and lay her hand on his arm.

Anna pushed away, saying, "I'm okay. I'll be at work on Monday morning. I'll see you then."

The look of hurt on his face hurt her too.

Softly, she added, "Thanks for being here."

Doug and Sammy were standing nearby, watching her with their mouths open.

"Can you guys wait for your checks until tomorrow? I need to get some cash and take care of Smoky and do other stuff. If you're free tomorrow, I'll come get you both and you can ride Smoky around our pasture all you want."

"Wow! That'll work!" Doug answered enthusiastically.

"Yeh, that'd be nice," Sammy concurred.

Anna hurried away calling back over her shoulder, "You boys call me when you're ready to ride." She hoped it wouldn't be too early, but rather expected it would be. After a few steps, she made an about face and asked, "Do you guys have a ride home?"

Both boys shook their heads "no".

"Just give me a few minutes and I'll give you a lift," she offered.

Gabe stepped forward, saying, "I'll take them. It's no trouble at all. I pass both their houses on my way home."

Their eyes met and held. Anna knew he saw the depth of gratitude in hers—gratitude and more she was unable to hide.

Chapter Eight

The excitement of the evening had Anna on an adrenalin high. She managed to gather her things from the fairgrounds and load them and Smoky into the trailer and was home within the hour.

Since she was almost out of gas and had stopped to fill up, she bought herself something sweet and a container of peanuts for Smoky. He loved them and he certainly deserved something special for all his efforts.

She unsaddled him and rubbed him down, then gave him his peanuts. He ate them with relish and nudged around, obviously looking for more. Instead Anna fed him some "Horse and Mule", a sweet feed mix with corn for horses.

This is the only way I know how to tell him how great he is and how much he means to me, she thought.

Later, after eating a sandwich and preparing for bed, she peeked in on her mother. Josey was snoring peacefully. Anna was glad her mother was able to sleep so soundly. Rest was important for recovery. She felt a stab of guilt. She had never been able to please her mother. It seemed life had never given Josey much happiness, making her perpetually crabby and hard to live with.

Which came first the chicken or the egg? Was she always crabby and hard to live with because she was unhappy or was she unhappy because she was so crabby and hard to live with— no one wanted to be around her and she found no joy in being alone?

Anna lay in bed, tossing and turning for quite some time, struggling with all the things that had happened that evening. Billy Freemont's accusation that Gabe had bedded Carla kept coming back to anger her. Little by little, the agitation transported her back in time, and she was remembering all that had happened way back then.

When she had unexpectedly found Gabe with his arms around Carla and then saw Carla kiss him on the mouth, she had thought she would die. That awful, dreaded feeling returned. It was almost as if it had happened only yesterday. Tears rolled down Anna's cheeks.

But Gabe had explained why it had all happened, and convinced her that Carla meant nothing to him. Carla had even promised to come to Anna the next afternoon and confirm Gabe's explanation. Josey had vehemently declared Gabe had to be a liar and that Anna was stupid to believe him. But Anna hung on and waited to hear what Carla had to say.

The next afternoon, when Anna had got home, Carla's car was in her driveway. Carla came out of Anna's house, crying, as Anna got out of her vehicle.

"What's wrong?" Anna asked.

Carla started crying harder than ever.

"I can't do this! It's so hard to have to say!"

"What is? What are you talking about?"

Carla didn't answer. A sick feeling had crept into the pit of Anna's stomach.

Josey had been watching from the window. She came running out the door, yelling, "I told you he was lying! She's carrying Gabe's baby not Billy's!"

Stunned, Anna had laughed. This was a joke of some sort. Realization of the seriousness hit her as she watched Carla sob.

"No! It's not true! Carla! It's not Gabe's baby! Carla!"

Carla had started running toward her car.

"Wait! Wait!" Anna had to know the truth. "Please, Carla, tell me the truth. This is my life! Please tell me the truth—whatever it is. It's not Gabe's baby is it?"

Carla was crying so hard she couldn't speak. Finally, she nodded her head "yes".

"No! No! Don't do this to me," Anna cried. "You lie!"

A vehicle was pulling into the driveway. It was Gabe's truck. Carla, wide-eyed with fear, started her car and raced away—narrowly missing Gabe—as he got out and started towards Anna.

"What's wrong with her?" he asked.

When he saw that Anna was crying and tried to put his arms around her, she pushed away, sobbing beyond control.

"What is it? What's so terrible? Annie, please tell me."

She fell to her knees, wanting to die.

After a few minutes of uncontrollable emotions that kept her from speaking, she finally managed to squeak out, "She said it was your baby!"

"No! Annie, no. That's a lie. Sweetheart, it's not my baby. It can't possibly be. Why would she say such a thing?"

Josey started yelling and screaming, "Git outta here! You're the liar! Don't ever come back! Go marry the mother of your child!"

A cry from Anna's soul rent the air as she heard Josey's command.

"No, I will not go! It is not my baby!"

Gabe was so upset that he turned on Josey, raising his voice he demanded, "How is it that you know so much? I did not sleep with Carla and I will not give up until she tells the truth! I will see her in hell before I will submit to this lie!"

Turning to Anna, he lifted her in his arms and said, "Annie, you must believe me! Please talk to me. We'll demand a paternity test. You'll see it's not mine."

She clung to him. He must be telling her the truth. A paternity test would prove it. He wouldn't take the chance if there was a possibility that it could be his child. Why had Carla lied?

Josey began again. "If you don't git outta here, I'll call the sheriff."

Anna turned to her mother. "Shut up and go in the house! I live here too and I'm an adult and I say he stays!" It was an unusually firm stand for Anna to take against her mother, but circumstances called for it.

Josey, shocked by Anna's retort went in the house, calling back over her shoulder, "I told you so!"

Gabe pleaded with Anna to believe him. "Sweetheart, I love you. You have to trust me. I wouldn't lie about something like this. Oh, Annie, Annie, please...you have to know I'm telling you the truth."

Still crying, Anna asked, "Why would she lie?"

"I don't know unless she has no other means to support herself and her baby. I'm sorry for her, but I won't be railroaded into this. I'll not give you up. I love you Annie. I have never touched her in that way."

Anna began to calm down. It did make sense. Maybe Carla's parents had kicked her out and she was grabbing at straws—any means of security she could hang onto. She must be in desperate need of help from someone.

Anna and Gabe sat in his truck going over what had happened, trying to make sense of it all and trying to figure out how to go about forcing Carla to submit to a DNA test on the baby. Could they do it now or would they have to wait until the baby was born? What would this do to their marriage plans? Should they go ahead and get married anyway? Anna didn't want any uncertainty marring her wedding. Could she be absolutely sure Gabe was telling her the truth? She wanted and needed to believe him. She prayed for proof.

What to do first? Gabe needed to confide in his parents. Maybe they'd have some good advice on how to proceed.

"I can't just leave you here like this with your mother spewing venom at every breath. If you listen to her, you'll not even speak to me tomorrow. Come with me. My mom will chaperone you," he chuckled softly.

Anna didn't know what course to take. Her sense of duty won out and she said, "I have things to look after—Smoky and Casey and the cattle. Please call me tomorrow."

"Yes, love, I will. Please, please don't listen to her. She'll ruin our lives."

"I'll try not to listen," she promised. She hoped with all her heart she could do that.

Gabe's parents had retained a lawyer who prepared papers for DNA testing to disprove Gabe's parentage of Carla's baby. But when the papers were to be served, Carla could not be found. Her parents had not known she was pregnant. They knew she had flunked several of her courses and had not graduated. And that Billy Freemont was the bad influence who kept her out until the wee hours of the morning—many times. They knew she had been gone for two days but had no idea where she had gone.

No one did. And for two months everyone had wondered what happened to Carla. Anna and Gabe especially had wondered and fretted, hoped and prayed that she would return and set the record straight. She did come back, but didn't straighten out the record—rather she complicated the issue.

Gabe had been right. Josey kept bad-mouthing him until Anna could think of nothing else.

She could not put her suspicions aside. Unable to eat, she lost weight. She refused to see Gabe and went into a severe depression, longing for her father and his comforting advice. The only peace she found was her time with Smoky and Casey. As days went by, her condition worsened. Gabe, after many attempts at reconciliation, finally gave up and left her alone. Her regular physician referred her to a psychiatrist.

"You can't keep losing weight. This can lead to serious consequences. Maybe if you can find a way to put all of this to rest, you can start to thrive again," he had told her.

He referred her to Dr. Gladys Mallory, whom Anna thought needed help herself. She was grim, rude and exceedingly suspicious of everyone and everything. She pounced on each word Anna uttered as though it held significant proof of an extreme malady or planned crime. Her sessions with Dr. Mallory worsened her depression until Anna finally gave up. She had to get away from Dr. Mallory, Josey, the friends and neighbors with all their well-meaning questions and suggestions—when they knew nothing at all about the real problem. She had to find peace somehow. It was imperative. She was heading into a colossal free-fall that frightened her.

Anna had searched the classified ads in the Daily Oklahoman and found a cabin for rent. It was cheap, had no running water or electricity and was located in a remote mountainous area close to McAlester, about 180 miles from Anna's home. It sounded like a place where she could lose herself—or just maybe—find herself!

She had hired a neighboring teenager to feed and water her pets and packed to leave.

Josey's reaction was what Anna had expected.

"I forbid you to leave! What will I do? Who will take care of the cattle, cut the hay, and all that? Why can't you do what you're supposed to and forget that no-good, lying bastard? You're not a very good daughter to abandon your mother this way."

Anna was so deeply depressed and upset already that she had no inclination to soothe Josey's feelings.

Though it was completely out of character, Anna said, "You figure it out, Mom. Just pretend I died." She had turned and left then—glad to distance herself from all the screeching.

After she found the place and unpacked, she didn't want to do anything but sleep—a lot. She tried to lose herself in books she had brought with her. Lying on the bank in the sun by a small clear stream in which she bathed, she tried to forget all her problems. It was impossible. But at least she didn't have to listen to Josey verbally slam Gabe.

It came to Anna that Josey had no way of knowing any more than Anna, herself, knew about Carla. And Anna definitely knew Gabe's character much better than Josey did. Josey had never even conversed with him—even if by happenstance they were found in each other's company for short periods of time. And her mother had done her best to see those happenstances never occurred. She had been dead-set against Gabe from the beginning. Anna knew she should discard any and everything Josey had to say about Gabe. It was worthless.

She also knew that Gabe had to be telling the truth or why would he submit to a paternity test? ...Unless, he knew Carla would be leaving and could not be tested. No! No! No! She couldn't think this way! She had to trust him. He had never been anything but good, honest and helpful to everyone who had ever dealt with him. He had to be telling the truth.

She was beginning to face her fears and sort out her misgivings. She was almost ready to go back home to Carnegie when she bought a newspaper, the Daily Oklahoman, and got the shock of her life or rather the second half of that life shattering catastrophe. The after-shock of the quake could prove more damaging than the quake itself.

Anna heard Josey calling—bringing her out of reliving her past—into the present. She picked up Miss Kitty, moving her aside so she could get out of bed. Wiping the tears from her cheeks, she went to check on Josey.

"Well, did you finally git home?"

"Sure did. I peeked in and you were asleep. Can I get you something?"

"Yeah, I didn't eat much. Make me a sandwich and bring me some coffee."

"Don't you want to get up and eat in the kitchen? I can tell you about the rodeo and how Smoky did?"

"Naw. I'll just rest and watch TV in here."

"Do you feel okay?"

"Yeah, I guess so. Just turn on the TV there."

Anna turned on the TV and went to brew a pot of coffee and make Josey a sandwich.

Miss Kitty came into the kitchen and rubbed up against Anna's leg.

127

"Uh-huh, I guess you want a snack too, don't you?"

Anna opened a can of tuna and gave Miss Kitty about half of it in her dish. Miss Kitty purred loudly and rubbed against Anna once more to thank her, before attacking her snack.

When Anna took Josey her coffee and sandwich on a tray, she asked, "Would you like to know who won the barrel racing trophy?"

"Nope! I already know. It had to be your durn horse. He ought to...as much time as you spend with 'em."

"Yes, he did and you should have seen his performance in the show. He was spectacular!"

"Okay. Okay. Shut the door when you leave. I can't hear what this guy is sayin'" Josey sipped her coffee and concentrated on the TV.

Anna thought it was strange that Josey was petrified of her leaving, but would not even converse with her or share thoughts and dreams. She just needed to know that Anna was at her beck and call. To Josey, Anna was just someone to count on, but not be bothered with.

The next day, Anna was exhausted. The adrenalin high was gone. She had slept fitfully when she finally slept and as expected the boys called early. She had cashed one of her checks at the grocery store and paid the boys as soon as she picked them up.

When they saddled Smoky, Anna noticed that Sammy seemed nervous.

"Have either of you guys ever ridden a horse before?"

Sammy hung his head and shook it "no."

Doug said, "Oh, yeah, lots of times."

"Where have you ridden?" Anna asked.

"My granddad had a horse and I use to ride him often, but he died."

"What happened to him?"

"Oh, he was just old."

"Well, Smoky is kinda spirited sometimes and he may want

128

to run. Do you think you can hold on if he does?" she asked Doug.

"Sure, I've done it before."

"Okay, let's just ride him around in the lot here for a bit, so you can get acquainted with each other. And don't try to get him to do any tricks. Okay?"

Doug wanted to be first and it seemed Sammy was good with that. Sammy's reluctance showed and he seemed to be embarrassed about it. Anna patted Smoky and told him to be a good boy. Doug mounted and flipped the reins. Smoky started at a trot. Doug bounced up and down and held onto the saddle horn. Anna knew he was not as good as he thought he was. She would have to be careful here and not let the boys get hurt. Smoky cantered around the lot. He also knew he had a novice on his back.

After a while, Doug offered to let Sammy ride. Sammy was scared but wanted to try.

"Would you feel better if I led him around the first time or two, since you've never ridden before?" Anna asked.

"Yeah, that might be better."

After a walk around the lot, Sammy reluctantly took the reins and Smoky cantered sedately round and round.

Though it seemed a long morning to Anna, it had been only a couple hours when Doug said he had to go. His mother was expecting relatives and wanted him there for Sunday dinner.

Anna unsaddled Smoky, gave him his apple and hugged him goodbye. She took the boys home and stopped off to wash her truck on the way back. She liked it nice and clean.

After an accounting, she discovered her checks from the rodeo covered all her clothing bills and the boy's earnings with some left over. She was more than pleased. The small greenhouse she had wanted for so long was now within reach. If things went well, she would have it constructed and operational before time to start spring plants. It would be good to grow her own garden plants and maybe some extra to sell. Why not? It was something she loved to do and it gave her a few extra dollars.

Anna bought a copy of the Sunday Gazette to read what they had to say about the rodeo. She removed that section and hid it from Josey. She didn't want any flack about Billy accosting her. Josey would probably say it was Anna's fault, that she had led him on by looking at him cross-eyed or some such nonsensical reason. She always had to butcher any feelings of accomplishment that Anna earned by blaming her for something else. Under Anna's picture, standing on Smoky's back carrying the flag, the Gazette had laid out in detail all of Smoky's stunts and how the crowd—a packed stadium, every seat filled—had roared their approval of the show. They did include facts concerning the arrest of Billy Freemont for his assault on her, but thankfully wrote nothing about his accusation against Gabe. And they didn't print her last statement to Billy. That alone would have given Josey a month's worth of excuses to bitch.

Monday morning came before she was ready for it, but Anna determined to make it a good one. She was reluctant to face Gabe even though she longed for that wonderful feeling she got when he pulled her into his arms. She needn't have concerned herself though. He didn't show up at all.

But lots of others did. It was good that she was caught up with her work. She felt she accomplished little all day. Everyone who came in wanted to tell her how much they enjoyed Smoky's performance. Several others, including Mr. Cummings and the mayor called to express their appreciation for her participation in the rodeo. It was good to be appreciated, but she felt she was shirking her duties. Talking about her achievements was not what she was being paid for.

Some fellow who claimed to be connected with the National Rodeo Association called wanting to buy Smoky.

Anna felt apprehension from the moment she picked up the phone and said, "Good morning, Whittier Enterprises."

"Put Anna Shelton on the line," he commanded.

"This is she." Anna said, wondering if he were military—giving orders instead of making requests.

"Hey, little lady, my names Pierce, Cleve Pierce, and I saw your performance last Saturday night at the rodeo in Carnegie."

His tone was condescending and the way he pronounced his name told Anna she should be impressed with it.

"Good morning Mr. Pierce. What can I help you with?"

"I'm affiliated with the National Rodeo Association and we've decided to buy your horse."

Was he nuts? Just because they wanted Smoky did he think the deal was done?

"Not a chance! We grew up together. I could never let him go." She answered without hesitation.

"Maybe you should hear what we're willing to pay before you decide." he said.

"Money is not a factor, sir. It doesn't matter what you'd offer, the answer is still 'no'. Thank you though," she said and hung up the phone.

What a creep. She could never let Smoky go, but to let that reprehensible person take him was incomprehensible.

At the end of the day, Anna felt rather tired, but took her list of supplies to the lumber yard and bought lumber, screws, door and window hinges and greenhouse vinyl to start on her construction project. It would be difficult not having anyone to at least hold the ends of the boards while she screwed together the other ends, but she would lay the frame on the ground and put as much of it together as she could, then raise it. It wasn't going to be that big anyway. Maybe Josey would hold a board or two if necessary.

Anna unloaded the building materials and took care of her animals before starting dinner. She could tell Josey had something on her mind.

"You got a call from a man who wants to buy yer horse," she finally said.

131

"Oh, he called here too? He called me at the office."

"You gonna sell 'em?"

"Nope!"

"Fifteen thousand dollars! That horse ain't worth that kinda money. Yer stupid fer not takin' it."

Anna slammed down her fork. Enough was enough!.

"I'm not going to discuss this with you, Mom! You have no idea what a horse like Smoky's worth! Besides, he's mine and he's not for sale at any price."

Josey looked chagrined, but offered one more reason for Anna to sell.

"If you sold 'em you could save all that feed money you have to spend on 'em."

"He's worth every penny. And it's my money. I said no!"

Josey let it go. Anna began to worry. What if Josey told Dugan about the offer. He might sell Smoky out from under her nose if he came back. What was she to do? ...She'd call Troy. Maybe somehow, they could track Old Charley and know if and when he returned. She sighed heavily. There was always someone around who had to ruin a good thing. Why had Josey ever taken up with that foul Dugan? How had she met him anyway?

The next morning, Anna talked to the sheriff about her offer for Smoky and her fear that Dugan might steal him if he found out how much she was offered. Troy said tracking Old Charley was beyond his jurisdiction as sheriff, especially since Dugan had not yet committed a crime—that he had proof of. He suggested she post two or three cameras in strategic places to record the license plate of any trespassing vehicles. Anna thanked him and would do that. But she must wait until she at least got her next check to do so.

Anna started working on the greenhouse, putting in all the extra time she could find. She decided to build it on the south side of her father's workshop. That would take care of the north wall of the greenhouse and she could run an electrical cord through the window of his shop to keep her plants warm if need be.

She had drawn up plans and began measuring boards to build the frame. She measured and remeasured to make certain she didn't make a wrong cut and ruin a board. Her father had a miter saw which made the angles easier to cut and they fit together fine. She had to use a long extension cord though, since the worktable for it set all the way across the shop from the electric socket. She worked for a couple hours every day after she finished her other chores and it went better than she had anticipated.

It was late on Friday before Gabe showed up at the office while Anna was still there. He had been coming in after work hours, leaving notes and letters for her to type and signed invoices for her to pay. Anna hated the thought he wanted to avoid her so much that he had changed his schedule to late hours in his own office.

I should resign and get out of his office, she thought.

Her resignation might give him back his peace of mind.

But, oh god, how can I possibly live without my job. I can't leave now. I would lose everything. I have to pay for my truck and Mom would really press for me to sell Smoky if I wasn't earning his keep.

She worried herself into a tizzy. When Gabe came in late on Friday, she was cleaning up the coffee bar in preparation to leave for the weekend. She hadn't heard him come in and when she turned and saw him standing there close to the table by the bar, she gave a small cry as her hand flew to her mouth.

"Oh, my! You frightened me."

"Sorry. I'm wearing my sneakers. Guess they're aptly named, huh?"

She tried to laugh, but just sort of choked.

"I just emptied the coffee pot. Shall I make a fresh one?"

"No. I'm just here to pick up some papers. He looked at her

for a few seconds before continuing. "I hear you got an offer to buy Smoky."

Surprised, she asked. "How did you know?"

"Troy told me."

"I didn't want it to get out because it makes him a prime target if everyone knows how much he's worth," she explained.

"We were trying to figure out what we could do to keep him safe and I haven't mentioned it to anyone else," he said.

Anna swallowed, "I appreciate that. I would hate for someone to take him."

"You're welcome to stable him at my place. No one has to know."

"Thank you. I'll have to think about that. It would be rather inconvenient for me to care for him though. I would miss him and—I know it sounds silly—he would miss me too. Besides, I don't want to bother you any more than I already have."

"That's not the way you bother me, Annie."

His steady gaze rooted her to the floor. She couldn't move or look away. He stepped closer and reached for her. His mouth found hers and before she knew it her arms were around his neck A hungry cry escaped her throat as he pulled her up close and whispered, "Oh, god, Annie!"

Someone entered the outer office and slammed the door. Gabe groaned and Anna turned, picked up the damp cloth she had been using and started wiping the coffee bar with it.

"Gabe?"

It was that beautiful, young thing that dogged his every step.

"I'll be right there. I just need to pick up these papers."

Gabe winked at Anna, reached out and gently pinched her nipple. Her breath caught.

He whispered, "I just couldn't resist." He kissed her once more, saying, "God, I love you Annie."

Then he was gone. So was she—gone from her body. She felt paralyzed, unable to move, dizzy, unable to think. She had to sit down for a few moments to clear her head. How could she possibly stay and work for him when he had such control over her emotions and yet was constantly with someone else. And if he loved Anna so much, why was he always with that other girl? She knew the answer to that one: because she had refused to marry him when he had asked—many times he had asked. She had been a fool. She had wanted it to be perfect with no suspicions or doubts hanging over their marriage. But now she wondered if that was ever true in any marriage. If he asked her again, would she turn him down? She didn't know. She needed him so desperately. Anyway, that was a moot point. He would never ask her again. He had found a new love or at least a playmate. But then, he had said he still loved her...hadn't he?

She closed her eyes and relived his kiss.

"Oh, god! I love you too, Gabe," she whispered.

After getting home and tending to her animals, Anna didn't feel she should try to work on the greenhouse. She was too disconcerted. She could think of nothing but the feelings she had when Gabe had kissed her. She was just wandering around in a daze unable to think what she should do next. She went to bed early, but didn't sleep. She lay there remembering his touch and wondering where he was and what he was doing now. Miss Kitty purred gently next to her feet.

The next morning at breakfast, Josey made another attempt to persuade Anna to sell Smoky.

"If you'se to take the money for that horse a your'n, you could quit workin' for that low-life and find'ja a nuther job som'ers else."

Anna gave Josey a hard look that spoke of rigid dissent, but said nothing.

Josey, disgruntled, knew there was no hope for it, but added in a small voice, "Well, he could just up 'n die and you'd lose it all anyway."

"Yeah, and *I* could die tomorrow too, but I'm not planning on it."

Anna left the table. Would Josey ever shut up and stay out of her business?

After finishing her regular chores, Anna went to work on her greenhouse. She turned on the lights in her father's shop and started to plug in the electrical cord that ran across the floor to his angle saw. It was already plugged in!

"Now, I know I unplugged that!" she muttered.

Anna never left it plugged in when she was not using it. Somehow it seemed to her a hazard, running across the floor like that. It was an ingrained habit and she wondered who had plugged it back in. As she stared at the cord, she realized it was not the cord she had been using. This one was orange and hers had been a dark red. She thought she had best check it out before using it, since her father had left several damaged cords that could be dangerous to use. She first unplugged the cord and started running her hand down the length of it, checking for cuts or frays. It seemed to be in excellent condition until she reached the end. There was no plug—only a frayed end with wires sticking out of it. Someone had deliberately placed her in a potentially fatal circumstance.

"Wow! What if I hadn't noticed? There could have been a fried Anna on the floor of Dad's shop!

Anna shuddered to remember what she had just said to Josey—"Yeah and I could die tomorrow, but I'm not planning on it."

Well she hadn't been planning on it, but someone else surely had. Someone wanted her dead! She couldn't deny it any longer. Every other suspicious occurrence could possibly have been discarded as an unfortunate accident or an oversight or something else maybe, but not this. This was deliberate without a doubt. But who and why? How could she ever feel safe again until she learned the answer?

She hurried in to call Troy, who drove out immediately.

As they discussed the situation, he asked what happened to the regular cord—the one she usually used.

"I have no idea." My dad always kept a box of old cords that he intended to repair over here in this box," she said as she walked across to the far side of his shop and lifted the lid on a large wooden container. There, coiled up on top of several others, lay the long dark red extension cord she had been using.

Troy stroked his chin. "This has become an extremely dangerous situation. How are we going to keep you safe?"

"Find out who's doing it! But how?" She shivered and wrapped her arms around herself. She had no clue.

After a moment, she asked, "Do you think Billy Freemont could be behind all of this? How long has he been back in Carnegie? Does he hate me that much or maybe he hates Gabe and thinks he can get to him through me? He's cowardly enough to do it that way."

"I have no idea, Anna. And yes, he could have done this. He's out on bail again. There's really no way to protect you without locking *you* up." He grinned slightly. I could assign a deputy to be with you at all times, but whoever is doing this could set you up anywhere you go—even in your own bedroom or bathroom. This is a very difficult scenario to defend. Because we don't know whom to suspect—or what they might do or when another attempt might occur—we have very little information that would let us form an intelligent plan for your safety." He wanted to talk to Josey to see if she had heard or seen anything suspicious.

"Do you suspect anyone else?" he asked Anna as they went into the house to find Josey.

"No. Not unless Dugan is back. He hates me, but why would he want me dead? He could steal my horse just as easily now, couldn't he?"

Josey let it be known she didn't want to be bothered until the sheriff told her what had happened and that it was obvious someone was trying to kill Anna. Fear flicked across her face and widened her eyes. She said nothing but continued to stare at Troy.

"Since you're here most of the time, we wondered if you might have seen or heard something suspicious."

Josey shook her head, "no." "I sleep a lot 'cause a my heart," she finally said.

"Can you think of anyone who might want to do such a thing?"

"No." She shook her head again.

"We were specifically concerned about Charley Dugan. Have you seen him lately or know anything about where he might be?"

"No," was the answer again, but her expression gave her away.

She knew something, but wasn't going to talk about it. Fear was evidently a factor. Anna knew Troy had picked up on that too.

"Well, if you do hear from him or learn anything at all, I would appreciate it if you would let me know."

"Okay." was all Josey said.

She stared at the TV in dismissal. Anna never expected to get any cooperation from her. Troy asked for a picture of Dugan, Anna had never seen one and if Josey had one she wouldn't admit it.

Troy thanked Josey. Anna walked with him to his cruiser.

"I will give all my deputies a description of Dugan and ask them to be on the lookout for him and especially in this neighborhood. They will patrol here as frequently as possible. But that is not good enough. That will not keep you safe. You are your own best protection. You must take every precaution and protect yourself every moment. Put up cameras and check them every day. It would help if you took a course at the gun range and got a 'concealed carry' permit. One of my deputies, Matt Kelly, is an instructor there and I'll have him to call you. I can loan you a gun if you can't afford it. So far this person has not threatened you face to face, but he may soon do that. You need to be watchful and ready to defend yourself."

Tears filled Anna's eyes. She knew Troy was at a loss and wanted desperately to help her. She agreed to do what he had suggested and promised to call him with any information she might come across that indicated who was behind the attempts on her life.

He hugged her before he left and apologized for not being able to do more to insure her safety.

"You could move somewhere else or stay with someone else, but they would eventually find you. However, it would take some time. Maybe with a little extra time, we can come up with a significant lead....Where's your dog?" he asked as if just noticing Casey's absence.

"He's here. I just fed him a little bit ago."

"He would surely have barked if a stranger were here." Troy thoughtfully offered.

"Yes, he would. He seems nervous lately and stays close to the house. Wants to come in the house, actually. I'm not sure what that tells me. Maybe that he's scared too."

Troy was reluctant to leave, but there was nothing else he could do at this point. "Call me anytime. Put my personal number on your quick dial. Don't take any chances and suspect everyone. Look before you take every step," he urged as he left.

Anna tried to be more alert. She looked for tracks around the yard and workshop. She noticed where things were and checked to see if they had been moved. Most of all she just tried to "look before she leaped,"—to considered any possible danger involved before she undertook a chore she needed to complete. It slowed her down, tried her patience and made her angry. It was not a fun position to be in.

She put Troy's personal number and the sheriff's office number on speed dial—9-1-1 she could dial as fast as finding it on speed dial. When Matt Kelly called, she agreed to take the firearms course and bought two cameras to mount for surveillance. She let Casey sleep in the utility room. But, what about Smoky? While he needed her special care, she wondered if

139

he were safe with her now.

Anna took Josey back to the hospital for further tests. Though an angiogram showed blockages that could be cleared with stents, Josey didn't want to go through the procedure. She would think about it, she insisted, and decide later.

Anna hated to leave her mother at home alone, but Josey refused help from anyone else. What else could Anna do? She buried herself in her work as best she could. She longed to see Gabe to tell him about her close call—wanted to feel his concern—a togetherness—but she knew she had no right. Anyway he never came into the office alone anymore while she was there. It seemed one of his colleagues was always with him. And he never stayed long. But that was one of the reasons she had accepted the job here wasn't it? That she would not have to be disturbed by his nearness? My! How things had changed. She felt alone and scared.

In the middle of the week, Anna happened to notice papers blowing across in front of their office door. She went to check it out. Sammy Grisham, one of the boys that helped her at the rodeo, was scrambling to catch them all. The wind was blowing fiercely and he was having a hard time of it. She rushed out to help him gather them and asked if he wanted to come inside.

He came into their office, embarrassed, smoothing down his hair.

"I was just trying to do my homework while I was waiting on my ride to school," he said.

"When are they supposed to pick you up," she asked?

"Not 'til about ten minutes after one, I think," he said. "I had some time and I sure needed to study."

"Well that's about an hour away. Why don't you go into our break room and study at the table back there? There's a big clock on the wall so you can keep tabs on the time."

"Okay, thanks." He seemed pleased.

It was time for Anna's lunch and she had brought some of

her special soup. She heated it up and made herself a sandwich. Sammy sniffed the air appreciatively.

"Boy! That sure smells good," he said.

"Have you had lunch?"

"No...thanks." He blushed. "I wasn't askin' for any."

Anna got another bowl and filled it for him. She made another sandwich as well.

Putting the food on the table in front of him, she said, "I want you to try my new recipe and tell me how you like it."

"Okay," he said as if he doubted it was a new recipe, but reluctantly started eating. "Oh, golly. This is really great." He ate as if he were hungry.

Anna watched his attempt at studying. He seemed frustrated.

"What are you studying?" she asked.

He threw down his pencil in disgust. "Algebra!" He shook his head. "I just can't understand it."

"Really? Maybe I can help. I used to be pretty good at it." Actually she had been a straight "A" student.

Sammy's eyes lit up, then he seemed to lose hope again. "I don't think I can ever learn it," he said. "It's story problems and they don't make sense to me."

"Well, let's have a look." She moved her chair around close to his and asked, "Which problem are we looking at?"

Sammy gave her his book and pointed to the first problem.

If a tree is 7 times as old as another tree, five years from now it will be 4 times as old—as that other tree. What is the present age of the trees?

"That's stupid! Who could know?"

"You can, Sammy. First of all, what do we know for sure? Just let X equal the age of the younger tree, Okay? Write that down. Now, if the older tree is 7 times as old write down the age of that tree."

"That would be 7X?" he asked.

"Yep." Anna agreed. "Now in 5 years, how old will that younger tree be?"

"Well, I guess it would be X plus 5 years."

"You're right. Write that down. Now, how old will the older tree be?" she asked.

"Would it be 7X plus 5 years?"

"Yep!"

Sammy wrote that down.

"Now, my fine friend, tell me what we know about the relationship between the two trees in 5 years."

"I don't know."

"Yes, you do. Read the problem again. It says in 5 years the older tree will be 4 times the age of the younger tree then. So if we took the age of the younger tree in 5 years—which you just told me would be X plus 5—and multiplied by 4, it would equal the age of the older tree in 5 years—which you said would be 7X plus 5— Right?"

"Yeh! Yeh!" Sammy got it.

"So you know what equals what. Just write out the equation and solve for X. Then plug your answers into that equation and see if it's true.

Sammy was tickled pink. The present age of the younger tree was 5 years and the older tree was 35. The younger tree would be 10 years old and the older one would be 40 years old, 5 years later. It checked out. He was all smiles.

It's almost 1 o'clock now. I need to get back to work. Don't be afraid of algebra. Think your way through these problems and find your equation, then solve for the unknown. If you need any help...well you know where I am."

Sammy left—hope shining in his eyes. Anna was gratified.

Everyone needs help and encouragement at some time or other. I could use some myself. Right now...before it's too late.

Chapter Nine

After the sheriff investigated the frayed electric cord, the next two weeks passed without any spooky episodes. Anna kept her nose to the grindstone and Gabe kept his distance.

Young Sammy Grisham came by from time to time with an algebra problem he couldn't solve, but he was doing much better. His teacher had even asked him to help a couple other students who were having difficulties. It gave Sammy's confidence a big boost.

Josey still wasn't letting the doctors do anything for her heart condition. She was grumpy and irritated most of the time and slept a lot.

Anna installed two cameras in hopes of identifying any trespassers. One was placed in a strategically located bush, close to the ground, to get a good shot of the license plate when a vehicle exited her driveway. The other was higher up, hidden in a tree and aimed at the yard and loading chute, to catch anyone attempting to load Smoky. She checked them every day and had not yet gotten pictures of any intruders. She had tried to be as secretive as possible to let no one, not even Josey, know about the cameras. But because Anna checked them every day, Josey soon learned about them and their whereabouts.

Every extra minute Anna could find was spent working on the greenhouse. It was taking shape. Anna was going to plant some tomatoes in large pots as well as various herbs to overwinter there. She had planted greens and turnips in the fall garden and was already enjoying some rewards for her efforts. Earlier, she had planted winter squash and late potatoes and had harvested a good crop. She loved to garden.

143

In addition to all her other activities, Anna went to the firing range twice a week and took lessons from Matt Kelly, Troy's deputy, on how to shoot a Beretta. Troy had left the gun there for her use, but she could not "carry" until she learned everything necessary and was certified. At first she was apprehensive about firing a weapon, but Matt was patient and gave her explicit instruction about the gun itself and how to handle it. Soon she felt more comfortable, was able to hit the target every time from any distance, and usually was close to "dead center". The hardest thing for her to learn was to slowly squeeze the trigger and not jerk it. Jerking pulled the gun off slightly and shot the bullet off target. Her final test was coming up soon. She was looking forward to getting her permit to carry.

Anna had asked Josey several times what had happened to her father's shotgun. She could use it on the farm, if the need arose, before she got her permit for the borrowed Beretta. Josey had no idea where the gun was, or so she said.

Everything was going smoothly—too smoothly it seemed. Had whoever wanted her dead just given up and gone away? Not likely. It was good not to have concerns about someone trying to kill her, but Anna still didn't feel safe. She felt as though there had to be a plan in the works for some last—maybe successful— attempt on her life. She was still carefully studying every path before she stepped onto it.

Anna was especially tired one evening and went to bed earlier than usual. She fell asleep quickly, but was soon awakened by an angry growl and loud bark close to her ear. Casey had come into her bedroom, barking and growling, running back and forth from her bed to the utility room door, wanting out. She jumped out of bed, pulling on her jeans. Grabbing a flashlight, she ran to open the door. Casey vaulted angrily across the steps and flew across the yard toward the center of the pasture that ran between the barn and the road. Loudly, he vented his anger and left Anna far behind, as she tried to get over the fence. She saw the figure of a man, barely within the reach of her light, running hard with Casey close behind. She wondered why on earth she had not called Troy first or at least picked up her cell phone.

The man stopped and picked up something Was it a rock? Anna turned off her light, hoping he couldn't see Casey well enough to hit him. But the moon was large and bright. She could actually see things in better perspective with her light off. So could the man, evidently. He threw something. Casey yelped and backed off, still angry and pursuing, but keeping a distance between them. The man ran into the timber that bordered the road. No doubt he had a vehicle parked close by. Anna called Casey back. He obeyed.

She had not been able to get a good look at the invader. She didn't know any more about who he might be than she had known before. She felt foolish. He could have had a gun. He could have shot her or Casey, maybe both.

I'm not very adept at protecting me or mine, am I?

Smoky neighed near the barn. She went to check on his welfare. Casey followed. Smoky was in the lot, rapidly walking back and forth, obviously agitated. Anna spoke to him softly and rubbed his neck.

"Sorry, sweetie, I don't have a thing to eat, but I'll bring you something extra in the morning."

Rubbing down his shoulder and across his back, telling him how pretty he was, finally calmed him down. Anna turned to leave. Casey barked and sprang forward again just as Anna saw a small light bobbing towards her.

"No, Casey. Come back!"

Her first thought was to run to the house for a weapon of some sort and to call Troy, but she knew she would never make it. It was too far away and the intruder would surely see and hear her running. Then hide! But where? The loft! Behind the pile of loose hay. Hurriedly, she climbed the loft ladder, grabbing a pitchfork before she went behind the stack. It was high enough to hide her well. She was shaking. Why had the man returned?

Casey was barking again. She heard a voice speak to him. He quietened. She had thought the unwelcome interloper had surely been Charley Dugan, but Casey would never let him approach without a challenge. Who then? Someone Casey knew and accepted. Maybe someone who wanted her dead, but had somehow managed to befriend Casey.

She heard footsteps enter the barn. She held her breath. A light flashed all around. She couldn't control her trembling. Footsteps retreated and went outside around the barn. Anna slowly let out her breath. That had been too close for comfort. She heard the man speak to Smoky, calling him by name. He returned to the barn and, snapping off his light, started climbing the loft ladder. Panic stricken, Anna had gripped the handle of the hay fork so tightly her hands were becoming numb. She was cold, but knew it was the uncompromising fear gripping her that caused her to shake like a leaf in the wind. Who was it that was invading her life, wanting her dead? And why? What would he gain if she died? Why was he now climbing into the loft of her barn? Had he been hiding there, watching what she did—looking for an opportunity to set another trap? She wanted to run, but there was nowhere to go. No escape could be had without facing the intruder and forcing her way past him.

But wait. There had to have been two of them. Casey had chased away one, but accepted the other. He would not have accepted the one who hit him with a rock. Anna crouched low, slowly letting out her breath. She had to know who this man was. What if she speared him hard with the weapon she held in her hands and he turned out to be friend not foe? Evidently, Casey found him to be friendly, but why would he be in her barn at night?

She opened her mouth to speak but couldn't find her voice. Still there was no way to avoid it. She had to know! She took a deep breath and slowly let it out and with supreme effort tried to control her trembling.

Before she could speak, another voice, low and masculine,

asked, "Anna are you in here?"

Anna almost fell to the floor with relief. Her breath expelled in a whoosh. Tears of deliverance from harm filled her eyes.

"Good lord! You almost scared me to death! What are you doing here?"

Gabe turned as she rushed to him from around the pile of hay.

"I saw someone pick up a man who ran from your pasture. A light was bobbing around and Casey came this way so I thought you might be down here checking things out. I chased them to the highway, but I couldn't tell which way they had gone, so I came back to see if you were okay."

After a moment's hesitation, he asked, "Were you going to stab me with that thing?" He motioned to the pitch fork she still held in her hand.

"Yes! I was going to demand your identity first though...when I got up enough courage."

She gave a half laugh. She had been sleeping in only a pajama top and no bottoms. She had just pulled on her jeans and stepped into loafers, so she was chilly and still trembling.

"Are you cold?" Gabe asked, putting his arm around her.

"Yes, a little."

"Did you get a good look at the guy?"

"No, I couldn't see him that well. The light was bouncing around and so was he. Why are you out here so late at night?"

"I had a cow who was having difficulty calving and I went to check on her. She's had her calf now so she's okay." He slid his hand under the back of her shirt at the waist. "No wonder you're cold. You have nothing on under that light shirt."

He took off his jacket and put it around her. He was at first tentative, as though he were fighting an impulse he would not give in to. Then he reached around her again and jerked her up hard against him, surrendering to a wish that could not be denied.

"Annie," he whispered, as he tilted her chin up to softly cover her mouth with his own.

147

She must have returned his kiss, since somehow her arms had found their way around his neck. His hands were under her pajama top, exploring the softness of her waist. Then he was gently kissing her all over the face, the corner of her mouth, behind the lobe of her ear and the soft hollow of her throat. She found herself kissing him back with the increasing fervor that drove his kisses for her.

He groaned and lifted her pajama-top to rub his cheek between her breasts. Her breath caught and a small cry escaped her as his mouth closed over one pointedly tightened peak. A jolt shot through her lower abdomen causing her to whisper his name and push closer to the length of him. That wasn't close enough. She needed more. So did he.

With one arm beneath her legs and the other behind her shoulders, he lifted her and carried her behind the stack to lay her on the soft, sweetly-scented hay. He stretched out beside her, kissing her softly once more, and again lifted her shirt, nuzzling, tugging and teasing—fanning into flame a yearning in her for what he had to offer.

Her fingers found their way through his hair, gently massaged his neck and shoulders, then his lower back. Her mouth returned his kisses, found his neck and teased the place between it and his shoulder, before moving down onto the furring on his chest—yet not finding that special something to alleviate the hungry ache within her.

He had unzipped her jeans and his own, before she was aware she could not control her need of him.

But someone else could. Josey's voice, loud and strong, yelled, "Anna!"

"Oh, crap! She must be psychic. Anything to keep us apart." Anna reluctantly zipped up her jeans and started to get up.

"Annie, the need of you is killing me." He sounded as desperate as she felt.

Gently, he pushed her back on the hay and covered her body with his. She could feel his need of her as he put his hands underneath her hips and pulled her as close as possible.

"Don't go sweetheart. Stay...let me hold you for just a moment."

A soft cry of joy mixed with yearning escaped her as she wrapped her legs around his waist. He groaned and pulled her up tighter, seeking to slake his hunger for her.

Josey's harsh yell rent the air once more.

"Damn her and her hateful intrusions." Gabe swore as he unwillingly released Anna.

Slowly, she rose and walked to the window in the loft and yelled back, "I'll be right there, Mom. I'm just throwing Smoky some hay."

Josey went back into the house.

With utmost tenderness, Gabe brushed the tears from her cheeks. His kiss was long and softly binding his spirit to hers. Here was the love of her life. How could she not join her life to his and give him all she had to give for as long as she lived?

"Annie, please marry me. I can't live without you. I need you. I love you. Please tell me you love me too."

"I do! Gabe, you know I do! You are in my every thought, in all my hopes and dreams. You know how much I want you. I am so stupid. Why can't I get over this fear that I will cause you grief and our marriage will fail if I don't know positively what happened years ago? It's a fear of my own inability to cope, I think—if things turned out to be other than what I had thought they were. What makes me such a coward?"

"You're not a coward. It just one special fear that seems to have taken root somehow. We'll work it out. Please say you'll marry me."

Before anything could be settled, Josey appeared at the kitchen door, again, yelling, "Anna!"

"Good lord! Guess I'd better go before she comes out here and drags me in," Anna said. "Why don't you stay here a bit before you come in. I need to call Troy and you need to tell him about the vehicle you saw."

149

"Okay, I'll run back to my truck and drive in." He smiled at her.

They embraced once more before Anna brushed the hay from her clothes and out of her hair, then climbed down the ladder.

She suppressed a giggle, turning back to Gabe as she handed him his jacket. "Maybe, I shouldn't go in with this on." she said.

"You are so right." He chuckled, as he spun her around and once more kissed her hungrily on the mouth.

"Be right back," he said and took off, jogging towards his truck.

Casey stayed with Anna and went back to the house.

"Where you been? What's that crazy dog barkin' bout? Can't nobody sleep with all that goin' on." Josey was contentious.

"Someone was out there, Mom. I saw a man running across the pasture toward the road. Casey took off after him and he hit Casey with something."

Anna started to ask Josey if she had seen Dugan lately, but knew she wouldn't admit it even if she had. Maybe if the sheriff asked her she couldn't lie about it without somehow giving it away.

"Who was it?" Josey squinted at Anna.

"I don't know, Mom. I couldn't see him well enough to recognize him."

Anna called Troy and reported a prowler.

"Casey chased him and he hit Casey with something and then ran through the timber toward the road."

"How long ago did this happen?" Troy questioned.

"Not exactly sure. Probably thirty to forty-five minutes ago. Smoky was agitated because of Casey's barking I guess, and I went to calm him down and fed him some hay."

"Guess it's too late to chase him now. Did you see a vehicle?"

"No. But...I thought I heard a motor start and go on west a little later."

She had almost said, "No, but Gabe did." She caught herself. "We'll come on out. Maybe we'll get lucky and find a clue of some kind.'"

He hung up.

Within minutes, Gabe's truck pulled up and parked just off her driveway. Shortly thereafter, Troy arrived and deputies in two other cruisers pulled up beside him.

Gabe talked to Troy and told him what he had seen. Anna listened carefully.

"I was just coming back from checking on one of my cows and saw this man run out of the pasture where the trees are and get into a truck waiting by the side of the road. The person driving the truck took off almost before the guy got into the cab. He drove like his hair was on fire." he said.

"What kind and color was the truck?" Troy wanted to know.

"It was dark—black, I'd say—and a Ford, I think. Extended cab. I chased them to the highway, but I could never catch them. He must have a souped engine. I wasn't even close enough to tell which way they went when they reached the highway—you know how the road curves there with a lot of trees. So I came back here to see if everything was alright."

Troy sent his deputies to run the highway in both directions, looking for a dark Ford truck with an extended cab and at least two guys inside. It was not promising, but what else could they do? Maybe they'd get lucky.

Gabe went with Troy to check on tire impressions where they had parked off the road.

Anna waited to see if Troy would have other questions, but no one came back. She finally went to bed to toss and turn and wonder what would happen next.

Her closeness to Gabe was a well of happiness in her bleak life, but it also raised questions in her mind. Why had she let herself become that intimate with him if she hadn't intended to marry him? She had always wanted to be his wife, but had let a small niggling of doubt grow—because of other people's

151

thoughts and actions—until she lost her convictions about his innocence. His worth and honesty and all the good things she knew about him were pushed aside. But somewhere in the back of her mind she must still intend to marry him. If not, why couldn't she walk away and forget him?

Guess I'm just waiting for some proof of his version of what happened to slap me upside the head! I wish that would happen soon.

She wondered about that pretty young thing who was constantly with him. Gabe couldn't be serious about her, could he? Not when he exhibited such ardor for Anna as he had done that night. Or was that just passion that could be assuaged somewhere else? She hoped not. It certainly was not that way for her. She wondered what their now admitted passion for each other might mean for the immediate future. Would he do as he had been doing lately and stay away from the office until she was not there? She knew it would not happen—but just for the sake of verifying her own true feelings—she wondered what she would do if he asked her to meet him in her barn again the next night?

I'm afraid I would not be able to think before eagerly asking, "What time?"

She realized she had just put herself in a position to spin even more out of control.

The next morning, Anna remembered to check her cameras. Why had they not remembered to do that the night before? The camera in the bush close to the ground was missing. Anna looked for tracks around the bush and on the side of the driveway. She found none. The other camera had blurry images of a man hurrying away from the barn, but they were not clear enough to identify. Anna thought it could have been Dugan. He ran in a crouching position—hoping to be less conspicuous, she supposed. But she had to admit it could have been any one of a number of persons.

Anna called Troy to give him the information and offered to bring him the video from the remaining trail camera. She hoped he would not want to see them. She and Gabe had been caught by that camera as well.

"Well, I don't think it will do me any good if they are not clear images. But hang onto them just in case," he had said.

"Did you get any good tire impressions?"

"Yes, we did. And there were very clear identical tread marks where they turned onto the highway. They went west into Carnegie, but we never found a truck matching that description."

"You know, Troy, Billy Freemont drives a black truck with an extended cab. I think it's a Ford F-150. I wonder if you could get his tire impressions?"

"I'll bet I can figure out a way to do that. But that wouldn't prove anything. There may be twenty or more black Ford trucks with tires like that right here in Mechlin County. But it would give us reason to watch him closely. We're going to be watching him anyway."

"It's harder than you would think to get to the truth isn't it?" Anna was thinking about past crimes that rode her mind.

"Sure is. Lots of criminals go free because of it. And not all innocent people escape strong circumstantial evidence. But it's the best we have. Thanks, Anna. And be careful." He hung up.

Maybe this is the lead they've been looking for. At least, they have a suspect to watch. Anna hoped something more definitive would show up.

Years ago, Anna's father was fond of saying, "Bad luck comes in bunches, like grapes." It still seemed that way to Anna the next morning. Gabe came into the office in a very somber mood. Anna knew immediately something troubled him.

"Is something wrong?" she asked.

"Yes, Mom and Dad had gone to a big Edward Jones & Company conference in Salt Lake City. Dad was hit late last evening by a truck while crossing the street. I'm driving up to be with them. He's in critical condition and I don't know how long I'll be gone. I've put Tim Callahan in charge with Bill Grant as back-up supervisor until I return. If you need me, call me at any time. I'll check in when I can."

He put his arms around her and kissed her gently.

"I'm so sorry Gabe. I'll keep you posted and please be careful. It's a long trip," Anna cautioned.

"Yeah, I know." He took a deep breath and continued, "I really should fly, but we'll need transportation while we're there and I might be able to bring Dad back with me if he has a swift recovery, so just thought I would drive."

His gaze held hers for a moment, and he sighed heavily. "Life's not ever easy is it?"

At that moment, the office door swung open. The lovely, sweet thing that shadowed him constantly looked lovelier than ever. She gave Anna a winning smile, saying, "Good morning."

Anna returned her smile and greeting, understanding how any man would want her constant companionship.

The girl reached out and slapped Gabe on the shoulder and said, "Come on Gabe! I'm hungry...and we need to be hittin' the road." Her actions and words indicated a special familiarity.

Gabe winked at Anna, squeezed her hand and raising it to his lips lightly brushed a kiss across her knuckles. He whispered, "I'll call you." And they were gone.

Anna's heart plummeted within her as she watched them get into Gabe's red Hyundai Santa Fe and drive away.

So the irresistible young thing was actually going all the way to Salt Lake City with him—alone! And she would be there with his parents during his father's convalescence. They had to be very close.

How can I be such a dunce?

The traditional old platitude "love is blind" took on new meaning for her.

I'm no more than a pawn! What does love mean to him? Certainly not a commitment! But he asked me to marry him!

154

Does he think he can have playmates on the side? Evidently he does. The fact that we were both in his presence—at the same time—bothered him not at all! It's a good thing Josey called me when she did last night. I was about to say "yes" to his offer of marriage—and more.

Their relationship from the beginning had been wonderful, harmonious, almost without flaw—until Carla and her accusations had ripped them apart and caused it to become a perpetual see-saw. It was exquisite joy for short periods and then torturous prolonged agony for a time. How could anyone endure such as that, especially for a lifetime? No! It would not be possible. What could she do? He would be gone for—who knew how long? She had some time to figure it out, but she already knew the answer.

Anna struggled with self-condemnation for days and wondered how she could have been so culpable. She knew she loved him totally. Some women put up with a wandering husband just to have what they could of him. Anna couldn't "put up with it". She would have to "put up without it." Put up with life without his presence, his love, his laughter, his wit and humor, his touch—everything that sparked and embodied the essence of her being.

The days went by and Anna worked like a zombie, keeping herself as busy as possible and her mind occupied—her emotions at bay. Gabe called several times and there was always someone there who needed to talk to him so his conversations with Anna had been short and all about business. Anna was glad. She could function as a business automaton.

No matter how short the conversations, Anna always asked about Gabe's father and how he was progressing. He was convalescing nicely and no longer in critical condition. He had suffered a broken leg, a concussion, one collapsed lung and a ruptured spleen. The accident had happened almost in front of Salt Lake City General, a "cutting edge" hospital, and had fortunately received almost immediate care. They still weren't sure when he would be able to travel.

Anna always called Josey mid-afternoon, every day, to check on her well-being. On Friday afternoon, Josey didn't answer. Thinking she may have been in the bathroom or just outside, Anna waited a few minutes and called again. After the third try, Anna left a message on her answering machine for anyone needing her to call her cell phone and hurried home to check on her mother.

As she approached her house, she saw a truck and trailer backed up to the loading chute and two men trying unsuccessfully to catch Smoky. She immediately called Troy.

"Troy, two men are trying to load Smoky. Please hurry. I've parked across the driveway by the house so they can't leave.

"Hang on Anna. We'll be right there."

Anna thought she should stay away from the barn until the sheriff arrived, but seeing the men hassling Smoky was too much. She hurried toward the barn.

One of the men, a tall, very skinny guy with a bushy mustache, wearing a western hat, turned when she angrily demanded. "What do you think you are doing with my horse?"

"He's not your horse!" The man retorted. "Cleve Pierce with the National Rodeo Association bought him and sent us to fetch him."

"He's my horse and no one else can sell him. I did not sell him so you have no right to take him."

"Ma'am, we didn't come hundreds of miles on a whim. Cleve Pierce bought this here horse and we aim to take him."

"You just stay right where you are and leave him alone. The sheriff is on his way." An approaching siren could be heard in the distance. Looking puzzled and somewhat alarmed, the two men looked at each other.

Thank God for sheriffs and law enforcement personnel! Anna felt an immense sense of relief.

Troy pulled up and deputies in two other cruisers pulled up

beside him. The two guys seemed more confounded than scared. The shorter, heavier one kept moving his ball cap up off his head then putting it back on. He was obviously feeling the tension. The sheriff walked calmly toward the two and asked to see their driver's license.

Why? Of course, identification and addresses, Anna realized. One of his deputies was quickly copying all the information on his report. The taller man wearing his western hat, complemented with jeans and boots, spoke up, "We just had instructions from Cleve Pierce with the National Rodeo Association to come pick up this here horse he bought. We ain't causin' no trouble."

"If he just bought the horse I need to see the bill of sale." Troy held out his hand.

"Uh," the men looked at each other. "Well, he didn't give us no bill of sale, but I'm sure he must have one. I mean he's a very respectable man."

"Who sold him the horse?" Troy questioned

"I don't know. We weren't privy to any of the particulars."

The man seemed to realize he might be in a jam.

"Well, why don't we just call Mr. Pierce and get the particulars?" Troy pressed for a phone number.

"Uh, well, he just left and went on vacation. He's gone on a cruise and I don't know how to get him, but I got his office number. Maybe his secretary can help."

Troy took the number and punched it into his cell. After a pause, he said, "Mr. Cleve Pierce, please."

After listening for a moment, he thanked the person on the other end of the line and hung up.

"Well, that number is a switchboard or answering service. Mr. Pierce's office is closed for two weeks and his secretary is on vacation as well. So...unless you can come up with someone else who can verify your story, you two will be guests in the Mechlin County jail for two weeks."

"Now wait a minute!"

"No, you wait a minute! This young lady owns this horse. I know that for a fact, personally. I know she would never sell for any amount of money, so until you show me a bill of sale or someone can corroborate your story and I know who sold you a horse that wasn't theirs, I have to act under the assumption that you were trying to steal him."

The shorter man fidgeted nervously. "Good god! I gotta wife and kids. I need to go home."

"Go ahead and cuff them, Stan," Troy instructed his deputy.

"Well, god amighty!" the tall man expelled in disbelief.

Troy told Anna he would have someone come, pick up their truck and trailer and remove them from the premises. The deputy taking notes took down the license plate numbers.

"You might need to keep tabs on Smoky until we get this straightened out. I think these yahoos really think they're legit so whoever sold them a bill of goods may have sold to several others...who knows." Troy cautioned Anna.

"It just has to be Dugan, but how?"

After a moment's reflection, Anna exclaimed, "Oh, my gosh! I left work and came home because I couldn't get Mom on the phone. I completely forgot." She started running towards the house.

"Wait a sec, I'll go with you." Troy hurriedly followed.

Anna needed to calm Smoky, but he would have to wait.

As Anna opened the door, she was greeted with the blaring noise of Josey's TV. Leaving the door open for Troy, she ran to her mother's bedroom, calling, "Mom, are you okay?"

Josey had apparently been asleep in her recliner. She lifted her head as Anna and Troy entered the room and Anna flipped off her TV.

"Well, what in tarnation! Can't a body take a nap in her own house?"

Anna wasn't sure Josey had actually been asleep. There was something, perhaps fear, in her eyes as she pretended grogginess. Troy had surely noticed as well.

158

"I tried to call you several times Mom! You didn't answer so I came home to check on you."

"Well, I didn't hear ya. Turn ma TV back on."

"No. If you don't mind I need to ask you a few questions," Troy interrupted.

Josey's eyes flashed something—fear mingled with anger and irritation—but after a moment's consideration, she stopped frowning and said, "Okay."

"Have you seen Charley Dugan in the last week or two?"

After hesitating, Josey dropped her eyes and said, "No".

"Be very sure. This is important and could give you some problems if we do not get the whole truth." Troy was being as gentle as possible in questioning Josey, being aware and considerate of her heart condition.

"I done told you, 'no'"

"Were you aware that there were two men outside just now attempting to take Anna's horse?"

Josey blinked her eyes several times and again said, "No".

"Do you know of anyone claiming ownership of Smoky and trying to sell him?"

Josey nervously rubbed her thumb across the pads on her finger before saying, "I don't know nuthin' 'bout that durn horse!"

"Do you have any idea how we can get in touch with Dugan?"

Josey hesitated a long time before answering, "Last time I heard he wuz sommer's in Texas."

"Do you know of anyone or any connection he might have with someone here in Mechlin County?"

Josey pursed her lips and tapped her fingers on the arm of her recliner. It seemed she wanted to tell something, but was weighing the ramifications. "Seems he has a nephew—lived round here close," she finally answered.

"Do you know his name or where he works or anything about him?"

"No, don't know nuthin' 'bout 'em."

Troy gave up, thinking that was all the info he would get from Josey. But maybe that would turn into something. It was a lead of sorts.

Law enforcement officers, it turned out, had difficulty getting access to a judge in order to set a bond hearing for the two men held in custody on the attempted horse rustling charge. It would be Monday, after the weekend, before a judge could hear the evidence. Since the men were from out of state and would probably leave as soon as bond was made, the prosecutor would ask for the bond to be set exorbitantly high. Mr. Pierce would most likely pay the bond, but if he could be reached and prove he had paid for the horse and told the court who had fraudulently sold him Smoky, the charges would be dropped with no need for payment of any bond. It looked as though everything would be on hold until Mr. Pierce had his say.

Anna thought—knowing what little she did about the man—that the situation would greatly massage his ego. He thought the world revolved around himself—waited on his input. What would happen to his ego when he found out that he, the big power broker, would never own Smoky?

Monday morning came sweet and blissful. Birds were singing cheerfully and the sun was shining brightly. Anna stretched luxuriously, absorbing the goodness of it, before she became fully awake. Then startled, she jumped from her bed and raced through the house, checking on Josey while pulling on the clothes she had laid out the evening before, after she had showered and washed her hair. She must hurry or be late and she was never late for work. The alarm hadn't gone off or she had forgotten to set it. She had only thirty-five minutes to feed Smoky and Casey, get ready to leave, grab a banana and drive to work.

"Mom can you get your own breakfast this morning? I'm running late. I'm so sorry."

"Well, I guess I don't have any choice do I. Why'd you sleep so late?"

"The alarm didn't go off."

Anna ran to slap on some makeup and take the rest with her. Maybe she'd get a break and be able to make some repairs.

She ran to the barn with two apples, putting them in Smoky's feed pan, along with some "horse and mule." "I'll see you later," she said, kissing him on the nose.

She noticed, in passing, Casey's food and water dishes were more than half full. That would be enough food for him until she got home again.

She got to the office with three minutes to spare. She had been glad Troy was not out that early—at least on her road. Well, not really, she never breached the speed limit by more than five miles per hour at most.

The rest of the day was not so hectic. Sammy Grisham came by, needing help with his algebra. He was more outgoing of late. She wondered if it could all be attributed to the newly found knowledge that he could lick those contrary algebra problems.

How wonderful if all children could get a similar boost.

She did manage to apply her makeup properly and teased her hair a bit in one or two places. Even added a touch of cologne. She felt better. She didn't want to look like a frump. She respected her job and would strive to present a respectable image to the public for herself and the office as well.

She had caught up with all her necessary posting, typing, billing, and paying of invoices by early afternoon and was making a fresh pot of coffee, when Bill Grant walked in.

"Hey! Anyone here?" he called.

"Yes, of course. Come on back, I'm just making fresh coffee."

"Great! I sure could use some. I also need to ask a woman's opinion on the house plans I've been working on for the last several weeks. I'm really pleased with it all...except the placement of some kitchen items. Seems when I get them exactly where I want them, they're across—or at a great distance from—

161

the water source. I need this to be absolutely perfect if possible. It's a great plan with lots of space and I'm trying desperately to keep the cost down. Maybe the location of the appliances, the sink and the ice maker in the fridge is not as critical as I'm thinking they are."

"Gosh, Bill, you're the architect. I know nothing about engineering a design."

"You don't have to. I just want an opinion from your perspective as a woman...as a kitchen user." He laughed.

"Okay, I'd love to see your plans."

They stood side-by-side with the plans spread out on the coffee bar. He pointed out several salient features and seemed extremely pleased with his latest achievement.

"You know, every time we build a new plan and we show it, I make a note of all the things the customers like and dislike. This house has all, but this one arrangement thingee, that 78% of the buyers said they liked or must have."

Anna was still studying the plans. "I love the way this house is laid out and the front elevation is beautiful. But I don't see how you can put these appliances where you want them, without laying a lot more water lines. Guess you can't have 100% perfection can you?"

"Oh, wait...wait...wait a minute! All you would have to do—if it doesn't matter or matters less—is not to mess with the kitchen arrangement, but change instead the utility on the other side of the wall. Just switch places with the closet and the washer. If the dryer will fit in the remaining space."

"Well, yeah, but that would leave the dryer on the left of the washer. Most people want it on the right."

"Would they consider stackables?" she asked.

"Some would. Most wouldn't."

"Well, even if you move the washer to the left, you would only need the width of the washer in extra waterline."

"Yep, and that's a lot less than the pipe necessary if I leave it as it is."

162

"I think that would be great," she said.

"I do to!"

The problem was settled. It had been too easy—too quick.

That goober! He had already made up his mind about that possibility before he ever discussed it with her. Anna felt sure.

"Thanks a lot for taking a look."

He gave her a big hug that lasted longer than was necessary, which heightened Anna's suspicions about his motive for being there. What should she do? Ignore it and let him think she thought she had solved his problem. That made her look like a thick-headed dullard, who was insensitive to nuances. Or should she mention his shabby cover-up and ask what were his intentions? Would that hurt his feelings? Anna decided to let him think her a dullard.

"Thank you for letting me look at your plans. I really like this house. How big is it?"

"Twenty-one hundred square feet. I think this one will really sell." he said.

"Looks like a winner," she agreed.

"Glad you like it."

He seemed happy that she approved of his work.

"The coffee is ready if you would like a cup."

"Sure would."

He helped himself to the coffee and sat with his cup in front of Anna's desk for about thirty minutes enjoying amiable conversation, before Gabe called. After a few minutes, Anna asked Bill if he needed to speak to Gabe.

"Yeah, let me talk to him," he said, reaching for the phone.

"What am I doing here?" he asked in answer to Gabe's question. "Well, I brought my almost finished house plans for your secretary's critical review and she solved my latest quandary. I think this house will be a real seller and not as costly as some we've built. The profit margin looks to be great." After a pause, he continued, "I would like a savvy, decorating wizard, preferably a lady, to help choose colors, textures, drapes, carpets

163

and furniture when it is finished to showcase it, if that meets with your approval."

He listened a moment and then continued, "Well, okay, sure, we'll discuss it when you get back. How soon will that be, do you know?" After a moment he added, "Okay, I'm anxious to show you these plans. I think you will like them. See you then."

Handing Anna the phone, he informed her, "He doesn't know yet how soon he will be back."

Later that afternoon, as Anna was on her knees cleaning out old files, Troy came into the office.

"Gracious girl! That looks like an uncomfortable position....I think you may want to have a seat. I need to give you some information that you will find disturbing."

"Of course. I was just looking for something to keep me busy. I'm caught up with everything else."

After they were both seated at Anna's desk Troy began, "Mr. Pierce, evidently called someone to check on whether or not his guys had delivered Smoky. He found out we had them incarcerated here in Carnegie so he called me, demanding their immediate release. When I demanded proof that he had actually paid for Smoky, Pierce faxed us a copy of his wire transfer for $15,000 to an account here in Carnegie. He was still waiting on a promised bill of sale in the mail. We checked with the bank and the money was still in the account. We immediately put a freeze on that account."

Troy hesitated. Apprehensive, but desperately needing to know, Anna prepared herself for a shock.

"Whose account?" she asked.

Troy's mouth tightened as though he would rather not say, but continued, "It's in your mother's account, Anna...deposited early on Friday morning."

Anna gasped. "No! I can't believe it. Mom just wouldn't do that to me."

Tears filled her eyes as she rose from behind the desk and

began pacing back and forth, trying to comprehend the traitorous deed perpetrated upon her by her own mother.

"I guess there's no possibility of any error is there?" she finally asked in a small voice.

"No, Anna, I don't see how. It's about 4 o'clock now. Would you be able to lock up here and go with me to arrest her? That is if you want to press charges."

Anna buried her face in her hands.

"How can I possibly do that. She's sick and just being in jail might kill her. What can I do? I just want to keep Smoky. The man will get his money back. So why should I..."

"Why don't we just go and talk to her. Find out what light she can shed on the matter. Maybe she was coerced by Dugan, which could leave her in the clear."

"Yes!" Anna prepared to leave. "Let's go see what she says."

Josey was watching TV and not particularly interested in the arrival of Anna and the sheriff, until Anna snapped off her TV.

"There have been some very interesting new developments in the attempt to steal Smoky. The sheriff needs some answers that apparently only you can give him. I suggest you cooperate to the fullest without holding anything back," Anna warned her mother.

She had begun to feel some resentment for the way she had been sorely used by Josey.

Troy took charge.

"As you already know, a Mr. Cleve Pierce claimed to purchase Smoky for $15,000. Well, this morning he managed to fax us a copy of the wire transfer confirming that is true. The $15,000 is in your account. Sent to Josey Shelton, and we have put a freeze on that account so you cannot spend any of the money. It has to be returned to Mr. Pierce, since you had no right whatsoever to sell Anna's horse."

Josey's eyes were brilliant with anger as she loudly denied any knowledge of the transaction.

"I didn' sell her durn horse and I didn' take any money fer

'em. You're a lyin'!"

"The evidence is right here."

Troy reached into a folder and handed Josey a copy of the wire transfer and a copy of the bank's deposit slip showing it had been deposited to her account.

"Facts don't lie. That the transfer happened can't be denied."

"Well, I didn' have nothin' ta do with any of it. I didn' know anything 'bout it a tall!" She was adamant in her denial.

"Did you talk to Cleve Pierce and agree to let him have Smoky for $15,000?"

"No! I just talked ta the man onct and that was when he wuz askin' fer Anna. He told me what he'd pay and I told him I thought it wuz a fair offer, but he'd have ta talk ta her 'bout it."

Troy hesitated and seemed to be considering a different possibility. He punched in a number on his cell and listened while it rang.

"Hello. I'd like to speak with Mr. Cleve Pierce please. This is Sheriff Henderson in Carnegie, Oklahoma. I need more information about his attempted purchase of a horse." After a moment he continued, "Yes, Mr. Pierce. Mrs. Josey Shelton denies even discussing the sale of her daughter's horse with you. Can you explain how you got her checking account number and why you think you had an agreement with her."

"Hell, yes, I can. No, I never talked to the girl. I talked to a man who said he was her dad and that she had been involved in a car roll-over and had broken some ribs or something. Said she was in the hospital and couldn't talk, but had changed her mind about selling her horse on account of she needed the money to pay hospital bills. Needless to say I was well pleased and when he gave me the name and account number and stuff, I questioned the name. I said, 'I thought her name was Anna.' And he said, 'It is. It's Josey Anna Shelton. She sometimes uses Anna, sometimes Josey, sometimes both. It just happens the account is in the name Josey Shelton.' Sounded good to me. I wired the money."

166

"Why wouldn't an astute business man, like yourself, wait on a bill of sale first, before sending that kind of money?" Troy questioned.

"I didn't think he's send a bill of sale without getting the money first and besides, I was boarding a cruise ship, I needed to leave."

"I guess you know by now that you have not bought a horse. The horse belongs to Anna Shelton, who is the daughter of Josey Shelton and no one gave any man the right to bargain for Anna in the sale of her horse. If you give me your banking information, your money will be refunded...minus any court costs or fees...any costs the judge may have assessed."

"Well, dang it! I still want that horse. Let me talk to that Anna girl."

Troy turned to Anna and asked if she wanted to talk to Pierce about a sale of Smoky.

"No! Never! Not at any price," she immediately responded.

"Mr. Pierce, Smoky is not for sale under any circumstances for any price. Any further attempt to contact Anna about it will be considered harassment. Do you understand?"

"Well, hell! Offering a better price is not harassment!"

"Do you understand me Mr. Pierce?" Troy firmly asked the question again.

Anna smiled to herself. She so appreciated his refusal to allow the overbearing, self-important egomaniac to aggravate her. She hoped that now she would not have to make a decision about filing charges against her mother. There was no proof that Josey knew any money had been deposited to her account for the sale of Anna's horse. And the prosecutor would probably not pursue any charges, especially if Troy added his comments about Josey's health and Anna's reluctance to cause her further trauma. But, somehow, Anna could not believe her mother was totally unaware of the transaction. However, Josey was exhibiting an extraordinary amount of shrewdness in maintaining her innocence through silence, if she were in fact guilty.

Anna walked with Troy to his cruiser.

She sighed a pronounced, "Whooosh!"of relief.

"I so much appreciate who you are and what you do," she told him.

He smiled, "Thanks, Anna. You're entitled to a little peace," he said and patted her hand before turning the key and starting his patrol car. "But please, be aware that your life could still, and probably is, still in danger. Stay alert and call me if you need me."

Anna knew the puzzle was still not solved, but maybe they were getting closer to putting the pieces together. She prayed it would happen soon.

Chapter Ten

Anna went about her regular routine with only half her usual attention. The other half seemed to be focused on the door and beyond, listening for any car parking next to the curb or a familiar figure darkening the doorway. She didn't know herself why she was so "wired" this Friday morning. No one knew when to expect Gabe back, so that probably wasn't why she had taken such painstaking care in applying her makeup and arranging her hair. Or why she had worn her new gray, circle skirt with the dark suede pumps that made her look tall and slender. And the soft, white, silk blouse with the light pink sweater—the pink that heightened the color in her cheeks. Or why she smelled of his favorite perfume.

Good gosh! Everyone likes to look their best at all times and it's my favorite perfume too, she told herself, trying to believe it was a normal day and that she wasn't hoping for anything special—just in case it didn't happen.

Bill Grant called as he often did of late. He asked her to lunch, but she claimed Sammy Grisham would be by to ask for help with his algebra. She would be tutoring on her lunch hour. She bragged about Sammy's latest achievement—about how he was actually tutoring other students who were having difficulty with their algebra.

"I can only attribute Sammy's success to your help, Anna. Well, okay, I'll call again late this afternoon, so make up your mind to go to dinner and dancing with me tonight. Please. At least think about it, will you?"

"Bill, I'm all tied up and usually too tired to dance. And I have to tell you I'm not interested in a relationship at this time, so maybe we should just remain business associates for now, huh?"

169

"Not if I can help it," he said "I'll call you later."

Anna tried to give all her attention to the few odds and ends she could find to do. She even dusted and polished Gabe's desk and credenza and ran the sweeper in his office, then burned a spice-apple candle. He probably wouldn't be in until sometime next week, but it might still smell nice—a little like apple pie.

Mid-morning, Troy called. "Morning Anna. Is everything okay with you?"

"Yes, as far as I know. What's up?"

"We tracked a Bill Freemont, presently living in Mechlin County, Oklahoma back though Ancestry.com and found his mother was Miranda Louise Dugan, sister to Charley, born in Galveston, Texas. So we went looking for Billy and when we found him, we asked him about Charley. He didn't deny the relationship, but said he had no idea where Dugan was at present. Swore he had not seen him recently. We are watching him closely so maybe we'll come up with a clue of some sort. We will probably put out an APB, all-points bulletin, if we don't get something on Charley soon. We can say he's wanted for questioning about the attempted theft of your horse." Troy sounded hopeful. "At least it's more than we had before."

"Were you able to get impressions of Billy's tires?"

"We're working on that. Should be in our hands late this afternoon."

Anna thought Troy seemed a little more upbeat than usual and after approximately another hour, she learned why.

Janice called Anna, who was delighted to hear from her.

"Janice, it's so good to hear from you. How are you?"

"Hi, Chiquita! I've missed you too, but I have to say my life has been so much more exciting, since I saw you last."

"Why is that? Have you learned to make apples pies without me?" Anna pretended to pout.

"Oh, way better than that. This gal learned to fish and caught the best catch of the season."

"What are you saying? Are you....?

170

"Yeah, buddy! He asked me to marry him."

Janice was so excited, Anna squealed in contagious delight.

"Oh, Janice, I'm so happy for you. When will you be married?"

"Tomorrow, if I had my way, but he's a stickler for order in all things, so guess it'll be next June. I would like to show you my promise of that blessed event."

"Do you mean your engagement ring?"

"Yes, Oh, Anna it's gorgeous. It's almost too much! And just think...I get to be 'Mama Trojan.'"

Anna laughed happily. "He's a super cool guy, Janice. And he has a really great partner in you. I know you'll be happy together. I'm so pleased."

A few minutes after her conversation with Janice ended, Anna found herself wiping tears from her cheeks. Was she crying in happiness for Janice and Troy or was it because she felt so lost and alone herself. It had to be a mix of both.

Sammy Grisham did indeed come by during her lunch hour for some help with his algebra, though she hadn't positively expected him. After finding the algebraic solution to his vexing problem, Sammy thanked Anna profusely.

"Boy, you have really changed my life and I thank you so much for helping me all the time."

"You're most welcome Sammy. It was fun for me to kinda brush up on my old skills."

Sammy looked at Anna for a moment before asking, "I see that guy in here quite a bit. Bill, I think his name is. When I asked the other day if he was your boss, he told me 'no'—he was going to be your husband. Are you going to marry him?"

Anna laughed, "No, that goose! I don't think we'd be a very good match, Sammy. He's just shootin' off his mouth."

Sammy stared at her for another moment before blurting out, "Well, he sure would be lucky if he married you. I'd marry you myself if I was old enough!" He blushed furiously, shocked at his own audacity.

171

Anna laughed delightedly. Who would have thought shy Sammy Grisham would say such a thing!

"Thank you for that wonderful compliment, Sammy. Whoever finally gets you will be a very lucky girl."

Sammy's embarrassment eased and he was smiling again.

"I'm going to make the honor roll this semester...thanks to you."

"No, Sammy...you earned your grade. I just gave you instructions on how to go about it. And I'm so glad for you."

His achievement and his expanding confidence warmed Anna's heart. If she gave up her job at Whittier Enterprises, maybe she should teach or just tutor on the side.

Bill Grant didn't call and Anna was glad. She didn't want to hurt his feelings, but wished he'd back off. As she was washing the coffee pot and cleaning the coffee bar, the outer door slammed and there was Mr. Grant in person.

"Hi, sweetie, I got held up and couldn't call earlier. I was 'just in the neighborhood' and thought I'd drop by instead. You are going dancing with me tonight, aren't you?"

"No, Bill, I'm too tired to dance and I need to go check on my mom and other stuff."

Anna thought she heard the door to Gabe's office close softly. She walked to the window and could see just the rear end of a red Hyundai Santa Fe. He was back! She struggled to maintain her composure. Why had he not come in to let her know? Maybe he needed a moment to unwind. It had been a long trip she knew.

Bill Grant evidently hadn't heard the click of the door closing next to the break room.

"We don't have to go dancing, just have dinner with me. I have something to discuss with you."

"Oh, really. I have a few minutes. Why don't we just discuss it here? Is it connected to the new house design?"

Perhaps he wanted her to choose the furniture and stuff to showcase it. Anna thought that would be fun.

"No, not really...but it is a...uh...a proposal that I hope you'll consider."

"Okay, what is it?"

He took a deep breath. "Marry me!. I want you to marry me before some other yahoo turns your head."

Anna laughed. "Marry you? Just like that! With no courtship involved whatsoever? Surely, you can't be serious."

"Yes, I am. Marry me and I'll court you the rest of our lives," he said, moving closer to put his arms around her.

She moved to the other side of the table.

"Bill, you don't even know me. Be careful making those kinds of rash proposals. You might get yourself into a lifetime of trouble."

"Yes, I do know you. I've watched you for months now and I know how you work, what talent you have, what you believe in and how you help others. I've never met anyone quite like you and probably never will again. I know what I want. Marry me we'll solve the problems—if we have any."

"Bill, marriage is not like a business proposition. It involves emotions deep down personal commitment and you don't just marry someone because you think you like who they are or that you're going to be compatible with them. There has to be feelings—emotional togetherness—love, if you will. And love is not a thing you can wish into being. It either happens or it doesn't. And if it's there you can't wish it away."

He held her gaze for a few seconds before answering. "What you're saying is that you have no passion for me, right? I know what *I* feel and I'm willing to bet you can—given time—feel it too."

Gently, Anna asked, "Willing to bet what? A lifetime of misery if it never happened? I'm not saying love doesn't grow and bonding get stronger by being with someone. It does. But to have missed that magic, ecstatic, to-die-for sharing of something so exquisite you can't put words to it, is not where I want to start my marriage."

173

His lips tightened. "The other half of your statement: 'You can't wish love away' is the real problem isn't it? It's Gabe isn't it? You love him, don't you?"

When she didn't answer, he nodded his head slightly. "I was afraid of that. Damn! I should have known he was telling the truth when he said you did."

Anna had been so shocked at Bill's proposal she had forgotten that Gabe was probably on the other side of the wall. She felt exposed. Her inner feelings viewed by an observer. Why had he not made his presence known? Would she eavesdrop on a conversation between him and his sweet thing? He flaunted their relationship under her nose constantly as though it was his right even though he swore love and devotion to Anna and had asked her to marry him. Now he had just heard her almost swear she could never ever love anyone but him and would never marry without feeling the love he knew she felt for him alone. She felt like a fool. Maybe she should turn the tables on him. Let him know how it felt to stand and watch someone you loved walk away with another. The hurt was almost unbearable. She wanted him to feel that—to know how it hurt. And he would feel it—if in fact he really loved her. Perhaps, she should go dancing with Bill. No, it wouldn't matter. Gabe knew she could never love anyone as she loved him, didn't he?

Answering Bill's question regarding her feelings for Gabe made Anna reconsider.

"My relationship with Gabe is not a subject for discussion—now or ever."

"Okay...okay, lovely lady. Just be my best friend. Go to dinner with me. I enjoy your company. You inspire me to be better than I am."

Anna laughed lightly. "In that case, maybe I will Where to and what time?"

Bill's eyes brightened. He smiled. "How about the Country Club. I'll pick you up at 6."

"Make it 6:30 and only if Mom is feeling fine and doesn't

174

need me. I might even dance with you."

Bill clasped his hands together with a slap and said, "Alright, sweetheart! I'll see you then."

He grabbed her hand and brought it to his lips. She pulled it away.

"Okay, but friendship only...a deal... right?"

He smiled and winked. "If that's what you really want!"

Anna felt somewhat disconcerted. This was not good. She knew Bill was not totally convinced there was no hope for anything other than friendship. But, she thought of Gabe and his relationship with that lovely thing always on his arm and said nothing further.

It took only a few minutes to gather her things and leave by the back door, avoiding Gabe's red Santa Fe and whoever might be inside it.

Josey was her usual self, watching TV and drinking coffee. Anna asked if she felt okay.

"How was your day, Mom? Do you hurt anywhere? How hungry are you?"

"I'm good. And no I'm not hungry. Just sumpin' light otta' do."

"Okay, how about a vegetable burrito, some fruit salad and yogurt. There's some apple pie left if you'd rather and of course a cup of coffee. Would you like to play gin after your supper?"

"Sounds good, 'cept no I don' wanna play gin. I'm gonna watch Lester Holt on Dateline, and Grimm, then that new show—Hannibal. It's a good night for TV."

"I'm glad you're feeling so good. I have been invited out to dinner and an evening of dancing at the Country Club, so if you're busy with TV, I think I'll go."

Josey seemed to feel bad all of a sudden.

"That Gabe Whittier is back I guess," she hissed.

"Now, Mom, we agreed that you would back off from any criticism of Gabe when I started to work for Whittier Enterprises.

175

I have to work and he's a good employer and the pay is great. Besides, I hardly ever see him. He's out supervising the construction on his houses. So stay off his back. And no Mom, Gabe didn't ask me out. It's someone who works for him. His name is Bill Grant and he seems like a nice guy. I'll bring him in to meet you if you'd like."

"No, I don' wanna meet 'em. Just git home early. I might git ta feelin' poorly and I couldn' call ya. What da ya have to go fer anyway?"

"I haven't been going out at all for a long time now. I thought it might be fun."

Anna hurriedly fixed Josey's supper and then tended to her animals. Then tried to get herself ready for a rare night out. While she was bathing, she contemplated what she could wear.

I don't have a frazzlin' thing to wear dancing!

After a few moments, she wondered if her prom dress might still fit—if it were still in one piece. After toweling off and slipping into a robe, she looked in the back of her closet to find the gown. On a shelf in a large box, still wrapped in acid-free tissue paper, untouched for years, it looked in perfect condition.

Now if it will just fit!

She truly hoped it would. What else could she possibly wear? Anna did her best to brush aside the nostalgia when she lifted it from the box and buried her face in its soft folds. It still smelled of Design, her favorite perfume. Poignant memories from the one and only happy time she had worn it filled her eyes with tears.

No! I can't possibly wear this!

But then she remembered the sweet, lovely thing that had captivated Gabe and knew she had to make a life for herself somehow. Maybe now was a good time to begin breaking the shackles that bound her—or at least attempt to.

The dress was soft and white with the feel of velvet, but was thinner and much lighter in weight. It had a halter top and full circle skirt that fell gracefully to her ankles. A small bolero type jacket made from a gold metallic lace covered her bare back enticingly. She searched until she found all the matching paraphernalia and when finally ready, she went in to say good night to Josey. She wore high-heeled, gold sandals and carried a matching small clutch. On her ears were tiny gold nuggets and golden butterflies encircled her left wrist. Her hair was in an up-sweep of large lustrous curls that added inches to her height.

Josey exploded when Anna entered her room.

"Good gawd! Did ya have to dress like Cinderella? He might git the notion ya like him a lot."

"No, Mom. Bill knows we're just friends. With regard to the dress—I really didn't have much to choose from."

"Doncha go out drinkin' or nuthin'. You come right on home."

"Sure, Mom. I don't intend to dance but one or two waltzes and then I'll come home."

She didn't mention she might have a cocktail with dinner.

"Oh, my god! You look absolutely fantastic!" was Bill's greeting when she answered the door.

He wore a nice dark suit with a dress shirt—open at the neck—with no tie.

"Did I overdo? My Country Club wardrobe is rather slim and outdated. Did you expect blue jeans?" Anna asked.

He laughed "No, I'm just amazed at how different you look. I mean you always look great but you 'clean up' so damned gorgeous!"

He took her arm and walked her to his car, a black, late model Lexus.

When they reached the Country Club, they were seated immediately. That told her he had made reservations early on, because this rarely happened otherwise, especially on a Friday night. After placing their orders, they were told there would be at least a 30-minute wait. Anna looked around the room and toward the dance floor. The band was playing softly and couples were already beginning to drift there. Her breath caught audibly. Bill

177

noticed and looked to see what had caught her attention. There several tables away sat Gabe with his back to them, alone, finishing his dinner.

"So Gabe's home again, is he?" he asked wryly.

Anna saw no need to reply. She must go and ask about Gabe's father. How could she not. As she rose, Bill also pushed back his chair and walked beside her toward Gabe's table.

"So the wandering wayward returns." Bill greeted him.

Anna wondered where the young girl was. *Must be home asleep. It surely had been a very tiring trip.*

Gabe turned, taking in Anna and what she wore at a glance. Something in his eyes told her he felt betrayed. She felt it too. It was a though a sacred trust had somehow been broken. The memories evoked by her wearing of the prom dress were the last of the good times they had shared and now she had treated them as though they meant nothing.

Gabe looked so tired. She ached to press his head against her bosom and tell him how important he was to her.

He took a deep breath. "Yeah, I got back a little bit ago. Everyone else went to bed. I had a few things to check out at the office and thought I'd grab a bite to eat before hitting the sack myself."

"How's your dad? He did come back with you, didn't he?" Anna asked.

"He's okay. Very tired, but much better. Yes, I brought him home with me."

Bill offered his hand and said, "It's good to have you back. We've missed you."

"Thanks," Gabe replied, "It's great to be back."

"I'm going to dance this young lady around the floor for a few minutes, then it will be your turn."

"My turn? I don't want to dance with you, Grant." Gabe grinned wearily.

Why had Bill made such an offer anyway? Did he feel sorry for Gabe or what? Anna felt like a pawn offered between

178

brokers. She wanted to snap at Bill, but held her tongue and went with him to the dance floor. Gabe avoided looking at her.

The band started playing an old oldie, a favorite of Anna's, as well as Gabe's. But at this time, she wished they had played something else—anything but the Tennessee Waltz. The haunting refrain, "And while they were dancing, my friend stole my sweetheart from me" filled the air and Anna's heart to bursting. She wanted to scream, "No! Turn it off."

When they returned to their table, Gabe was gone.

The rest of the evening Anna fought despondency. She tried to be companionable and not show how much she wanted to get away. What had she been thinking? But she had no idea Gabe would be at the Country Club. She had wanted him to hear her plans not see them in action. Somehow it seemed much more hurtful. Had he come just to let her know that he knew? Was it okay with him then? It certainly had not helped matters as far as she was concerned. She felt much worse.

Bill had been very attentive and complimentary all evening and when he opened the car door and walked with her to the front steps he said, "I hope I didn't walk all over your toes tonight."

"Of course not. You're a very good dancer and an excellent host. Thank you for the evening. I enjoyed it."

"Anna, please don't give up on being my best friend."

"I'll always be your friend, Bill. *Best* I couldn't say. But you need to go find someone and *now* who can return what you have to offer. Don't get more involved in a hopeless maybe hurtful situation."

After a moment's hesitation, he said, "I'm not sure I have anything to offer someone else."

"At least give yourself a chance. Change your thinking while you can and actively pursue the idea that you're looking for someone out there that can make your heart sing. I'll bet you find her."

She kissed him on the check and went into the house.

Sounds of an engine starting then slowly fading into the night left Anna feeling more alone than ever. She buried her face in her hands and sobbed softly—praying for some relief from all the problems that consumed her.

After checking on Josey, who was in bed fast asleep with the TV on, Anna flipped off her mother's TV and prepared for bed herself. She finally crawled in between the sheets to lie awake with Miss Kitty purring contentedly at her feet.

She couldn't fall asleep and found herself searching for reasons that had put her where she was. Soon she was remembering that awful day when she was at the cabin near McAlester, ready to return home and read an appalling story in the Daily Oklahoman written under the headline "Missing Carnegie Girl Found." Anna hurried back to Carnegie. If Josey was glad to see her, she didn't mention it. She was too busy blaming Gabe for what had happened to Carla.

Carla was back in Carnegie. No one knew where she had gone, what she had done or why she came back, but someone had killed her and left her body in the city park.

"He killed her! I told you that bastard was no good. She came back to take that polygraph and prove it was his baby. He'd have to marry her then. So he killed her like he said he would."

"Mom, Gabe never said he'd kill anyone. Besides even if she's dead, they can still test the DNA of the baby. But she was no longer pregnant, so that could not have been an issue."

Anna could hardly speak. Wasn't sure if she actually had spoken. She might be dead herself. She felt nothing. All Anna knew about Carla's death was what she read in the papers. Some children, playing in the city park had found her body, near the duck pond. She had been badly bruised and apparently run over by some vehicle that left cuts on her back in a special pattern of lines parallel to each other and about one foot apart. A blow to the back of the head, severe enough to actually crush her skull was determined to be the actual cause of death. She had no papers on her. No purse was found—not a scrap of anything to indicate where she had gone or what she had been doing for the last two months. And she was no longer pregnant.

Finally, Anna wept. She wept for Carla and the lost child. She wept because of knowledge denied her. Now she would never know positively who fathered Carla's baby. Josey was strung higher than ever. Constantly yelling and swearing about that no-good bastard, Gabe, who had sworn to kill Carla two months before and had now done the horrible deed.

Anna tried to get her to shut up and leave well enough alone, but Josey was frantic to see that he be punished for what she thought he had done. Josey relished the thought of Gabe being in prison. Did she hate him that much? Or was she just that determined to get him out of Anna's life for good.

"I told ya he was no good, didn' I? He even killed 'er to keep 'er quiet!"

"Carla's accusations that Gabe was the father of her child are public knowledge. So keeping her quiet was not at issue there. And especially since she was no longer pregnant. Maybe, she never was. Maybe she just wanted Gabe or some money or who knows what? Who will ever know for sure. Just leave it alone."

"Somebody killed 'er. They'll keep lookin' 'til they find out who! And who else woulda done it?"

"I don't know. Maybe Billy Freemont. Maybe it was an accident. Someone may have accidentally run over her on the highway and was afraid to come forward. They are sure her body was moved."

"Yeah, but Gabe said he'd kill 'er and that's just what he done."

"Mom, Gabe never said such a thing!"

"He did so! I heard 'em. He said he'd find 'er and send 'er to hell. He was standin; rat out yonder. You wuz there. You heard 'em too!"

Anna didn't remember any such thing. She had been so distraught over the one thing said—which had so wounded her

181

soul—that nothing else penetrated her conscious mind.

Little by little, story by story, the papers informed Anna that Carla had indeed been pregnant. An autopsy showed there had been an abortion not too long before her demise. Anna forced herself to go to Carla's funeral. The doctor had given her some tranquilizers and she left the chapel as soon as decently possible. It had still been almost unbearable. Carla's mother had hugged her tight and said, "I prayed that Carla would have kept your company and not taken up with Billy's crowd! But there was no controlling her. She had to have him."

I'm so sorry it came to this. But how could we have changed it?" Anna replied, wanting to leave, feeling inadequate to help Carla's mom deal with her loss.

Later the statement, "She had to have him" was a big factor in convincing Anna to lie on Gabe's behalf—saying she remembered what he had said when she really hadn't. For if Carla "had to have Billy," it didn't follow that she would have messed with Gabe and besides Gabe was more honorable than that. Wasn't he? Soon everyone who knew Carla was called in and questioned by the authorities about any and everything they knew concerning her and her activities. Anna was questioned at length and so was Josey. Anna felt it was Josey's screeching and accusations that eventually prompted a judicial inquiry to determine if there was enough evidence to try Gabe for the murder of Carla Spencer. Devastated, Anna knew in her heart Gabe never said he would kill anyone, but how could she convince an august panel of skeptics if she couldn't even convince her own mother.

Subpoenas were issued and received. The date was set and Anna grew more apprehensive while Josey became more gleeful that she could send Gabe away—out of Anna's life forever.

The day finally arrived. Anna was again prescribed tranquilizers, but she was careful not to take too many. She needed her wits about her.

Lots of people testified as to Carla's downfall—her good

attendance changed from never missing a day of school to rarely coming at all. Her grades plummeted from honor roll to failing. Friends became non-existent except for Billy Freemont and his crowd—from church going classmates to boozing junkies, who swore with every breath and were constantly trying to pick a fight. No one had heard that she was pregnant except Gabe, Anna and Josey. Billy Freemont wouldn't admit that he had any inkling he was to become a father. His alibi at the time of her death was substantiated by two of his close friends who swore they were with him in Houston, Texas—just kickin' around. No one could prove otherwise.

When Josey was questioned, she became very loud and accusatory. "That no-good louse said, 'I'll find 'er and send 'er to hell' and that's just what he done. Found 'er and killed 'er. He's probably mad 'cause she ruined his precious reputation and he didn' want no brat runnin' round with his name. He should pay fer his fun with 'er. He ought to take care of his kid—not kill it." She was almost screaming when she finally shut up.

Gabe was very confident on the "hot seat." He was angry and indignant, anyone could tell, but he kept his composure well.

When asked, "Where were you on the night Carla was killed?"

"I was in Oklahoma City. I had taken a load of cattle to the stockyards for sale and stayed overnight to watch them sell the next day and picked up my check. I have a motel receipt and also the check stub with the date of issue and deposit dates. I deposited it the day I picked it up, which I could not have done if it had been mailed to me."

"Is it possible you could be the father of Carla's unborn child?"

"No, absolutely not. I never knew her in that way."

"Do you know why she would say it was yours?"

"No, not unless she couldn't get Billy to marry her and she was desperate to make someone else do it. Or maybe she just thought she could scare me into giving her money for the abortion she wanted."

"Did you have anything to be scared of?"

"No, but no one wants that kind of a story out about them and maybe she thought I would give in just to keep her from creating a scandal."

"Would you have married her?"

"No, of course not. I was engaged to Anna Shelton and we planned to marry soon. We got a court order to demand a paternity test, but couldn't find Carla. She had run away."

"Do you have any idea where she might have gone?"

"No, none."

"Mr. Whittier, did you have anything whatsoever to do with the death of Carla Spencer?"

"No, absolutely nothing."

"It has been told to this panel that you were heard saying you would find Carla and put her in hell before you would marry her. Is that true? Did you threaten her life?"

"No, I did not. What I said was, "I am not the father of her child and I will see her in hell before I will be railroaded into a marriage with her.""

"What did you mean by, 'I'll see her in hell first'?"

"It's just a phrase meaning—to me—that I would spend eternity and even go to hell before I would give in to that lie. I never threatened her physically."

Anna was the last to testify. She knew that she herself had been briefly considered a suspect, but she had grocery and gas receipts with dates that put her in McAlester on, before and after the date of Carla's murder. Besides it seemed unlikely to the authorities that she could have physically inflicted upon Carla the trauma that had caused her death.

"Ms. Shelton, you have heard the testimony of your mother that you were present when Mr. Whittier threatened to send Carla Spencer to hell. Did you hear that threat?"

Anna took a deep breath feeling Gabe's future hinged on her next few words. It was imperative that she not make conflicting statements.

"I was present and heard everything that was said, but he did not say he'd send her to hell. He said that he would see her in hell before he would submit to Carla's lies."

"What do you think he meant by that?"

"Well, if I had said it I think I would mean I'd never—in this lifetime ever give in to being manipulated by her untruths."

"Why didn't you and your mother hear the same thing, do you think?"

"Mom wasn't all that close and I'm not all that sure she could actually hear what he did say. But I am sure that if she heard anything that could be construed to be a threat she would hang onto that and expound it as gospel."

"What do you mean? That your mother has lied."

"Not intentionally. But she has always been against our marriage and would be happy to find anything to keep us apart."

"Why is she against your marriage?"

"She would be all alone and she has a desperate need to keep me there to help, no—to run—the farm for her. She is incapable of doing it herself."

Anna was sorry to say that about her mother in front of such a crowd, but it was the truth and needed to be told.

"Ms. Shelton, do you believe Mr. Whittier is the father of Carla's unborn child?"

"No, she even told Gabe it was Billy's and he wouldn't marry her. She asked Gabe to help. She wanted money and the name of a doctor. Gabe said he couldn't help with either and cautioned her to be very sure that was what she really wanted."

"Why do you think she later changed her story and named Gabe as the father?"

"I think she couldn't find anyone else to help her and thought she could force Gabe to at least help her with money or whatever. It didn't work so she left before we could prove he was not the father. She knew the paternity test would prove her a liar. And isn't that extortion. She could be in legal trouble."

"Ms. Shelton, one last question. If you believed Gabe, your

then fiancé, was innocent, why did you call off the wedding?"

Anna had thought that might be a question they would ask. She was committed to do her best—not overelaborate—just indicate.

"Well, Gabe is a very good and considerate person and would allow everyone to believe that I called off the wedding. But, just let me answer this question with a question. Would you like to face a lifetime of yelling and screaming accusations from a mother-in-law in residence?"

A smirk appeared on several faces. One person even voiced a subdued "Whooh!"

Anna never looked at Gabe or anyone else. She hated to have to go home and listen to what Josey had to say, but face it she must.

Findings of the hearing were announced in the headlines of papers all across the state the following day. "Insufficient Evidence to Indict For Murder" was found word for word in every paper Anna had seen. Relieved that the legal proceedings were over, Anna still had to deal with her own misgivings, questions without answers and less than forthright actions on her part that were constantly and severely criticized by Josey. Anna desperately needed positive proof of all that happened to assuage her feelings of complicity with a testimony that was less than truthful. She knew she would never find the proof to substantiate the truth now that Carla was gone. How was she to live a lifetime with suspicions that wouldn't be put to rest and a guilt that she could have possibly been mistaken in her heart-felt certainty that Gabe was innocent. She had effectively taken the law into her own hands. But it had been the right thing to do. Justice had been served. Hadn't it?

Chapter Eleven

Five times the trigger was squeezed. Five times the gun fired and all bullets penetrated the center of the large circle. The clip was empty.

"Very good! Now put five more shells into the clip and see how many you can center in the upper right small circle."

Anna did as she was instructed. All bullets left holes in the indicated circle. The instructor, Matt Kelly, repeated his request until all circles on the paper target were riddled and Anna had not missed once. "Excellent," Matt said. "I have watched you handle your weapon and you do everything correctly. You understand how to determine if there is a bullet in the chamber and what to do about it. You know how to drop your clip and fill it properly. You do not sweep a gun with live ammunition in it. All this of course is elementary, but necessary. Your written exam showed you know when you are allowed to use deadly force with it and when and where you can legally carry it. It shows you to be an informed and capable gun owner. I see no reason you should not be certified." He smiled at her, signed the certificate showing she had successfully completed the course and handed it to her.

"Thank you. I'm delighted to be done with this, but I want you to know that I will always endeavor to be responsible handling any weapon. It's been a pleasure to be in your class, Mr. Kelly. Thank you again."

"The pleasure has been mine, Anna. Troy has mentioned your problem and though you are not cleared to carry a weapon concealed or openly, he has asked me to go ahead and let you take his Beretta home with you so you can at least have some protection there. You will, as you know, have to take your certificate along with your application to be fingerprinted. OSBI, the state bureau, will do a background check on you and if all is okay, issue your permit. It usually takes about ninety days. Your case, however, is unusual and may warrant special attention. I'm not sure Troy has enough clout with OSBI to hurry the process. If he can, I'm sure he will."

Anna accepted Troy's borrowed Beretta and a partial box of shells. She checked the gun carefully to see that it was not loaded then smiling at Matt said, "I'll keep them separate while transporting in my vehicle."

"Good girl." Matt smiled. "Again I wish you good luck and if I can be of assistance in the future just give me a call."

"I will. Thank you so much and have a wonderful day."

Anna put the shells in her glove compartment and the empty gun in a briefcase in the back seat of her extended cab. She would need to handle the gun more before she would feel really comfortable with it. She was glad Troy had also lent her its holster. Carrying it while doing chores on the farm presented a problem unless she had a holster.

Several uneventful days followed. Gabe rarely came into the office while Anna was there. If he did, it was with a co-worker and he was usually there for only a few minutes. His demeanor was very businesslike and no observer would have guessed there had ever been any emotional ties between them, let alone imagine the passion that—as little as a month ago—held them in its relentless grip and forced itself, in rare moments, to be exquisitely recognized.

Well, if that's the way you want it! She wanted to say, but kept her thoughts to herself and behaved as he did.

Hurt, but knowing she was complicit in creating the present situation, she chastised herself severely.

Well, what in heaven's name did you expect? You must be some kind of an idiot.

She had no clue what she had been thinking. She just knew

something had to change—and quickly. All the stress and uncertainty were wearing her down, driving her mad. She feared it would shortly become so overwhelming she could no longer hide it. Janice was a ray of sunshine when she bounced in one day unannounced saying, "Hey, Chiquita, take a gander at this." She held out her left hand that supported on the third finger a rather large, marquis-cut, diamond engagement ring. "Maybe you should put on your sunglasses first."

Anna was so glad to see her, she fought tears.

"Janice! How lovely.! It's everything you said it was. It's perfect. You're so lucky!"

"What's luck got to do with it?" Janice laughed. "You make your own luck, sweetie, and you need to do a better job of it." Seeing the stricken look on Anna's face, she backed off. "I'm sorry. I can be tactless, I know. Hey! Come have lunch with me. I need to express my happiness before I burst."

Anna was glad to go and have a "happy hour" in the middle of the day. Janice brought sanity to her life. Anna embraced it with joy and wished for more. Gabe had asked Anna to gather certain papers and plans for him to take to a meeting of the Builders Association. Because he wanted to keep abreast of all new laws, proposed laws, codes and happenings in the housing industry, he had joined the local association. They were holding their monthly meeting in Oklahoma City to consider a joint venture with other associations in neighboring counties. He told Anna he would pick up the materials at 11 o'clock before leaving for his luncheon meeting in Oklahoma City that was expected to last most of the afternoon.

Anna had all the requested papers in packets, according to topics, lying across his desk so that he could arrange them as he pleased for his personal presentation. He arrived at his office at approximately 10:45 to assemble his portfolio. She explained what information was in each stack and gathered other incidentals as he requested them: a small tape recorder, special highlighters, small and large clips and numerous pens.

As they were about to finish, they both reached for the same packet. Their hands touched momentarily. Anna caught her breath sharply, audibly. They simultaneously stiffened and looked at each other. It was a first for Anna—to feel such a jolt of pure passion at the mere touch of their hands. She had seen the same in his eyes before she quickly looked away.

Hesitating for a fraction of a moment, he quietly hissed, "Damn!" before turning back to finish his task.

"I was wondering if it would be okay for me to leave an hour or so early today? Mom has been so fretful and hard to live with lately I thought I could take her to dinner and maybe alleviate her boredom. It will take some time to convince her I'm sure."

"Of course. I trust you to know when you can afford to take the time you need. You know that."

"Thank you. Yes, we are all caught up at present. Good luck with your meeting."

He looked at her as though he wanted to say something but decided not to.

"Thanks," he said, "I hope your mother appreciates what you do for her. Enjoy your dinner."

He was gone. Anna as always felt a loss as he left.

How can I love this man so much and not throw everything else to the wind. Janice was right. Things sometimes needed a nudge in the right direction. But what was the right direction and how to nudge? She herself needed the nudge.

She prayed for guidance.

Anna left work early knowing it would probably take some time to persuade Josey to go out to dinner. When she was almost to the clump of trees in their pasture that border-lined their farm and hid their house from view, Anna saw an old cattle trailer hooked to a black Ford truck parked on the side of the road. No one seemed to be near it. Anna was immediately suspicious. It looked like Billy Freemonts's truck. Were they after Smoky? She hurriedly took down the license number and rushed home.

Before she had reached her driveway, Anna saw two men

trying to lead Smoky across the pasture. Smoky was unstable on his feet, stumbling and wobbling around. Casey was doing his best to thwart their efforts, barking and nipping at their heels. One man kicked at him and picked up a small limb and started chasing him. Casey ran but as soon as the man returned to Smoky, Casey was back—running interference again. Anna gunned her engine and was smack up against the fence in a few seconds. She slammed down on her horn blasting her objections. She jumped out of her truck and yelled for them to leave her horse alone. They ignored her and was jerking and pulling harder than ever trying to get Smoky to hurry.

Anna remembered the gun. She grabbed the shells from the glove compartment and the Beretta from the back seat. She hurriedly put a few bullets in the clip. She needed to let them know she had a gun and would use it.

Well, I'm on my own property and even though I can't shoot to kill I can fire my weapon. Not into the air. A bullet in the air has to come down somewhere.

Without further ado, Anna pointed the gun at the ground and fired...there should not be anything underground to cause a problem. No gas or water pipes even close.

Both men turned Smoky loose and started running toward the parked truck and trailer. Anna wanted to fire another shot or even to chase them down, but her concern for Smoky won out. Why was he falling down. He had to be hurt somehow.

She crawled over the fence and ran quickly to where he had fallen. A tranquillizer dart was still sticking in his flank. Thank god her cell was in her pocket. She hurriedly call 9-1-1.

"I need a vet in a hurry. Dr. Emit Daniels if you can get him. Someone used a tranquillizer dart on my horse trying to steal him. I don't have any idea how much he had. He is still down.

"Where are you located?" asked the operator."

Thinking the operator might just know of her and Shelton farms, Anna said, "I am Anna Shelton at Shelton farms and we are located..."

191

Before she could finish, she was interrupted, "I know where you live Anna. Just hang on, I'll get you some help."

Anna listened while the switchboard got Dr. Daniels on the line and told him of her emergency.

"I know where she lives and I'm on my way," he said.

Anna breathed a sigh of relief. "Thank you so much. I'd just die if I lost Smoky," she told the 9-1-1 operator.

"I know he must be like a member of the family. I really enjoyed him at the rodeo last month. Good luck, Anna. I have to go." She disconnected.

Anna called Troy. "I'm so sorry to bother you, but I just used your gun to stop someone from stealing my horse. Don't worry I just fired a shot into the ground and they took off. They used a tranquillizer dart on Smoky and I have a vet on the way. I hope they didn't give him too much. He is down and flat out." Anna was wiping tears from her cheeks as she reported everything to Troy.

"Did you get a good look at the guys?"

"I'm not sure I could positively identify them. One could have been Billy Freemont. The sun was shining right in my face so I can't be sure, but I did get their license plate number and it was a black Ford F150 like he drives."

"Good girl. Give me the number and I'll put out a BOLO, be on the lookout alert, especially for your area."

Anna did as he asked and apologized profusely for not calling him immediately.

"I'm so sorry, Troy. I should have called you first, I guess, but I was so concerned about Smoky I called the vet first. I'm afraid I cost us at least 10 minutes."

Troy hesitated, "Well at least we have a license number. That's more than we've had before. I'm on my way out there now. Where was the truck parked?"

"Just down the road west, where the first clump of trees hid it from the house."

"Okay, I'll check there first and then stop at your house."

"Thanks, Troy. See you then."

When the vet arrived, he knew immediately based on the dart, how much and what kind of tranquillizer Smoky had been given—if that had been the only one they had shot him with.

"If this is the only dart used, your horse should begin to revive in about 30 minutes. I really need to know if more were used."

Anna was trying to control her rising panic.

"I'll go all the way back to the barn by the path they took and look to see if I can find any that might have dropped off. What else can I do?"

"Nothing really. I'll stay here and keep tabs on him while you search. Let me know as soon as you find another dart, if you do. I would guess they were careful not to overdose since he's no good to them if he's not salable...if they knew what they were doing. But it seems obvious that they weren't experts because they gave him enough to put him down when what they really wanted was for him to walk to their trailer."

Anna hurried away, looking carefully along the pathway back to the barn. Hoping there were no extra darts and praying the thieves knew enough not to dispense a lethal dose. She searched thoroughly and systematically. She had found nothing and was about to return to where Smoky lay when she saw a tranquillizer gun on the hood of her tractor parked in the barn. Beside it were two unused darts. She reached to pick them up, but stopped herself in time. There might be fingerprints on them. She would leave them for Troy's expertise. Maybe the gun could be traced. Not everyone had access to tranquillizer guns and darts.

By the time she had reached Smoky and the vet, Troy had pulled into her drive and gotten over the fence. When he was within a few yards of them, he held up a tag with the number Anna had given him over the phone.

"Guess the license plate number is not going to do us much good," he said. "They took it off and threw it in the weeds, but I

193

could see it from my cruiser. It must be stolen."

"Well, maybe you can track them through fingerprints on the tranquillizer gun and darts they left in the barn. I didn't touch them so I didn't ruin any prints that might be there." Anna told Troy.

Smoky was beginning to move and struggling to raise his head. Anna knelt beside him and rubbed his head and neck. She talked to him quietly, but he seemed to struggle even more. Casey whined and licked Smoky's nose.

"No, Casey. Come away."

Casey came to her and lay on the ground at her feet. He had run to the house when she fired a shot. Not knowing what to expect, she guessed he had decided not to take any chances. But he was back now and she wondered if he thought she had shot Smoky.

"He's going to be okay, I think." the vet said. He may be groggy for an hour or so, but he is trying to get up so he's less sedated than when I got here. The drug is beginning to wear off."

Before Dr. Daniels left, he gave Anna his personal cell number in case Smoky took a bad turn, though he didn't expect that to happen. Troy told her he would let her know if they came up with any information that could positively identify a suspect. He suggested that she get a smart phone so she could monitor Smoky's barn and paddock at all times.

"You could check on him as many times as you want and if anyone were trying to take him, you could just call me and the "long arm of the law" will do the rest. You can monitor Smoky from anywhere 24/7. I think it would give you peace of mind and you need that—what with everything else going on. And you just might catch someone else prowling around...someone who has set you up for a fall."

"That sounds like a very useful tool. I will check into it, but I'm almost certain it is out of my reach financially."

Troy left and Anna stayed with Smoky until he was stable enough on his feet to walk back to the barn. She curried him down and fed him his rations, all the time telling him how pretty he was and how much she appreciated him. He nickered low when she left.

Anna apologized to Josey, "I left work an hour early so I could take you out to eat, but it's so late now. Would you still like to go?"

"What in tarnation wuz all that noise? Thought I heard a gunshot! Then I saw the sheriff. What wuz wrong with yer horse?"

Anna told Josey the whole story.

"Looks like they're aimin' to get yer horse one way er t'other," Josey commented.

"They're not getting Smoky if I have to start sleeping in the barn," Anna declared. "Do you want to go out and eat?"

"No, I dun ate some cold chicken and tater salad. And I done drunk all the tea. Ya need ta make sum more."

"Okay, Mom, but sometime soon I want to take you out to eat. You never get out of the house. I don't see how you can stand it. It would drive me crazy."

Josey didn't answer. She was already involved in a TV show. Anna thought it was NCIS. Josey was talking back to the characters as though she were involved in the plot.

Anna fed Casey and brushed his coat. She told him he was a very good protector and meant every word of it. Each time Anna fed Casey of late, he made noises deep in his throat—with an occasional high note thrown in—as if he were speaking to her. He also licked her profusely all over the hands and arms—the face if he could reach it.

"You're welcome, Casey. You're a good boy and you earn every bite you get." Anna guessed his antics were in appreciation of the food he was receiving. She laughed when he jumped up and tried to lick her face, wiggling all over and waging his stub of a tail. He'd been born with only a vestige of one. Anna thought it made him cuter than any other Old English Sheep dog she had ever seen. He was a very special dog. He even tolerated Miss Kitty.

195

On Monday morning, Anna checked through the yellow pages of the phone book for companies offering security systems for homes with remote access. She chose "Safe Home" that offered one day installation and remote access to monitor Smoky's barn and small pasture from a mobile phone or laptop.

After getting all the details, Anna sighed, "It's pretty much as I expected. It's just out of my price range," she said, "but I had to check. Someone is trying to steal my horse and Smoky's too important for me not to try, but I thank you for your time and the information." She started to hang up.

"Wait, wait, don't hang up. You said Smoky...are you Anna Shelton?"

"Yes, I am."

"Okay!...We may be able to help you on the financial end. By the way, I loved your show at the rodeo. What I wanted to say is, we're getting set to run some special ads and if we could set up your system and we do catch the criminals, would you be willing to do an ad for us with Smoky for advertising purposes?"

"Sounds great, but what if we don't catch them?"

"That would be okay. We understand that just because you have a system installed, there is no guarantee that a criminal will break in." The sales lady laughed. "Let me check and I'll get back to you."

"One other thing," Anna added. "I would only need the system for a short time. That is until the crooks are caught. I really can't afford a monthly bill in that amount for an extended period."

"That's okay. We'll take all of that into consideration." replied the Safe Home sales person. "I'll get back to you. By the way my name is Chris...Chris Andrews."

"Okay, thanks a lot." Anna was dumbfounded.

Hah! Sometimes even a blind pig picks up an acorn! she thought. It was a phrase her father often used when some unexpected piece of luck fell into his lap.

As Anna was leaving the office for a rare lunch out, she

noticed Gabe's red Hyundai parked next to Bill Grant's truck and the pretty young thing—who was always with Gabe—was standing talking to Bill. The door to his truck was partially open as though he had started to get out, but was blocked by her presence. She seemed to be speaking earnestly and Bill seemed irritated, as if he wanted her to move. He glanced up and saw Anna. She looked away and hurried on to her truck. She thought she heard him call out to her, but ignored him just the same.

After she was seated in the Carnegie Diner and had placed her order, Bill walked in the door and headed straight for her table.

"Are you expecting someone else or can I sit and have lunch with you?"

Anna laughed softly. "No, I'm not expecting anyone and yes, you are welcome to sit with me."

"Why didn't you wait up?"

"What?"

"I was coming to take you to lunch, but I got hemmed in. That little chicky wants to decorate the first house built off my new plan and use it as a showcase."

"Oh? Well, that sounds like fun."

"I wanted you to do that and I told her so. Told her I didn't want any flighty school girl messin' up my select design. Think I made her mad."

"You need to be careful. Gabe has the final say and she seems to have the inside track with him."

"Yeah, well, she's got a mouth on her too. Said I needed to know more about her before calling her a flighty school girl and that I might like what all she could do."

Anna had no doubt about that. And maybe it would be a good thing for Bill—might even be a good thing for Anna too—if the sweet, young thing and Bill learned to like each other—a lot.

"Bill, she's a beautiful color coordinator. You can tell that by the clothes she wears and if you needed someone in the house for walk-throughs she'd be a winner."

He placed an order with the waitress who had just approached their table, before resuming their conversation. He seemed to be considering Anna's comments about Gabe's girl and finally agreed.

"Well...I guess you're right as usual. Maybe I shouldn't be so hasty. She might fit in pretty well at that and as you say Gabe does have the last word. That is if you're not interested."

"I think it would be great fun, but I pretty much have my hands full at the office. Thank you though."

Anna thought she could handle it fine, but maybe Bill needed to take another look at the "flighty schoolgirl." Maybe she would take another look at him. Who knew what might develop.

Anna Shelton, you are such a dork, she told herself. Even if something did eventually develop between Bill and Gabe's girl, Gabe had such a cavalier attitude about their relationship, perhaps she was just *E pluribus unum*—one of many.

Mid-afternoon, Anna received a call from the security company concerning the protection plan she had inquired about. They wanted her to come by their office and discuss further the possibility of the trade-off Ms. Andrews, the sales person, had mentioned.

Their offer was pretty much as Ms. Andrews had indicated. "We think it would be great advertising and yes, we'd like to do it immediately if you are willing. We spend a lot on advertising and get unpredictable results as you can image. We think this will grab the public's imagination in a very positive way," she said.

"What if they steal the cameras? They have already stolen one of mine."

"We are pretty good at camouflaging our stuff, but you will not be held responsible for any equipment loss."

"Sounds great to me. If you'll draw up the contract, I'll have my attorney give me the go-ahead. I need his opinion for fear I might overlook the obvious in my need to hurry and get this done. Okay?"

"Certainly, we understand. We'll have these ready first thing in the morning. I know you are in a hurry for as much protection for Smoky as possible."

"Yes, he means so much to me I couldn't bear to lose him. If you will call me as soon as they are prepared, I'll come by and pick them up. Thank you so much. You have given me hope when I thought there was none."

"We can fax them to your attorney if you wish. That will save you a trip and be much faster."

"Great! Just let me contact him first to see how soon he can get to it. I'll call you with his fax number if it's a go." she concluded.

Anna spoke with Jed Garrison, her father's attorney, and explained the circumstances. She asked if he would check out the contract with Safe Homes for her as soon as possible.

"Of course, Anna. I'd be glad to. You were a small tyke when I last saw your father, but I've been reading about you in the papers and I know he'd be very proud."

"Thank you, Mr. Garrison. I'll have Safe Homes fax the contract to you and if it's okay, then you can fax it to me with a bill and they can have the cameras set up by tomorrow afternoon. Will that work?"

"That'll work. I'll call you before I send it with any words of caution and I wish you good luck. Hope you catch those horse thieves."

"Thanks, Mr. Garrison. That's very kind of you."

Anna had not seen Gabe since his meeting in Oklahoma City. Several days had passed and she wondered where he was and how things were going for him. One morning, however, there he was—all alone and in a great mood.

"Good morning, Anna." He was smiling and seemed to be the old Gabe she knew so well and loved immutably.

199

Anna's heart fluttered. "How was your meeting?"

"Wonderful. My presentation went over well. Everyone was 'gung ho' to start new projects—large, newly proposed projects—of public interest. Projects that would be funded by the state or federal government or bonds issues, such as: a new agriculture center in Grandfield County, new fairgrounds and a courthouse annex in our own county, a new library in Gravin County and new docks and a state owned lodge in Clevan County at the lake. Contracts will be let on all of these within the next five years, but of course not all at the same time. We figure if we can get the bids,—or at least some of them—it will keep us all busy for that length of time and profitably so. There were only four firms really interested so maybe we can all come together reasonably. We have to take the jobs as they are okayed by the county officials so our county will let bids for the first project. Mechlin County has announced they have the funding now accessible and want to accept bids soon. With all of us working together we should be able to complete each job rather quickly and be ready when the next job will become available. This is of course just projections. We hope we can make it work out good for us all."

"Sounds exciting."

"Yes, it is and one thing that worried them was traveling to the job sites and interim housing. I offered to set up several portable houses on or near the job site here to start the ball rolling. Can't do it for free, but I can do it for cost. Everyone was happy about that."

"Will you build those portables or buy them?"

"I can build them cheaper, but it depends on how soon we need them—if we get the contract here. These bids have to be exactly right. That's the tricky part. Even if there is no politicking involved, we have to be pretty close to the low bid, but we still have to have a reasonable profit margin. It does get sticky."

"Sounds like things are all falling into place for you," she said.

His expressions sobered. His eyes searched her face. She trembled but couldn't look away. He took a deep breath. There was a flicker and a softening in his gaze before he said, "Yeah, *some* things are."

She wanted to climb right over her desk and jump into his arms to hold him—so close he'd think they were one. But she could only stand rooted to the spot, saying, "I'm so glad for you. You deserve it all. You've worked diligently and non-stop and your work is of the best quality. You've a right to be proud."

He blinked a couple times, then became the boss again. "Thanks, Anna. Those were some very fine compliments. What is this?"

He reached for the smart phone on her desk. The one Safe Homes had lent her. She had just dialed and was remotely connected to Smoky's paddock. Anna explained the situation and all that had happened to her and Smoky.

Gabe seemed to be concerned. "Maybe now there'll be a resolution to this mystery and you and Smoky will be safe again. I sincerely hope so."

Laying some papers on her desk, he said, "Here is a lot of info concerning bids, prices, dates and also numbers of workers and supervisors available for the first bid we want to make. I need it in the format indicated as soon as possible. They will be sent to the other three firms for their input and of course there'll be revisions. I'm sure you'll have questions concerning some of the content, but please check with me anytime and do not hold up the process for a minute because you have unanswered questions. Okay?"

"Got it!" Anna answered. "This project is top priority. I will call you at midnight or demand you get out of the bath if I have a question."

They both laughed.

"Yes, it's that important," he said. "I know I can count on you."

Anna made a promise to herself at that moment—he would

201

get it all in tip-top shape and fast. She could work overtime now that she could check on Smoky at any time from her office desk.

Sammy Grisham came into their office while Anna was on her lunch break several days later. She had just checked on Smoky and was examining each camera location just to make sure no one was lurking about.

"How did you do that? That's Smoky and that's your barn. He's moving around. It's live!" Sammy could see Smoky on the phone and was excited to know just how that worked. Anna explained the whole setup and told Sammy why and that she might be making an ad for TV with Smoky.

"Golly, that's cool!" Sammy was grinning from ear to ear. "I hope you catch those guys who're trying to steal Smoky." He paused and stared at Anna for a few seconds. "I heard down at the Ford place that you're in danger. What did they mean?"

She hesitated not knowing if she wanted to tell Sammy the whole story. Better he know than get caught unawares...he was around her quite a bit. Finally, she said, "Someone wants me dead, Sammy. They're trying to kill me."

His face went stark white, his mouth fell open and his eyes grew large with fear. "How do you know?"

"Well, Sheriff Henderson has done some investigating and determined several things that happened to me couldn't have been accidents and he has lent me his gun to protect myself. I've been certified to carry a concealed weapon, but have to wait 90 days for clearance. But, I can carry on my own property."

"Why would they want to kill you? I mean you're just about the best person I know. He must be a crazy man!"

"I don't know why, Sammy. If I knew why, I'd most likely know who it is. But so far I have no clue. Whoever it is has just set up situations to hurt me, but he has not threatened me face to face yet. Sheriff Henderson thinks that may happen soon. I'm almost wishing for it. This waiting and tiptoeing around is very stressful."

"Gosh, I wish I could help." Sammy was still wide-eyed and fearful. "I'll watch and listen for anything about you. It's not much, but sometimes big guys say things around us kids like it doesn't matter. Maybe, I'll hear something."

Anna smiled at Sammy. "Thanks a lot Sammy, but don't put yourself in danger of any kind. If they know you're listening they might want to hurt you too."

"I'll just act like a dumb kid. I gotta go. But be careful. You're real important to me and my algebra grade."

They both laughed. Sammy scurried away—a frown on his face.

The next time Anna saw Sammy was noontime two days later. He burst into her office, breathless, his face as white as a sheet.

"Anna, two guys are messin' with your truck!"

Anna immediately grabbed her phone and punched in Troy's cell on the quick dial.

"Troy, Sammy says there's two guys messin' with my truck here at work."

"Be right there, Anna! Stay inside."

Anna wanted to go check on her truck, but knew Sammy would follow, so she hesitated. It was only a matter of minutes when Troy pulled into the parking lot and hit his siren. Two deputies were close behind. Anna tried to see what was going on from the windows of the office, but could see nothing concerning what was happening to her truck. She went outside. She wanted to see if she recognized either of the two. The guys ran in opposite directions, zigzagging in and out among cars in the parking lot and then across the street and behind the buildings. Anna only had a glimpse of ball caps as they bobbed here and there. Deputies followed on foot at first, but returned to get their cars and followed in hot pursuit. They found Billy Freemont three blocks away sitting in a small cafe drinking coffee. His ball cap and shirt were the right colors, but he swore he didn't know what they were talking about. The restaurant owner said he had only been there a few minutes, which proved nothing.

Billy was not arrested, but was given warning that if he had left fingerprints behind it would go bad for him—worse if he had lied to the deputies. He didn't seem concerned. The other man was never found.

Troy had inspected Anna's vehicle and found a pair of cutters on the ground just under the end of her truck. There didn't seem to be any damage done to anything, but the sheriff surmised they had intended to cut her brake lines. Troy called the Ford dealership and asked that a mechanic be sent to Whittier Enterprises to examine Anna's truck for damage that he might have missed.

Sammy was still wide-eyed, but silent. Anna bought him a soft drink out of their machine. He gulped it down. Troy came in and asked Sammy if he had recognized either of the men.

"Yeah, one was the guy you arrested for hitting on Anna at the rodeo, but I didn't know the other one."

"Oh gosh, no, Troy! Don't let anyone know Sammy's a witness. If they're the ones trying to kill me, Sammy will be in danger too."

"No, we'll not make this public knowledge. And son," he spoke directly to Sammy, "don't mention you saw this to anyone. Okay?"

"Yeah, I won't breathe a word." Anna knew he wouldn't either.

Troy explained to Anna he wasn't going to arrest Billy. "All we can charge him with now is suspicion of tampering with a vehicle. He'd be out in a heartbeat. We will watch him closely and maybe get him on a more serious charge."

Anna was skeptical. "I hope it's not murder," she wryly offered.

She went back to the smart phone and checked on Smoky. Casey was laying in the shade nearby while Smoky grazed contentedly near the barn. She thanked God and Safe Homes for the wonderful tool that had been placed in her hands to offer such tremendous relief. She thanked Troy for his quick efforts and Sammy for his sharp-eyed observance. Both were sorry it could not have been more.

After Troy left, Sammy was still watching Anna check all cameras in and around her barn.

As she clicked on the one showing the inside of one tack room, Sammy jumped to attention. "What's that?" he asked. He could see a pile of hay covering some lumpy things and one even protruded from under the hay.

Anna laughed. "Did you think it was a thief hiding under the hay? Kinda looks like one doesn't it? Those are watermelons. I always save them at the end of harvest. I lay them on hay and cover them with hay as well. They keep astonishingly well. I even have my own melons for Christmas."

"Really? Golly, that's neat! I can't believe they'd keep that long."

"Would you like a few?" Anna asked. "I probably have at least twenty in there."

"I sure would. That would be great. I love watermelon and Mom and the kids would like it too. That is if you really want to give us some."

"Of course, I do. It's the least I can do to repay you for spotting those guys messing with my truck. One day this week, when you've told your mother where you're going and you can meet me here at 5 o'clock, I'll take you out there and you can pick out a few. I have some other things in the garden like: squash, radishes, all kinds of greens—plus onions and potatoes in the cellar—stuff you might take to your mother if you would like."

Sammy grinned. He had just earned some melons. It was not a handout.

"Gee, thanks a lot Anna. It will probably have to be Friday evening. Is that okay?"

"Sure is, Sammy. See you then."

Sammy left happy, but watchful.

205

Chapter Twelve

The first thing Anna noticed when she returned home that evening and went about feeding her animals was that Casey's food dispenser was not empty as it usually was at this time of day.

Must have found something else to eat, was her first thought.

She wondered what it could possibly have been. Some dogs catch a rabbit or a squirrel for an occasional meal, but not Casey. He would never eat raw meat. He had never been fed anything uncooked. If any raw bit of hamburger or steak happened to be dropped while barbequing, Casey might sniff it, but would walk away. He didn't consider it edible fare.

Smoky seemed to be nervous, pacing back and forth and looking toward the road as if he thought something menacing lurked there. Anna noticed a dark stain on the barn at the side door. It appeared to be fresh.

"Oh, god! Is that blood? Not Casey again! But he was here about 3 o'clock and everything was fine. I saw him on camera!" She exclaimed aloud to no one.

The Safe Home cameras don't really get a good view of this side door, Anna realized and went to check her field camera. There she had captured the image of someone fighting with Casey. She was sure it was Dugan.

Casey bit him several times on the legs and hands and when Dugan ran into the barn, Case gave him a good bite in the seat of his pants. Old Charley came back out of the barn with a hoe and dealt Casey a severe cut to the left hind leg, which caused him to withdraw, limping badly. Dugan chased him as Smoky appeared on scene, then Dugan left the viewing range of the camera. He had to have run toward the road. What was he doing here? What was he after? Had he set up another pitfall for her?

Anna looked around the barn to see if she could find other clues. There were none, except a shovel that had been left at the corner of the building—stuck in the ground. What was Dugan going to do with the shovel? Dig her grave or Casey's? Anna felt a chill sweep over her as she called Troy and reported what she had found to the much used and appreciated sheriff of Mechlin County.

Troy came out to investigate once again.

"I know you must be getting tired of all this." Anna commiserated.

"Not nearly as tired as you are I'm sure. But now with these photos, maybe we have something to arrest him for—trespass at least and cruelty to animals. And when we get him into custody we'll get his fingerprints and check them against those we have gathered at other places where crimes have been perpetrated against you—if we can just find him now."

Troy took the photo card from the trail camera, asking Anna if she needed more shells for the Beretta.

"No, Troy, I don't and I will replace all your bullets when I return your gun."

"Take every precaution. Things seem to be heating up," he said before rolling up the window on his cruiser and starting the engine.

Anna was desolate. She had to go and find Casey. He was hurt and it had looked like a very serious blow. He must need attention. On camera it had appeared he ran back toward the house, which he instinctively did when hurt or scared. Anna looked for traces of blood moving in the directions she thought Casey had taken. She searched every building, nook and sprawling bush until it was too dark to see anything. She had called out to him repeatedly, but to no avail. Casey was well hidden or too hurt to respond. Anna returned to the house to face Josey's wrath about a late supper.

"Where'd ya go fer god's sake? What wuz that sheriff doin'

here agin'? Seems like he lives here now."

"Mom, someone—looked like Dugan on camera—was here for some reason. He got into a fight with Casey and finally hit him with a hoe. Looked like a bad cut to Casey's leg. I called Troy and gave a report and I've been looking for Casey ever since."

"Well, hurry up and git supper ready, I'm about ta starve ta death. And bring me a big glass of tea now. My favorite shows comin' on TV rat this minute."

Anna sighed heavily. She wanted to say, "Get your own damned tea." It would serve no useful purpose and only cause an argument. She wearily did as she was bidden.

The next morning, Anna was out looking for Casey at first light. She went in the opposite direction from her previous search, carefully watching and calling every few minutes, but found no trace of Casey. She went to work, worried, not knowing what else she could possibly do to find him. She checked on Smoky more frequently during the day, hoping that somehow Casey would find his way back home.

Gabe came by for a few minutes and was pleased with the progress Anna was making on all the reports he needed for the Builder's Association groups.

"You've been working overtime to accomplish this, haven't you?"

"A little, yes. Doesn't matter, I couldn't sleep anyway."

She looked up at him when he didn't answer. Their eyes met and held. Anna tried to control her breathing.

Gabe, himself, took a deep breath, "I hope this situation resolves..."

Before he could finish what he was going to say, the gorgeous young thing—who had been obviously waiting in his car—burst through the door.

"Hurry up, Gabe. I'm starving and I can't be late for my meeting." After a pause, she continued. "Oh, hi, Anna, how are you?"

"Fine, how about you?"

"I'd be fine if I could get some food." She laughed.

Gabe rolled his eyes and said, "Guess I'll run. You're doing a great job here. Catch you later."

They were gone and Anna was left alone with her problems and an ache that wouldn't go away.

Before 5 o'clock, Anna had decided she would get on her tractor and slowly and systematically search every inch of their farm. If Casey were there, she would find him. He just had to be there. She hurried home and spent the rest of the daylight hours combing the pastures, checking out the creeks and gullies, carefully looking behind every bush and clump of grass. There was no sign of Casey. Where on earth could he be? He of course knew no property lines. Maybe he was just over the fence, somewhere close by on neighboring farms. She would start there tomorrow early. He couldn't have gone far.

Three days passed Anna had not been able to locate a trace of her beloved pet. She had to admit the possibility that he could be gone for good this time. It was morning again and time to get up, but Anna was despondent, not wanting to face another day, when she thought she heard a muffled bark. She jumped out of bed and ran to the window. Seeing nothing, she listened intently, but heard nothing further. With a protracted sigh, she walked away.

I'm hearing things. Wishful thinking, I guess.

Then she heard it again and realized it was coming from under the house. How was that possible? Had Casey been there all along—too hurt to make his presence known?

Hurriedly, pulling on her jeans and boots, she ran outside and around the house to a crawl hole with a door that was supposed to always be locked shut. Sure enough, Casey was just emerging, dirty, dried blood in several places and noticeably thinner. Anna was beside herself with joy. She tried to pick him up, being careful of his injuries, but was unable to do so. Casey wasn't being too cooperative, himself. He wanted to lick her face and get about on his own. He seemed okay except for a limp and the need of a good bath. They managed to get to the back patio where Anna put some food in his dispenser and filled his water bowl. He ate ravenously.

"Not too much, buddy. I'm going to fix you steak and eggs." And she did. He ate it all—even though he had already had a goodly portion of "Kibbles and Bits."

She called the office and unbelievably Gabe answered the phone.

"I need to come in an hour later this morning if that's okay. I just found Casey and he needs some attention. Okay?"

"Of course. I'm glad you found him. Is he alright?"

"I think he will be. Thank you. I'll be there soon."

Anna hung up and began working on Casey. She trimmed the dried blood from his wounds, a large one on his leg, one on his head and several smaller places across his body. She filled an old tub with warm water and doggy shampoo. Casey was going to get a bath. That was no problem for Casey. He loved water and all the attention as well. Anna thought he even felt ashamed to be so dirty.

After he was bathed and dried, Anna took him into the utility. She had closed and latched the small door under the house. The latch needed to be replaced. She would do it soon.

"Mom, you'll have to get your own breakfast. I'm late already and I don't have time."

"Hah! "Ya spend your time on a dog and let your mother do without."

"Yep, if that's the way you want to see it." Anna was fed up with all Josey's grumbling. "I want Casey to stay in the house today. His wounds look like they're healing fine, but they're clean now and I put some ointment on them so I don't want him to get them dirty again."

Josey said nothing, but harrumphed her way to the kitchen to make a pot of coffee.

Anna's day at the office went better. Casey was back and they knew whom to blame for his injuries. If they could just locate Charley Dugan and get a confession, a large part of her stress and worries would be over. She prayed it would happen soon.

Anna's prayers were answered sooner than expected, but not in the way she would ever have imagined. After getting to work and settling into her regular routine, Anna soon had everything in order. She called Troy to report that Casey was found and to ask about any news concerning Dugan.

"Great! I'm so glad for you. Where did you find him?"

"He was under the house. I think he may have had a concussion and been out of it for some time. He had a cut on his leg and one on his head. He's going to be okay, I think. I will take him to the vet tomorrow. Do you have any new information on Dugan yet?"

"No, we picked up Billy and tried to get him to tell us where Old Charley might be, but he won't talk. We told him we have Dugan on camera and it's only a matter of time before we have him in custody and we'll have his fingerprints to compare with many others from all the crimes he has perpetrated, including attempted murder. We also told him he might be facing charges of aiding and abetting. He pretended to be unconcerned, but I could tell the seriousness of it registered with him."

"What if Dugan just runs back to Texas?"

"We're watching Billy closer than he would ever guess. If Dugan does leave, we think Billy will be the one to take him. Billy doesn't want Old Charley caught because he could implicate Billy as an accessory, so they'll be trying to help each other avoid us where possible."

"I hope you get them soon. This is almost too much to handle anymore."

"I know, Anna. Hang in there. I think we're close."

Sammy came by a few minutes before 5 o'clock.

"Sammy! I almost forgot about our melon gathering."

211

"Oh...well, we can do it some other time if you're too busy."
Sammy seemed disappointed.

"No, no. I've just been so busy I forgot. I'm glad you came
by."

After closing the office, Sammy and Anna went to her farm.
Anna pulled her truck close to the barn.

"Not so far to carry melons," she explained. "You go ahead
and get three or four while I run to the house and change into my
jeans. Okay? They're in that tack room on the left there with the
horseshoe above the missing door."

When Anna returned, Sammy had put three melons in her
truck.

"How big is your family, Sammy?" Anna asked.

"There's four of us kids and Mom," he answered.

"Why don't you get a couple more? I'll never use all the rest
and I usually have several left after giving away a few others,"
Anna suggested. "And if I still have some left at Christmas and
you don't, I'll give you a Christmas melon. Okay?"

Sammy grinned. "I'm sure these won't last 'til Christmas,"
he said. He seemed pleased to comply and got two more melons.

"There are some plastic bags in the door pocket of my truck.
Why don't you take several and go over there and gather some
garden produce. Just take any and all you think your mom might
use." She pointed to a fenced-in area closer to the house. "I'm
going to clean out Smoky's stall a little bit while you do that.
Okay?"

"Sure. I'll be right back."

Anna got a pitchfork from its place hanging on the wall and
started pitching out hay and other "unwanteds" from Smoky's
stall, where he stood to eat his grain. After a few moments, she
heard a low snarl and then ferocious barking. She jumped and
turned to see Dugan with a steel pipe raised over his head,
walking in her direction. Casey, limping, but too mad to let it
stop him, started nipping at Old Charley's heels.

"Oh god, no! Get away, Casey. Casey, no!" she screamed as

Dugan turned and took aim at what was bothering him the most. Casey backed off, but didn't seem very stable on his feet.

"No, Case! Go home." she shouted.

Casey didn't seem to hear. He still wanted a piece of Dugan.

With the poised hay fork in her hand, Anna yelled at Dugan, "Okay, you low-life, here I am. You tried many times to kill me, here's one more chance!" She had to attract his attention from Casey.

Old Charley turned back to face Anna. He sneered, "I knew I'd git the job done. Just had ta keep tryin'." He moved cautiously toward her.

Anna, thinking of how he had hurt Casey and Smoky, wanted to spear him so badly he'd never walk again. She sprang to the side and poked. Dugan swung and missed. She ducked and thrust at his mid-section. She nicked his wrist. Casey was furious. Dugan turned to swing hard at Casey, but Anna intervened.

She yelled, "No, Case," and ran between them with her fork raised in front of her. She hit Dugan a glancing blow—just enough to fork him painfully across the ribs. But he was already in full swing and had slammed a ripping blow to Anna's shoulder, knocking her to the ground. Anna's concern was still for Casey. How to get him to leave? She remembered her gun and reached behind her to flip open the holster, as Dugan drew back for another swing. She knew she'd never get off a shot in time. Why had she not thought of the gun before?

"Oh, God, please no," she prayed. A shot rang out before her gun cleared its holster.

How? Who? Baffled, Anna wondered what on earth had happened.

Dugan dropped his pipe. Blood spilled into spots that appeared on his shirt and he slowly sank to his knees.

Sammy was running towards them, screaming Anna's name.

Cursing and sputtering, Old Charley yelled, "Ya filthy bitch! I'll tell on ya like I said I would."

Anna wondered what on earth he was talking about. Had he lost his mind?

Then she heard from behind her, "Go 'head, ya bastard. It's all over now anyway. And 'bout time I'd say."

Anna turned and saw Josey standing some distance away—with the shotgun Anna had been asking her about—still pointed at Dugan.

"No, Mom. Not again. He's down...not a threat to us any longer. Don't shoot!"

Dugan desperately wanted to impart some information before he was shot again. "Josey killed Carla! I saw her dump her body in the park," he screamed. "I have proof. It's buried in an old tool box at the corner of the barn." He indicated the corner where Anna had found the shovel stuck in the ground. Then looking at Josey as though he was pleading for clemency, he continued, "Ain't no need to kill me now. I can't hurt cha anymore. They already know everthang."

"Ya rotten son-of-a-bitch! Just in case ya might pull through, here's another fer all the hell ya put me through."

Josey pulled the trigger. Massive blood stains appeared in the middle of the now shredded shirt covering Dugan's chest before he fell face down in the dirt. Red sprinkles appeared on Anna's blouse and arms. She scrambled to move away while Dugan's hand caught at her sleeve as he fell.

Anna reached into her pocket and grabbed her cell. She punched in Troy's quick dial number. Immediately, she felt a moment of panic. Would Josey shoot her next? If she had killed Carla and now Dugan, when would she stop? Why had she done it anyway?

"Troy, oh, god! Send an ambulance to our house and hurry. Mom just shot Dugan. I think he's dead. Hurry and bring your troops." Knowing Troy would need the information she now had if Josey shot her next, Anna said, "Wait, wait! Dugan said he had proof Mom killed Carla. It's buried in a tool box at the corner of the barn."

"Hang on Anna! We're comin'."

Josey lowered her shotgun. Sammy came running and helped Anna to her feet. He hugged her hard, sobbing, "I thought they had killed you dead!"

Anna held him and brushed damp hair from off his forehead. "It's okay, Sammy. I need you to help me with something. Okay?" Sammy nodded, wiping tears from his cheeks onto his sleeves. "Casey ran to the house when shots were fired. Would you go and find him and keep him there if you can?"

"Yeah, I will." Sammy was glad to be useful.

Anna wanted him far away in case Josey had second thoughts or lost her mind or who knew what might happen.

Paramedics pulled up to the paddock a few minutes before Troy, followed by two other cruisers who always seemed to have his back. Dugan was still alive and Troy dispatched a deputy to escort the ambulance to the hospital and then stand guard over Dugan until further notice.

Anna retold everything she knew. Troy had the deputy handcuff Josey. He told her what her rights were and took the shotgun as evidence. Then he dug up the tool box from the corner of the barn—right where Dugan said it was. He locked the box in his patrol car without opening it.

Josey had been silent, but now told Troy that she would not speak one word about anything if Anna were not required to be present. Troy knew how silent she could be.

"I don' wanna have to tell all this crap but just one time!" she said by way of explanation.

"When will you question her?" Anna asked.

"The sooner the better. She may change her mind if we wait," Troy said.

"I need to run Sammy home, then I'll be right there."

"That'll work," Troy answered. Are you going to be okay with this?"

"I hope so." Anna was trembling. It was still unreal.

Anna heard Troy on the phone as she was leaving, "Ask my

best interrogator—that would be Fred—to take witnesses and tape recorders to the hospital and do their best to get statements from one Charlie Dugan there. We especially need statements about the culpability of his nephew, Billy Freemont, in the plot to kill Anna Shelton. Fred needs to get out there ASAP and be sure to read Dugan his rights. He's is on the verge and probably won't make it through the night. He's most likely in ICU and you'll have hell trying to get in to see him, but try anyway."

Anna, rubbing her aching shoulder, told Sammy of her plans. "Sammy, I have to go and sit in on an interrogation at the sheriff's office. So take what produce you have gathered and I will drive you home. Then when all this has settled down, you can come back and get some more stuff if you'd like. Okay?"

"Sure." Sammy was still staring, as if he were in shock.

"I'm so sorry you had to see all this happen, Sammy. I know it's quite upsetting."

"Yeah, it was really scary too, but it weren't your fault."

"I should have known it might happen, but no one knew when. This guy has been after me for a long time now."

"How come?"

"I still don't know, Sammy. Maybe I'll find out at the sheriff's office."

"I can't believe your mom killed Carla and then killed that guy!"

"He's not dead yet. But yeah, I can't either. She must have had a good reason."

When they reached Sammy's house, Anna helped him carry in the melons then hurried back to the sheriff's office.

Troy, two of his deputies, Anna and Josey were all seated around a table in the small interrogation room. Troy didn't usually conduct the questioning of suspects, but his officer in charge of that department was at the hospital with Dugan...or he had better be. And as Troy had told Anna, they needed Josey's testimony before she changed her mind.

After setting up the tape recorder and making sure it was

216

working, Troy asked Josey if she wanted something to drink.

"Yeah, I could use a cup a coffee. Lots of cream and sugar."

One deputy motioned to the glass window and soon a secretary came in with coffee—a carafe full—and extra cups with several packets of sugar and creamer on a tray.

Anna asked if the secretary could bring her a couple aspirin or some kind of a painkiller.

"What happened? Did you get hurt?" Troy was concerned.

"Yeah, I got a real whack in the shoulder, but I don't think anything is broken."

The secretary hurried off to get Anna something for pain.

Troy turned on the tape recorder and stated who he was, who he was interrogating plus the date and time. He read Josey her rights and asked if she understood.

"Yeah, I guess so."

"Yes or no? Do you have questions concerning your rights?"

"No."

"Okay," Troy continued, "You have been accused of murdering Carla Spencer. Did you in fact kill her as charged?"

"Not really. It wuz a accident."

"Would you just start at the beginning and tell us exactly what happened?"

Troy turned up the volume on the tape recorder in order to get Josey's statements more clearly.

"Well, she just come back ta town and come out ta see me. She went back on her word ta me. It made me sa mad I slapped 'er...real hard, I reckon. She jumped back and fell. She hit 'er head and it killed 'er."

"Where were you when this happened?" Troy asked.

"I wuz in the loft of the barn getting' a kitty for Mrs. Swartz's grand baby when Carla come lookin' fer me. She climbed up in the loft to see the kitties too. We wuz on the extra high tier in the loft. It's like two stories high."

"Carla had cuts in parallel lines all down her back. Can you explain that?"

"Yeah, she fell on 'er back on the disk that wuz parked in the barn at that time. She hit 'er head on the front bar of the frame and that's what they said killed er."

"Why were you mad at her?"

Josey glanced furtively at Anna and remained silent for a time.

Troy repeated the question. "Why were you mad at her, Mrs. Shelton?"

"She promised ta do me a favor and I give her money for an abortion and ta live on fer a few months. She got the abortion and since she didn' need my hep any more she backed out and left me holdin' the sack. She used ma money ta solve her problem then wudn' help me with ma problem."

"What had she promised to do for you?"

"That don' matter none. Didn' have nothin' ta do with 'er fallin'"

"I'll be the judge of that. What was the promise?"

Josey again glanced at Anna who was holding her breath, waiting for the answer.

"I had 'er to say Gabe wuz the daddy of 'er baby instead of Billy."

Anna tried to muffle the heart wrenching cry that escaped her throat. She fought to control her emotions covering her mouth with one hand, while the other found its way to her heart.

"You made her lie to get money for an abortion and she came back after getting the abortion and wanted to tell the truth?"

"Yeah, she paid me back some of the money and had a note all notarized and all—showing what she owed me and how she wuz gonna pay it back in payments ever month. She used me ta git what she wanted and then cheated me outta what I had paid fer. Said she cudn' live with what she done. I cudn' believe it mattered that much ta her. She just killed her own baby."

"Did she come to you for help or did you contact her first?"

"She come ta see Anna ta swear it was *not* Gabe's baby. I

218

didn't believe her anyway. Anna was not home yet so I offered to help her if she'd tell Anna it was Gabe's kid not Billy's like she told me it wuz."

Anna remembered Carla coming out of her mother's house that horrible afternoon, sobbing she couldn't do it. "It was too hard to say," she had said. Then Josey had taken over and yelled that it was Gabe's baby. Even yelled at Gabe telling him to go and marry the mother of his child. Anna had thought Carla couldn't admit to seducing her one-time-best-friend's finance. But no, it was even worse.

"*Oh, Gabe, I'm so sorry.* Her soul apologized as her heart broke. She struggled to keep control of her emotions. She had to hear it all. She had waited so long and prayed so hard for the truth. *The truth...will it really set you free?* flashed through her mind.

Troy, in deference to Anna's feelings, asked if anyone needed a break. Anna shook her head, "no."

"What did you do when Carla fell from the loft?"

"I hurried down the ladder. Didn't even take the kitten I went after. She wuz dead no doubt about it. She wuzn't breathin'. Her eyes were open and her head was all bashed in."

"Then what did you do?"

"Well, I cudn' help her none then. And if I wuz to report it, I'd get in trouble fer bribin' 'er, I reckon. That wudn' help her any no how. Since I cudn' git ma money back then...well, I thought it wud sorta be like she'd kept 'er promise if I never reported it."

"What you're saying is that if you never reported what actually happened and never told why Carla came back, everyone might still believe the lie you had paid for. Is that right?"

"Yeah! Well, she wuz already dead. I cudn' change that none. And I still hadn' got what I paid fer." Josey acted as though she were insulted that anyone would fault her for taking advantage of the opportunity that had availed itself.

"So then what did you do?"

"I wrapped her in a tarp so I wudn' get my car bloody. Took all the papers she give me—the loan and a letter she writ me—but she decided to come in person and brung it with 'er. I took 'er ta the park and drug 'er out on the ground near the duck pond. I didn' see no one around. It wuz in the middle of the night."

"How did Dugan find out about Carla's death.?"

"Sometime later, he come and stood by my car until I finished buyin' my groceries. Then he just got in ma car and told me he seen me drag Carla out of it and leave 'er in the park. He had got ma license number and just kept lookin' 'til he found me. Said he needed a place to stay and if I didn' let 'em live with us he'd report me ta the police. I didn' know what else ta do so I let 'em stay, hopin' he'd leave rat away, but he didn'."

"How did he manage to get all of your papers and stuff in the tool box?"

"He wuz a bastard of the worst sort. He'd bite the hand that fed 'em. He just kept lookin' 'til he found somethin' that would prove his story. I had left it all under a hay bale in the barn. I wuz gonna burn it when I got the chance. He found it first. Then I wuz caught fer good. Nuthin' could be done 'bout it after that."

"Did you know he was trying to kill Anna?"

"Not at first. I kinda suspected 'e might be. He wanted us to marry. I knew 'e just wanted my farm and stuff. I kept holdin' out. If Anna died and we wuz married, I'd be next, but if Anna could stay alive then I was still safe, I reckoned. Be no point in killin' me then, she'd git it all if she wuz still alive. Long as I didn' marry him I thought she'd be purty safe. But I reckon he didn't care if she died before he forced me to marry 'em. Must a got tired a waitin'."

"Did you know he was trying to steal her horse?"

"Yeah, I didn' fight it. I thought if 'e could sell him for $15,000, it might be enough and 'e'd leave."

"Why did he leave and go to Texas?"

220

"I don' know fer sure. Ya got ta sniffin' round and scared him off or maybe 'e just wanted everyone to *think* 'e went. Sort of like settin' up an alibi. If 'e really went 'e got back real soon, cause that's when all them things started happnin' to Anna."

"Did you and Dugan take Casey away that first time?" Josey looked quickly at Anna. "Yeah, I begged 'em to let the dog be, but Casey didn't like 'em and was always barkin' when Dugan planned somethin' in the middle of the night. I cudn' stop 'em. Anyway, Casey's just a dog."

"Weren't you afraid he would eventually kill Anna?"

"He might have...sooner or later. But she's mighty smart and I kept hopin' he'd do somethin' and git caught first. Ya gotta know 'e wuz threatenin' ma life too!"

"Was Billy Freemont helping Old Charley in any way to set up Anna?"

"I don' have no proof of it, but Billy was always carryin' 'em around when 'e needed to go some'ers. Especially after Anna kicked 'em like she done at the rodeo. He paid Billy, but I always thought he'd made bigger promises. I can't say fer sure."

"Was there anyone else that you thought might be helping Dugan?"

"No, I don' think so. Nobody wanted anythang to do with 'em. He was a sorry bastard of the worst kind. I'm glad I shot 'em. He deserves ta die."

"If he does, you could be facing murder charges. You shot him again after he was no longer a threat to you or anyone else."

"I don' care. I'm done with this 'er life. Anna ain't gonna forgive what I done. She'll marry that Gabe guy and I don' have no one to take care of me so nuthin' matters no how."

Troy asked the deputy to book Josey.

"On what charge?" the deputy asked. "All of them? Talk about throwing the book at someone....It would be a book!"

"Just hold off on the charges. We can hold her for long enough without them and we'll see if Dugan makes it. Otherwise we'll have a murder charge too."

"That'll work." The deputy gathered the tape recorder and tool box of evidence.

"Lock those up immediately—without fail!" Troy was adamant. He put his arm around Anna and asked, "Do you need someone to drive you home? This has been a harrowing experience for you, I know."

She felt like a zombie. Nothing made sense. She seemed to be walking behind herself, not knowing what to do or where to go.

Finally, she managed to say, "No, I'll be okay."

Anna needed someone to talk to, someone to hold her while she sorted out all the details of the ignominious and illegal acts her mother had committed. Josey readily admitted what she had done as if it were perfectly rational behavior. It was mind-boggling and Anna hadn't the slightest notion how to start "unboggling."

Possibly the worst pain of it all came from the realization she had been wrong. She'd not stood staunchly behind Gabe and supported him as she should have. She had thereby deprived them of years...no...a lifetime of togetherness by constantly refusing his marriage proposals. She deserved to be alone!

And Carla. She had been trying to do the right thing in the end—trying to correct a past mistake. Why did things happen that way? It looked to Anna that punishment, if that's what it was, should have been meted out when Carla consciously decided to hurt Anna and Gabe to gain money with which to resolve her own problems.

Were there no good answers? Did she even know the questions? She needed peace. She had thought it would come when those who sought to kill her were caught, but it was still as elusive as ever. She knew in her heart, however, wherein it lay..
It could be found in Gabe's forgiveness, in his arms, in the knowledge that he still loved and wanted her. She also realized with bitterness that it was too late. And to add more bitterness to the mix, she had to admit to herself that she was to blame. She

had deserted him...not the other way around. She thought she knew how Josey had felt earlier when she had said, "I'm done with this 'er life." What was there left to live for?

Anna wanted to know what Dugan had divulged to the sheriff's department. Had he lived? She had thought to go to the hospital to find out, but decided she had heard more than enough. She could handle no more details at this time.

She went home and took care of her friends. Smoky was as welcoming as ever. She had to admit it was most likely the apples she carried to him. Casey wanted to stay close by and she was glad. Miss Kitty purred in her lap as Anna sat and stared at nothing for hours—going over all she had learned that day.

How could she have lived with Josey every day as it had all unfolded and never, ever suspected her mother of doing the horrible things she apparently had done. How could her own mother, knowing how much Anna had loved Gabe—have caused her such anguish—almost to the point of losing her mind? Because of Josey's lies, a network of fabrication grew—leaving asymmetrical tangles of questions never quite meshing with offered answers—causing constant, uneasy speculation. Suspicions, unproven, could not be accepted as truth, yet not quite discarded as lies. It had been an unending, hellish nightmare that chewed at Anna's soul until—like a wooden structure infested with termites—the integrity of her whole being was in jeopardy of collapsing.

Anna shuddered to think the woman was her mother. Josey's way of solving a problem was so bizarre it approached insanity. Why the obsession with losing Anna and being alone? Had she just wanted attention from others and refused to assume responsibility for herself until she had reached the point where she felt she could never do so? Had her grandparents and her foster parents felt sorry for her and done everything for her—not requiring her to assume responsibility for herself even? Had the circumstance of being an only child caused her to acquiesce and not fight for what she wanted? What had caused her to assume that others should supply her every need? Anna would never know. It was more than disconcerting.

As much as Anna longed to talk to Gabe and apologize, she was too ashamed to face him. Yet, she must. First she had to have a small interim of time in which to straighten her thoughts—hopefully, gain a sense of direction—before owning her disgrace in front of the person who mattered most.

Anna sat for hours, letting all the facts bombard her as they would, trying not to make sense of any of it for the time being. Finally, she began to cry. She didn't know for whom she wept. Was it herself? Gabe? Her mother? Carla? Carla's baby? The whole crazy, mixed up world? Did it matter? It seemed the hurt was all encompassing. She cried until she could hardly see through swollen eyes or breathe through her stuffed-up nose. She cried until her body wore itself out and then she slept.

When she awoke the next morning, Miss Kitty was purring next to her cheek and Casey snuggled in her bed, behind her knees. At least she wasn't completely alone. She tried to fathom Josey's fear of it. Being alone could be terrifying if one dwelt upon it, she supposed.

Anna dragged herself to the bathroom and washed her face.

"God! What a sight! No...a fright!" She said as she looked into the mirror.

She wasn't hungry and just brewed a pot of coffee. She fed Miss Kitty and Casey then went to take Smoky an apple and feed him his grain. She'd check the cows later.

Anna returned to the house and poured herself a cup of coffee then buttered a piece of toast and went out onto the patio to munch while listening to the birds. It was a peaceful time of day. Anna wished she could soak it up.

Not wanting to do anything, Anna knew she should notify Gabe and ask for time off. Just a few days, maybe. While she sat there, postponing the inevitable, a car came down her driveway. Anna answered the door and discovered a rather subdued Janice, staring at her with questioning eyes.

"Hey, Chiquita! You okay?"

"Janice! Come in. Sorry I look like a disastrous train wreck." she said.

"Yes, you do. But I love you anyway," Janice said as she gave her a hug.

"Wow! Now that's true friendship. A smash and grab all in one statement." Anna tried to be less morbid than she felt. "How about some coffee?"

"Yeah, I'll have a cup."

"Would you like a piece of toast with it or maybe breakfast?"

"No, I've had breakfast. I was up all night. I worked the night shift at the hospital."

"Oh. Let's go out on the patio. It's rather nice there right now."

As Janice seated herself in a stuffed lounger, Anna asked the question she had wanted to ask from the beginning. "Did Dugan make it?"

"No, he passed early this morning."

"Did they get anything from him about Billy?"

"Well, it's a long story. Troy's guys couldn't get anything out of him, but he did want to talk...to me. I couldn't give him his rights or anything like that, but I did just casually ask what his name really was and got stuff they needed on the wire I was wearing—all the time puttering around like I was his private nurse."

"Janice, you're something else!"

"Yeah, I know. When I asked if Billy Freemont was his nephew, he said,'Yeah, and I got 'em into trouble I guess. I didn' mean ta. I just needed some help and didn' have anyone else'."

"What kind of trouble did you get him into?" I asked.

"Well, he tried to help me steal a horse and then we tried to cut the brake lines on a girl's truck and he got caught."

"Was she that Anna Shelton girl?" I asked.

"Yeah," he said, I needed to git rid of 'er and he took me to 'er house several times. But, the last time I got shot and he left

225

me there. Guess he cudn' do nothin' else."

"Did he know you were trying to kill her, do you think?"

"Oh, yeah. He knew, but he hated her too. She treated him bad once."

Janice finished her coffee as she was finishing her narrative. "Then Dugan got sort of quiet and went to sleep. He never woke up. I don't know if this can be used in court or not, but it might be enough to get a confession out of Billy."

"I hope so. I don't think he should get off scot-free. If for no other reason than—if he had taken responsibility for his own child, none of this would ever have happened." Anna concluded.

"Yeah, you're right, Chiquita." Janice looked at Anna for a long moment, before continuing. "Sweetie, I hate like hell to be the bearer of bad news, but I have to give you some. Can you handle any more right now?"

Anna stiffened. What else could possibly have happened. "Oh god! Not Gabe! Is he okay?"

"Yes, yes, he's okay. It's not Gabe."

Anna slowly let out her breath. "What then?"

"It's Josey. She had a heart attack last night and apparently died in her sleep. They found her early this morning."

Anna stared. She didn't know what she felt. She was still in shock, she guessed.

"Maybe now she'll have some peace." Anna reflected. "And thank God, she won't be subjected to a trial or prison. Thank you, Janice for letting me know. I'll have to make arrangements..."

"No," Janice interrupted. "Let me do that for you. You're to zonked out and exhausted."

"No, Janice, I'll do it. It'll be the last thing I can do for her. She'd have wanted it that way."

"Yeah, probably. But it's what *you* want now."

"I know, but I need something to occupy my mind—to keep it from going off the deep end. Okay?"

"Alright, but, please let me help where I can."

"I will, Janice....where is she now? Still in the jail?"

"Yes. They can only release her to someone authorized to accept responsibility for her body– like a close relative or funeral home or coroner, I think."

"I'll call the funeral home immediately and have them to take care of her."

"Okay, I'll go then, but please call me if I can help in any way possible."

"I will Janice. You're a peach and I love peaches."

"I do too." Janice laughed.

After Janice drove away, Anna started making arrangements for her mother's funeral. Though it was not the most pleasant of tasks it did occupied her thoughts. Work was the best anesthesia Anna knew of. She wished Josey could have found such a helpful antidote.

Chapter Thirteen

After Anna talked to the Peaceful Haven Funeral Home and coordinated her needs with their schedules, she called the Carnegie Gazette to place an obituary and a notice of Josey's upcoming services. It would appear in their Sunday edition. Not that Anna expected many to attend the funeral, but just in case she had old friends who might wish to pay their respects, she had followed protocol. Josey had no other relatives that Anna knew about. She surely had some somewhere, but Josey never seemed to care about tracking them down. Not having anyone else was perhaps part of the reason she was loathe to let Anna marry and leave her. But she had so much more to gain—Anna's children and grandchildren eventually. She could have had a large family. Had she ever considered that? Anna wondered if it had mattered.

Anna still hadn't called Gabe to ask for a few days off. She kept postponing the task. How could she tell him how sorry she was for not totally believing in his innocence. Before she had gathered enough courage and the necessary words, he called her.

"Hello." Anna's voice sounded calmer than she felt.

"I just wanted to call and offer my condolences for the loss of your mother, Anna."

"Thank you. It was quite sudden and a big shock."

"Yes. And I understand several things have come together at one time that must have created a lot of stress for you. I'm sure you need some time to get it all together, so if you'll tell me how much time you think you might need, I'll arrange for someone else to take over here."

Anna supposed she should have felt gratitude for his thoughtfulness, but right then her thoughts questioned how easy it was for him to replace her.

"I hate to take time off when I haven't quite finished all the work on your newly planned projects."

"That's alright. You were almost finished and Mrs. McClusky has already called and volunteered to come in for as long as you need to be off."

"That was nice of her." Anna tried to sound grateful. Why did she feel she was too easily replaced. Was she slipping as off center as Josey had become? Forcing herself to act—if not feel— positive, Anna continued, "I think three days will be sufficient. I really do better if I can keep busy."

"Fine. We'll expect you to come in then on Thursday unless you call and need a few more days."

"I'll be there...and thank Mrs. McClusky for me."

"I will. Take care and call if we can do anything at all for you."

"Thanks," she replied and hung up.

Anna felt desolate. He sounded so cold and businesslike She needed him. Needed to be close to him and feel his support for her.

Good lord! You fool. What did you expect him to do? Say, "Anna, all opposition to our union has now evaporated and positive proof of my innocence is now evident. Let's get married next week? Anna, you fool! she chastised herself. *Yes! Yes! That's exactly what I want,* her whole being cried to be heard. *But, no, I know better than to hold onto such foolish hopes.*

He had been cool as a cucumber and she had no right to expect more.

Work. That was the answer. She needed to do something before she dropped into a deep pit of depression. She would drive into Carnegie and buy a nice outfit for Josey's finale. As she started to get into her truck, she paused beside her mother's Lincoln. She got a peculiar mix of emotions, realizing it was probably hers now. She would not feel comfortable driving her mother's car. The cattle, all the equipment, even the farm was now totally her responsibility, she supposed. That caused no emotional upheaval whatsoever. She had always taken care of it all anyway.

Anna searched department stores and dress shops for a couple hours, trying to find just the right dress for Josey—one she knew her mother would have chosen. She finally purchased a pale orchid dress with a graceful drape from the shoulder to below the breast line. Josey's darker skin tone and dark hair would be enhanced by the pale orchid of the dress. She knew her mother would be pleased, although she probably would not have said so.

She went home after delivering the gown to the funeral parlor and called Josey's hairdresser to ask for her mother's final "do".

"I'll be happy to take care of it, Anna, and this last one is free. I'll make sure she looks real nice."

"Thank you so much, Cindy. I know she'd appreciate it very much...and so do I."

Anna was appalled at the high cost when she was given the total price of all the arrangements plus the burial site and headstone. She sought to cut a few corners if she could, but the savings amounted to very little.

Concerned about how she was going to pay for all the expenses, she wondered if Josey had perhaps had an insurance policy. She began to search through all of her mother's papers and dresser drawers and finally located a life insurance policy with herself as beneficiary. It was paid up and in force. The amount paid all of the funeral expenses and burial costs with enough left to pay off Anna's truck. It was unbelievable. She considered how very little she really knew about Josey. It caused her some feelings of guilt, but then she had never been able to converse with Josey no matter how hard she tried.

It was almost as if she were an "island unto herself," Anna thought.

Disconsolate and anxious, Anna decided to take a walk.

Maybe a little exercise and fresh air would help. Casey must have thought that was a good idea. He happily bounced along after her. She walked toward the paddock and saw Smoky at the far end grazing peacefully. The grass was still green and lush and he seemed to be enjoying it immensely. Anna stopped in the shade of a huge elm tree and leaned against the corral fence. A chaparral ran quickly from a bush nearby and flew upon the railing. He teetered awkwardly for a moment, before hopping down and disappearing into the shrubs.

Wish I could just disappear into the shrubs or somewhere, she thought.

Worrisome thoughts that she had considered many times before came back to bother her. She had to find some peace or lose her mind. She had to do something! She must make some changes—get out of the rut she was in. Exactly what to do and how to go about it were always elusive or at least hard to decide. After due consideration, Anna began to think she had only one choice if she were to ever gain any peace in her life. She needed to leave Whittier Enterprises and stay totally away from Gabe, the passionate love of her life, who was and would always remain—out of reach. She could pay off her truck now and if she could find another job, she would take that first step and set her feet on a positive and constructive path.

Does out of sight, out of mind really work, she wondered. Nothing else seemed to have had the slightest impact on her feelings for him.

She bought the Sunday Gazette to look through the classified ads. Headlines blared the whole story of Josey's revelations and Dugan's death. They also pointed out the irony of Josey's death on the same night. Anna didn't want to read about it, but couldn't leave it alone. It was all there in sordid detail.

How in the world did they get all that information. Who would have told it anyway? Reporters are very astute and ingenious at grubbing information from unsuspecting sources.

It could have been anyone connected with the sheriff's

office. The hospital staffers or even Sammy could have given them some bits of it. What did it matter? Josey was no longer aware. She couldn't be hurt by the release of all the information about her dishonorable deeds. In fact, it didn't seem that Josey had considered them to be dishonorable. But it bothered Anna. And she was very much aware.

Carthage University had an ad in the classifieds. They needed someone to teach their evening classes in algebra, trigonometry and accounting. She would apply on Monday if she could get an interview. Working evening hours would allow Anna the whole day, every day, to take care of the farm and all the animals. It might work out well.

Before she accepted another job, she wanted to go to Gabe and offer him apologies for her failure to trust in his honesty and integrity when it had mattered so much. Also, to tell him how much she had appreciated his help when she had so sorely needed a job. To tell him all that and then disclose that she had accepted employment elsewhere seemed somehow incongruous, if not dishonest. Maybe she could catch him at the office early on Monday before her appointment at the university.

Neighbors and co-workers, friends from the past and ex-classmates of Anna made a steady trek out to the farm. And as was customary, they voiced their condolences and left a special offering of something edible. Anna had no idea what to do with all that food, but finally decided to invite Troy and Janice—and all of the sheriff's department to dinner. She sent plates of leftovers to all who would take them. Most were happy to do so. Still there was quite a bit left. Anna bundled it all up and took it to Sammy's mother. Mrs. Grisham was extremely pleased.

"Sammy thinks you're the greatest. I know he's right. I'm so glad he met you. Thank you for all you have done for him."

"It has been a pleasure to help Sammy with his algebra. He's a mighty fine young man."

"I'm sorry about your mother. I know it was hurtful," Mrs. Grisham continued.

"Yes, it was very shocking." Anna said her goodbyes, not wanting to linger and left right away.

Time...that ever present, equivocating component in all our lives—rushing away the good times and crawling imperceptibly through the difficult days—was true to form. Anna tried to keep busy but there were hours when it seemed the old tormentor stood still. She needed to find something or someone to be with when life kicked her in the butt—someone to love and support her and always be there when she needed a kind word or kiss on the cheek. She was missing her dad.

Anna had not expected many at her mother's funeral. Josey had no real friend and no relatives except Anna. But, the chapel was packed. Lots of neighbors, Anna's friends and reporters and quite probably some curious onlookers, Anna presumed.

Josey looked lovely, soft and delicate, not at all like the harsh, miserable harridan she really had been. Anna hoped she could remember her as she looked that day. There were no tears and the eulogy was short and uplifting.

Troy and Janice sat beside Anna. Gabe sat with his family and that beautiful, young girl—who looking more beautiful than ever—was wearing black, no less. Bill Grant came and asked Anna if he could sit beside her. She was so glad to have him there. Gabe's girl kept giving him the eye.

What is her interest in him? Anna wondered.

Not many went to the grave site. Anna placed flowers on the top of the casket as it had not yet been lowered into the ground nor the headstone set. The verse on it would merely read, "Rest in peace, Mother." The minister said the final prayer and it was over.

On Monday, Anna made an appointment for an interview at the university. She was pleased that her favorite professor, Dr. Veatch was conducting the interview. It was scheduled for 10 o'clock, so Anna had time to catch Gabe at his office and tell him what she needed to. Maybe it would rid her conscience of some of the guilt she carried around with her. She hoped he would be alone when she reached his office. It would be hard to control her tears and she had hoped not to make a spectacle of herself or expose her emotions to anyone else, especially pretty, young competitors.

Anna drove by the drugstore to get a box of tissues...just in case. As she pulled up and parked, she saw the very person she did not want to see, running toward Gabe who was just getting out of his car. Waving a copy of the Carnegie Gazette in her hand, she was obviously crying—crying and laughing at the same time. Gabe stopped and dropped the box he was carrying. He opened his arms wide to embrace her. She threw herself into his arms and he hugged her tightly, kissing her, then swinging her round and round like a child. Anna, who had come to congratulate him on the new evidence revealed—that proved to the world he was innocent without a doubt—could not then approach him. She sat very still—until Gabe and his beautiful friend, who obviously loved him, left—and then she hurried away.

Anna had extreme difficulty dealing with self-deprecating emotions after getting proof positive that Gabe had indeed been telling her the truth. She had been so wrong not to continue trusting and believing in him. She had never known him to be anything but honest and kind and she had loved him so much. Where were her senses? She would never be able to forgive herself for failing him.

She still owed Gabe an apology and congratulations for hanging tough through hard times to win in the end. And she would gather her courage and go to him to ask his forgiveness, even though she didn't expect that he could forgive her. She would have done what she needed to do. Her sorrow was now doubly painful. She had lost—no, thrown away—that precious, exuberant love that he had now given to another. How could she survive this awful sickness that enveloped her? The loss had been her own fault. She had endured much, but wondered if this might be more than she could live through.

Desolate, but determined, Anna kept her appointment with Dr. Veatch at 10 o'clock.

"I'm so sorry to hear about your recent problems," he began.

"Thank you. It may well be the ending of a lot of long time problems," Anna said before she thought.

"Oh? Well, we're glad that you are considering employment with us. I know firsthand about your math skills and work ethics. Are you still employed at Whittier Enterprises?"

"Yes, I am. I just thought I might like to try teaching. I have a high school student that I have been sort of tutoring on the side. And I find it rewarding to teach him algebra. He's a good student after all."

"Anna, I'll be honest with you. There's no reason I know of that would keep you from getting this job, but we have to keep taking applications for as long as there are applicants—just in case you might change your mind or something. So I can't hire you today, but I'll let you know."

"Thank you Dr. Veatch. I fully understand."

Anna felt the job was probably hers, but instead of being elated, she felt a sense of loss.

She still needed to speak to Gabe and make her apologies before accepting the job at the university. She didn't feel up to it at the present. She would try to catch him on Tuesday morning.

The phone rang shortly after Anna returned home. Troy had some information he thought she might be interested in.

"How are you holding up, Anna?"

"Okay, I guess. I'm too numb to know for sure."

"Shock does that for you. I have some information you might want to know if you can handle any more right now."

"Yes, go ahead. If it's about Billy, I would like to know rather than wonder and fret with guessing."

"Okay, then. Based on the information Janice got from Dugan, we picked up Billy and told him Dugan had implicated him in attempted murder and we had it all on tape. We also had his fingerprints on the cutters under your truck and on your ladder as well. After thinking it over, he caved and made a full confession."

"He didn't even ask for an attorney?"

"No, he thought his statement that Dugan had given up on trying to kill you and taking Josey's farm—plus the fact that they hadn't gone there the last two times to do anything but dig up the tool box—would exonerate him."

"You mean Dugan was going to take the evidence that Mom was implicated in Carla's death and just split?" Anna couldn't believe Old Charley would quit so easily.

"Well, almost. He claimed that Dugan wanted to take the stuff to Josey and demand $20,000 for it and the promise he would leave her alone."

"I don't think Mom would have trusted him to keep that promise. Do you?"

"Hard to say. Knowing him as she did, probably not."

"I guess it complicated matters because Casey wouldn't let Dugan get the job done," she reflected.

"Well, yes and no. If he had gotten the tool box of evidence and made a deal with Josey and kept his promise, you would never have learned the truth and Gabe would never have the joy of all that positive energy circulating on his behalf. Like they say—it's an ill wind that doesn't blow some good."

"That's so true," Anna agreed. "So does that mean Billy is free to pester every girl on the planet?"

"Lord no! He was in the process of committing a felony or aiding in one. Under the murder felony doctrine, because Dugan was in fact killed in the commission of a crime, Billy's guilty as sin. He is also guilty of attempted murder on at least two other attempts on your life. Billy will spend a lot of time behind bars. And the best part is that he has already confessed to it. And we have it on tape—all wrapped up in a package and tied with a bow that has 'legal' written all over it. We took great care to make sure it was done right so he wouldn't be able to get off on a technicality."

"That's really good news, Troy. I'm so thankful for all you've done and come next election, you can bet I'm going to vote for you again—twice if I can." They both laughed.

"I'm glad to have been able to help you. It had me worried for a time or two and we had some setbacks. I know you suffered a loss when the truth came out, but as everyone says, the good lord never closes a door without opening another. I hope you will have a much happier future."

"Thank you so much. You're a treasure and Janice is lucky to have you. Give her a hug for me."

"That will be a pleasure." He chuckled as he said, "Goodbye."

Anna fed her animals and was once again letting Casey stay in the house overnight.

"You're going to think this is a permanent arrangement if I let it go on much longer," she said as she brushed his coat. He wiggled his stubby tail and tried to lick her face. He was getting around much better. The slight limp was hardly noticeable now.

Miss Kitty rubbed up against him before she leaped upon Anna's bed.

"Lord, I'm being overrun." she cried, thankful to have them there with her. "I guess if I had invited Smoky when I fed him, he'd be right here in my bed too, wouldn't he?" She laughed as she narrowly dodged another "Casey-face-lick."

The next morning Anna did her chores with determined effort. She had to go and face Gabe and it wouldn't be easy. She was not sure what she could say. Wasn't even sure she could say anything, but was certain she had to make the effort to say something.

When Anna arrived at their offices, several people were just leaving. She remained in her vehicle until they had all driven away. She recognized Earnest Galloway, publisher of the

Gazette, John Campbell the mayor, Hollis Pruitt, president of the First National Bank, Joe Southerd, the city manager, Sheriff Troy-the Trojan, and Clay Richards, pastor of the First Baptist Church. And there were others she didn't know. Some were carrying cups of—she supposed—coffee. They had all seemed very pleased. Anna knew they must have gotten together for a surprise we-knew-it-but-it's-good-to-prove-to-the-world congratulatory coffee klatch for Gabe. She remembered how strongly the publisher of the Gazette had believed in his innocence from the very beginning. The others must have too, for their very presence and stature evidenced—even without iron-clad proof—that he had been an accepted and trusted member of the community.

She entered the building, closing the door softly behind her. Opening the top drawer of her desk, intending to leave her purse, she decided not to. The tissues folded inside it might be needed. She forced herself down the hall to the closed door with "Gabe Whittier, President" printed in black letters on the glass panel and knocked lightly. A moment later as Gabe opened the door, Anna saw the beautiful, young girl, who—yesterday—had showered him with love and affection.

"Oh, I'm sorry to interrupt. I'll catch you later." She turned to hurry away.

Gabe reached out and caught her arm. "No! Don't go. I need to talk to you and it's important." He seemed—what?—angry?

The young girl quickly rose. She threw her arms around Gabe and kissed him on the cheek. "I love you dearly, Gabe Whittier and I'll see you later."

"I love you too." He laughed, "Just don't wreck my car."

Anna felt a dull thud in her middle. A feeling of despair engulfed her. She didn't want to hear this. She must get away.

The girl smiled at Anna, wishing her a "good mornin'."

Gabe followed her to the outer office and Anna saw him swat her on the butt before closing the door.

Upon his return, Anna began again to apologize, "I didn't

238

mean to interrupt."

"She was just leaving anyway. Have a seat," he said rather curtly.

"No, I won't stay long. I just wanted to tell you how happy I am that you finally have concrete proof those accusations leveled against you years ago were all false."

"Thank you, Anna. I hope this turn of events will wipe away the cloud of guilt that seemed to follow me the past several years, even though I was completely innocent. It was not an easy thing to deal with, but I had no choice. I had to..." A wry half-smile fleetingly appeared. "I had to endure and prevail." He chuckled "However, I am sorry it dealt you such a blow—that someone so close to you became the accused."

She felt tears fill her eyes and strong feelings threatened to undermine her determination, but Anna knew she had to finish the long overdue apology.

"The accused was guilty and admitted it. ...What did you need to discuss with me?" She wanted desperately to postpone her reason for coming.

He stared at her for a long moment. "I want to know if we here at Whittier have done you any disservice?"

Taken aback, Anna wondered at the question and his almost accusatory tone.

"No, of course not. You have been most helpful in all instances. Why such a question?"

"Are you upset with anything in particular concerning your job or surroundings?"

"No, Whittier Enterprises is a great place to work."

"Are you being paid a fair wage, do you think?" He was relentless and seemed angry.

"Everyone always wants to earn more, I guess. But I don't think I could beat it elsewhere. It's more than most companies pay beginning accountants. Why all these questions?"

"Because, damn it, I have been told that you're applying for a teaching position at Carthage University. I want to know why?"

Anna was aghast. Confused, she wondered who had told him and why they would do such a thing.

"How did you find out?" she asked feeling as though she had been caught with her hand in the cookie jar.

"It doesn't matter—someone who thinks you should stay here is all I can say."

Could it possibly have been Dr. Veatch? Anna knew he had also been Gabe's instructor in several classes and that they were good friends. She also knew Gabe would never betray that confidence.

"It's not that I don't appreciate all that you've done for me. And you have done so much. It just seems that under the present circumstances, it would be better...if I sort of move on."

"And what would those circumstances be?" he asked rather harshly.

Anna was at a loss for words. She couldn't say what she wanted to—that he loved someone else and it was killing her to see them together day after day. Instead she faltered and stuttered around, finally saying, "I feel so guilty for my lack of support for you when you needed it most. Please accept my apology...no...I don't expect you to accept...I mean I'm so sorry...I didn't...I..." She couldn't finish her sentence for fear of falling apart. She needed desperately to escape.

Someone entered the outer office and Gabe left for a moment.

"We're closed for the day," she heard him say. "There's been a death in the family." Well, that was true. He hadn't said which family. He apologized and she heard him lock the door after it closed behind whoever left.

He came back and staring at Anna, began again where they had left off. His eyes narrowed and his lips tightened as he asked, "Are you saying that you're leaving because you now know without a doubt that I was innocent all along? And because you feel you didn't support me as you should have back then— that now the right thing to do is to desert me?"

240

"No, no it' not that altogether...it's just that I...I can't find the words to tell you how much I regret..." Covering her face with her hands, she wished she could die rather than confront the guilt and agony she felt, but with extreme effort and grim determination, she finally managed to say, "Oh, god! Please forgive me Gabe. I was so wrong. No, I can't expect you to forgive me. Just know that I am so desperately sorry. I will never be able to forgive myself. And if there is any way I can make amends..." She was crying uncontrollably now. Tears streaming unheeded down her cheeks.

He reached for her and gently pulled her to him. "Don't, Annie, don't. I understand completely." His voice broke with the remembered torment they had shared. "The lies that were told were very convincing and circumstantial evidence seemed to support them. Only my alibi and your testimony saved me and some still could never believe they were the truth. We were both victims, you and I. We were cheated out of our right to work toward and fulfill our dreams together. I do not blame you, but your mother and Dugan, even Carla were guilty and have received their punishment—just rewards, I should say."

Anna, still crying, felt his arms go around her. A surge of long-ago happiness momentarily swept over her, but it was too late. She pushed away from him and dabbed at her cheeks with a tissue.

"I would like the day off if it's okay with you."

"Wait a minute! We're not through here! You want to run away from a good job here just because you can't face that you made an error in judgment back then? You had a lot of 'convincing' thrown at you constantly. It's over now. Don't you see that?"

Anna couldn't answer without him thinking her foolish. She couldn't say, "I can't bear to lose you to someone else—and still stay to see her making you happy—every day for the rest of my life." It would defeat her completely.

Gabe looked puzzled and more than a little upset.

241

"Alright, let's get to the bottom of this! You now have the irrefutable proof that you needed of my innocence. So you can now rest assured that what you said in my defense at the hearing was true, even though you weren't sure at the time. What you did was right...or at least justice was served. You most likely saved my butt from prison. You can't feel guilty about that anymore. Now you have no reason not to marry me...unless you just don't want me!"

Anna still couldn't say, "I can't share you with anyone else." Instead she said, "I really have to go now and I know that young lady is waiting for you."

She turned to go, feeling empty and lost. The door seemed so far away. Would she collapse before reaching it? He caught her arm.

"What? No one is waiting for me!. Slowly, he seemed to comprehend her dilemma. "Oh, god! Anna, that young lady you're referring to is Joni! Don't you remember Joni, my baby sister? She's quite a bit younger than I. She's been away to prep school and we don't see her often. She has changed a great deal. Now I know why you treated her like a stranger. I'm not surprised you didn't recognize her." Anna staggered. He caught her. Stunned and relieved beyond measure, she was crying again.

Joni! Of course, that freckle-faced little hellion—always in rag-tag, holey jeans—that had breezed in and out when least expected as we studied for mid-terms or finals. Always on the move, she never stayed around long. And what had happened to all the freckles, and that slight gap in her front teeth...her hair was not the same shade either. Oh, yes! She had indeed changed a lot! That's the reason Gabe never introduced her to me...he thought I knew who she was!

Gabe put his arms around her, gently pulling her close. "I love you, Annie." His voice roughened with emotion. "I always have and I always will. Please don't go. Tell me we still have a chance at the happiness we once had. Don't let those fools keep us apart forever. I think you still love me. I need to hear you say

242

it."

Anna lifted her gaze to see tears glistening in his eyes. He swallowed hard. She knew without a doubt he truly loved her. Her spirits soared. She threw her arms around him crying, "Gabe, oh, Gabe, sweetheart, I have always loved you. I died a little every day without you. And I do, I do want you. I need you and I will spend every day—forever—making up for all the unhappiness I have caused both of us by not completely trusting the love of my life."

His eyes brightened. He pulled her roughly to him and held her close until she stopped crying.

"Anna, being here with you like this makes me feel that a hole in my very soul has been filled." he whispered. Finally Gabe pulled back and looked at her. Solemnly, he said, "I've waited for years with this god-awful need gnawing up my insides. I have a fury in my belly that's driving me mad. I need you Annie."

Slowly, her senses warmed to the man who held her. The man she had dreamed of night after night...for years. A sense of longing, that was almost painful, made itself known with an urgency that would not be denied and she knew exactly what he spoke of. Her breath caught. A tightness in her throat threatened to release a hungry cry that would tell him she felt the same fury. Her hands trembled as she held his face tenderly and softly caressed his lips with hers. He pulled her up snug against him. A wave of tightening muscles in her lower abdomen made her hug him even tighter—wanting to get even closer. She never wanted him to let her go. She couldn't fathom one moment of her life without him. She felt his breath on her cheek. His lips touched hers lightly, then hungrily, again and again, declaring his burning desire for her. She was no stranger to that desire. She returned his kisses with equal ardor. The need was tearing her apart. Nothing mattered except to satisfy the longing that crushed her with a ferocity that would not relinquish its hold on her. She desperately needed to meld together with him, to become and actual part of him, so that they would become one and no one or nothing could ever separate them again.

"Oh, Gabe, sweetheart, I love you so much."

A soft groan escaped him as he push up her blouse and bra, his fingers ever so lightly swept back and forth over tiny tips that caused her to gasp. A small cry escaped her. He buried his face under her shirt. His mouth was warm and wet as it covered the delicate phenomenon his fingers had awakened. He had given her a promise of waiting paradise.

With a firm, decisive grip, he picked her up and carried her into the back room of his office. He relinquished her for a moment and locked the door, then threw the pillows off the couch. It opened into a large bed. He reached for her. Kissing her softly, he unzipped the back of her pants and took a deep breath as he watched them slip to the floor at her feet. He unbuttoned her blouse and it too fell by the wayside. She was wearing those beautiful lace panties and bra with thigh-high stockings he had briefly seen her in that morning she had answered her door thinking it was Janice knocking. It was a vision that had haunted him and stalked through his dreams often and he told her so in soft whispers punctuated by tender kisses and gentle roaming hands.

When all their clothing lay here and—somewhere about them—they stood close, skin to skin, mouth to mouth, absorbing the warmth of each other.

"You are my life, Annie. I love you. I need you and you will be my cherished wife forever.

Her arms found their way around his neck and his reached around her tiny waist to pull her up close. She ran her fingers through his hair and caressed the back of his head and neck. His kisses were soft and plentiful. His hands found their way to sensitive places and charged her body with an yearning she could never have imagined. She rubbed his lower back and as he lifted her up, her legs wrapped securely around his waist. Groaning, he pulled her close, the small erected buds, he had aroused earlier

244

became more highly charged than ever as they touched his chest. She relaxed and let her buttocks rest across his tummy. She felt the strength of his body even though he held her gently. Recognizing a toughness in him, an intensity and a goodness—even nobility of character—her heart filled to overflowing. How completely she loved this man. She never wanted this to be over.

He must have felt the same way, for he gently whispered, "My precious Annie," again and again.

His loving caresses created a frantic search in her for a special closeness.

Gabe, oh, Gabe, I've needed you for so long and I desperately need you now."

His groan told her that he too felt that urgent need and was more than glad to let it possess him. He carried her to the bed and they lost sense of all else save each other and an all-consuming togetherness. He was finally as close as she wanted him. She was swept up in a euphoria that defied description, running her fingers through his hair, while pressing his face between her breasts. Her breath caught as he with a deep and firm thrust very deftly made them one. A small cry escaped her as she clung to this man she loved so completely and savored the moment she had longed for but never expected to experience and now knew she would never forget. A low, vibrating growl emitted from somewhere deep inside him, proclaiming that he was granted the long awaited passage to a soul satisfying sweetness that only the gods should enjoy. It was the most beautifully satisfying experience of Anna's life. She hoped and felt it was the same for him.

"My sweet Annie. I love you, I love you, I love you." he whispered.

After she recovered from his honoring of her request, she whispered back, "You are the love of my life. I can never live without you and I love you, I love you, I love you too." She laughed softly and kissed his mouth again.

Warm, happy, content and clinging to his strong, virile body, she felt safe, loved and protected. Relaxed and sleepy, a prayer for the future took shape in her mind.

God, please bless this union. Thank you for this man and help me to know how to support and keep him happy for a lifetime. Grant us health, knowledge, little Gabes and Annas and keep filling his heart with the same overwhelming love that I have for him. I positively know his character and worth and I shall always honor his ability to endure and prevail.

"We'll get a marriage license tomorrow," he said. "I want to tie you to me as fast as possible. I can't lose you again. If you need a large wedding, we will do that, but I just want to wed you and soon."

"Gabe, I don't want a large wedding. Married in the church would be nice, but with only the minister, the maid of honor—Janice, if her woo-hoos are not too loud—your best man and any of your family you wish to invite...and soon is good for me too."

She snuggled close as he kissed her lightly on the cheek and hugged her to him. Filled with so much love and happiness, she felt she actually glowed. Tomorrow was another day. Anna would make it a good one for Gabe as she would try to do every day for the rest of her life. Because good for him was good for her, as well.

Josey must have been lurking in the wings, for Anna could hear her condemning their exquisite coming together.

"This union has been joined together by God and no man shall ever—with all their papers, notaries, blessings or admonitions or whatever else, put it asunder!" She strongly answered back. And she truly felt it was a union blessed. All the rest that would follow were man's requirements and they were good. Good to keep track of who fathered or mothered whom and all that, but a blessed union was of premier importance—else a lifetime of misery or worse. Should God's blessing be made to wait until man has blessed it first? Anna knew that was a knotty question. A "no" answer could be fraught with serious lifelong problems. But, Anna knew for herself that she had no life without Gabe. This love of her life was there for her. A wonderful "knowing of rightness" bubbled up within her. She had lots of planning to do for her immediate future and it was a glorious feeling to contemplate jumping in with both feet and kicking up lots of long awaited joy and happiness.

He smiled as he watched her. "I know you are sleepy. I understand. I wasn't able to sleep last night either." He kissed her softly, saying, "This is our day, Annie. Sleep 'til you wake, but I must warn you...I feel about you the way John Denver did about his Annie. I died a little every time I heard him sing her song. Because you fill up my senses...and you must assuredly come and fill me again."

"Again and again, sweetheart," she answered softly. "Anytime you feel empty. And if I'm not immediately available, please don't fret. Just do what I shall be doing—endure...and we shall prevail."

Rachael Stratford

Rachael Stratford's life mirrors that of some of the characters in her books: a professional career woman, she has always possessed an unquenchable allegiance to the farming life of her youth. After a lifetime of working, studying human nature and writing, at last she has begun to share her literary gifts. Now Stratford's second work of fiction, *Endure and Prevail*, reveals her marvelous ability to spin a tale, drawing her readers into the lives of well-drawn characters and living with them on the farms, towns and rodeo grounds of today's Oklahoma.